M T

"Ten years is a long time for a man to go without a woman or a woman to go without a man."

Johnny's lips were achingly close to hers, and Marissa fought the desire to lean forward.

"It's still there, isn't it, Marissa?"

"What?" she asked, knowing exactly what he was talking about.

"Passion. Desire. Physical want," he whispered.

"It doesn't matter if it is or not." With enormous effort she stepped back from him, her voice shaky with emotion. "There's no going back, Johnny. At least not for us."

She desperately wanted to give in, to be Johnny's girl once again. But she had a son to consider. *They* had a son. With that thought she said, "Not tonight, Johnny," and closed the door....

Dear Reader,

I'm always getting letters telling me how much you love miniseries, and this month we've got three great ones for you. Linda Turner starts the new family-based miniseries, THOSE MARRYING McBRIDES! with *The Lady's Man.* The McBrides have always been unlucky in love—until now. And it's wedding-wary Zeke who's the first to take the plunge. Marie Ferrarella also starts a new miniseries this month. CHILDFINDERS, INC. is a detective agency specializing in finding missing kids, and they've never failed to find one yet. So is it any wonder desperate Savannah King turns to investigator Sam Walters when her daughter disappears in *A Hero for All Seasons?* And don't miss *Rodeo Dad,* the continuation of Carla Cassidy's wonderful Western miniseries, MUSTANG, MONTANA.

Of course, that's not all we've got in store. Paula Detmer Riggs is famous for her ability to explore emotion and create characters who live in readers' minds long after the last page is turned. In *Once More a Family* she creates a reunion romance to haunt you. Sharon Mignerey is back with her second book, *His Tender Touch,* a suspenseful story of a woman on the run and her unwilling protector—who soon turns into her willing lover. Finally, welcome new author Candace Irvin, who debuts with a military romance called *For His Eyes Only.* I think you'll be as glad as we are that Candace has joined the Intimate Moments ranks.

Enjoy—and come back next month, when we once again bring you the best and most exciting romantic reading around.

Yours,

Leslie J. Wainger
Executive Senior Editor

Please address questions and book requests to:
Silhouette Reader Service
U.S.: 3010 Walden Ave., P.O. Box 1325, Buffalo, NY 14269
Canadian: P.O. Box 609, Fort Erie, Ont. L2A 5X3

RODEO DAD

CARLA CASSIDY

Silhouette®
INTIMATE™MOMENTS®

Published by Silhouette Books

America's Publisher of Contemporary Romance

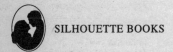 **SILHOUETTE BOOKS**

ISBN 0-373-07934-6

RODEO DAD

Look us up on-line at: http://www.romance.net

Printed in U.S.A.

Books by Carla Cassidy

CARLA CASSIDY

is an award-winning author who has written over thirty books for Silhouette. In 1995, she won Best Silhouette Romance of 1995 from *Romantic Times Magazine* for her Silhouette Romance novel *Anything for Danny*. In 1998, she also won a Career Achievement Award for Best Innovative series from *Romantic Times Magazine*.

Carla believes the only thing better than curling up with a good book to read is sitting down at the computer with a good story to write. She's looking forward to writing many more books and bringing hours of pleasure to readers.

Prologue

She had never been in a prison before. The outside of the Montana Federal Penitentiary had been daunting. The interior was terrifying.

Marissa Sawyer had taken the bus from her hometown of Mustang to the prison. There had been a dozen stops along the way, the bus picking up all kinds of mothers, sisters, lovers and wives of inmates.

The man Marissa intended to visit was not her brother or father, her husband or lover. He was her past, and she hoped by coming here, by talking to him, she could keep him there.

She walked with the others through a metal detector, then stowed her purse and jewelry into a locker as they had been instructed. As she closed and locked the door, she tried to ignore the fluttering nerves that assailed her stomach.

What would he look like? How had he changed? What

physical and emotional trials had he undergone through his time in this place?

The other women stored their personal items, not speaking to each other, not making eye contact at all.

That was fine with Marissa. She wasn't here to make friends. She was here to make certain her past didn't collide with her future and destroy what she had managed to build in the last ten years.

"Okay, ladies." A uniformed guard clapped his hands for attention. "Let's form a single line right here."

He indicated where he wanted them and they fell into place. "Now, before I take you into the visiting area, I'll remind you of the rules." He spoke in the monotone of a man who'd given the spiel a thousand times before. "You will go inside and sit across from where the inmate is sitting. There is to be no physical contact, and you will keep your hands on top of the table at all times."

As he opened the door to escort them into the next room, Marissa drew a deep breath, trying to still the anxiety that made her feel half-nauseous.

The room they were led into was large, with columns of tables on each side. The inmates sat, one per table, facing the visitors. Each man was clad in a gray jumpsuit, an orange patch across his chest, identifying him as an inmate.

Marissa saw him immediately.

Johnny Crockett.

He sat at the last table on the left side, as if he purposely chose to sit alone rather than follow standard procedure.

He didn't look at her. He appeared to be disinterested in the group of visitors who had come in. Instead he stared up at the ceiling, as if bored.

As the other women made their way to loved ones,

Marissa drew a deep breath, seeking the courage that had brought her this far. She concentrated on putting one foot in front of the other, bridging the distance in long, determined strides.

He hadn't changed, she thought as she drew closer. Ten years in this hellhole hadn't stolen any of his attractiveness. His hair was longer than she remembered, but still shone with the same blue-black lustre it had when he'd been a teenager.

She stood within three feet of his table and he tilted his head down. His eyes locked with hers. Ice-blue eyes that should have appeared cold, but instead burned her with intensity.

She'd been wrong. He had changed...changes she couldn't even begin to imagine.

For a long moment neither of them spoke. And in the space of that infinite moment, a million memories raced through her mind. The memory of his arms wrapped tight around her, the way his body had felt against hers as he possessed her as no other man had before or since. The final memory of the look in his eyes as he'd been led away by the sheriff.

"What in the hell are you doing here?" he asked, his deep voice barely audible in the babble of conversation from the other tables.

"I...I need to talk to you." She cleared her throat and edged closer to the chair opposite him.

A derisive smile lifted one corner of his mouth. "After ten years, you decided you suddenly needed to talk to me?" He gestured toward the chair. "Sit down, you're making the guards nervous."

She slid into the chair and folded her hands on the tabletop, grateful that by folding them she stopped their nervous trembling. She cleared her throat once again. "I understand you're being released in three weeks."

"Three weeks, one day and fifteen hours." His voice was flat, his gaze not wavering from hers. Once again a mocking smile curved his lips. "Checking up on me? Waiting for my return? Ah, Marissa, I didn't think you cared."

She flushed, stung by his sarcasm. "My father got a letter from the warden announcing your release date and your intentions to return to Mustang."

"How is the good mayor?"

"He's fine. Johnny, please don't come back to Mustang." She blurted the words in a desperate flurry.

His eyes flared, then narrowed. "Why shouldn't I come back there? Mustang is my hometown."

"Johnny, the people in Mustang have long memories." She stared at the table, finding it easier to look there instead of into his burning, angry eyes. "Even though it's been ten years, nobody has forgotten you...or Sydney Emery."

The name hung in the air, which had suddenly become too thick, too heavy to breathe. She looked up to meet his gaze once again. Hot. Angry. His eyes bore into hers with the intensity of burning blue fire. He leaned forward, his fingers inches from touching hers. She instinctively curled her fingers into her palms.

"Do you think I've forgotten?" he said, his voice dangerously soft. "I've had ten years of lonely nights and endless days to remember." He leaned back in the chair, his hands still resting atop the table. "Let me guess. Your father sent you to try to talk me into settling someplace else. He's afraid my presence in Mustang will make his constituents uncomfortable."

"My father doesn't even know I'm here," she pro

tested. "I just know if you come back there's going to be trouble."

"You're damn right there's going to be trouble." He leaned forward again, this time his knuckles brushing against hers. "I just spent ten years in prison for a murder *I didn't commit.*"

"Johnny, please think about it," she replied, desperate to change his mind.

"I've done *nothing but* think about it. I'm coming home, Marissa, and there's nothing you or anyone else can do about it. I'm going to find the person who killed Sydney. Then I'll thank those people who always believed in me, and I'll make sure those who didn't pay."

A chill of despair swept through Marissa. "Johnny, I…"

"Guard!" he yelled and pushed away from the table. "Get out of here, Marissa. You're wasting your time and mine. I'm coming home to Mustang. I'll see you in three weeks." As one of the uniformed guards led him away, he didn't look back.

For a long moment Marissa remained seated at the table, unable to move, unable to do anything but think about what would happen in three weeks' time.

Johnny's return would reopen old wounds, renew the anger and divisiveness that had once ripped the town apart. But more frightening than any of these things, was the knowledge that when Johnny returned, Marissa's nine-year-old secret would be exposed.

In three weeks, one day and fifteen hours, all hell was going to break loose in Mustang, Montana.

Chapter 1

Three weeks later

The door to the flower shop burst open, the bell ringing discordantly as a plump blonde flew to the counter. "Guess who's back in town?"

Marissa Sawyer clipped the end off a pink rose and added it to the floral arrangement she was putting together. Leaning against the counter, she smiled at her friend, Lucy. "Let's see, it's almost three-thirty and the one and only bus that stops in Mustang must have just pulled in. I guess Johnny Crockett is back in town."

Lucy's expression of eager anticipation in sharing a secret fell away. "How did you guess?"

Marissa picked up another rose. "Bad news travels fast. I knew he was getting out today. The prison warden sent Dad a letter letting him know the day of Johnny's release."

"I can't believe he would dare come back here," Lucy exclaimed.

Marissa shrugged with feigned nonchalance. "Where else would he go? At least here he has a ranch to live on."

"Yeah, if you want to call that broken-down old shack a ranch."

"It's not Johnny's fault that the place fell to ruin while he was in prison." Marissa shoved the rose into the arrangement, trying to still the sick dread that rolled in her stomach.

Johnny was back. Here in Mustang, Montana. Hopefully he would stay out on his ranch and never venture into town. Hopefully his and Marissa's paths would never cross and he would never find out about the secret she'd kept for ten long years.

Yeah, right, a small voice said dryly…and tomorrow pigs will fly. She shoved these thoughts aside, unwilling to face her fears until necessary.

"Who's the arrangement for?" Lucy asked, touching the pink ribbon that wove through the roses and greenery.

"Elena Richards. Trent came in and ordered it for their anniversary."

Lucy pouted. "How come all the good guys in Mustang are already taken?"

Marissa laughed. "You seem to do all right. You have a date with a different guy every weekend."

Lucy tilted her head and gazed at her friend. "And you never have a date. Why is that?"

Again Marissa shrugged. "Who has time? With Benjamin and this shop, by the end of a day, I'm too tired to think about love."

"Ah, but love is in the air. Prom is just a couple of

weeks away and the Summerfest Dance will be here before we know it.''

''I know, I've already let my supplier know to stock up on roses and baby's breath for the prom, and I haven't decided yet what flowers I'm going to use for the table centerpieces.''

''Roses and baby's breath, the stuff high-school proms are made of,'' Lucy replied.

Marissa frowned, remembering her high-school prom. There were no memories of baby's breath and roses, only memories of the murder of a young girl and the arrest of the man Marissa loved.

''I'd better get back to the café. Stella told me if I was late from my break she'd make me wait on every creep that walked through the door, and this time of year we get plenty of cheap, nasty cowboys drifting through town.'' With a wave of her hand, Lucy started out the door, colliding with Marissa's nine-year-old son, Benjamin.

''Whoa, cowboy,'' Lucy said as she leaned down and kissed his cheek. ''See you guys later,'' she said, heading back to work.

''Hi, Mom.'' Benjamin walked over to the counter where she was working.

''Hi, honey.'' As always Marissa's heart swelled with pride as she gazed at her handsome son. ''How was school today?''

''Okay.'' He stowed his books beneath the counter. ''I got a B-plus on my math test.''

''Hey, that's terrific,'' Marissa replied. ''I know you were worried about that test.''

''Yeah, but it wasn't too bad.'' He leaned against the counter and watched her for a few minutes.

His dark hair was longer than Marissa liked, but she

had to admit the style emphasized the features that every day seemed to be losing childhood and galloping toward manhood. Although he had Marissa's thin face, his blue eyes and the cleft in his chin were all his father's.

"Can I go over to Billy's house? He got a new computer game."

"We'll see after your chores are done." Benjamin was saving money for a computer of his own. He and his mother had agreed that after school each day he would help her in the flower shop for an hour or two and she would pay him a reasonable hourly salary.

"The floor in the backroom needs sweeping and the sink needs to be scrubbed," Marissa said.

"Okay." With a whirl of boyish energy, he disappeared into the backroom.

A smile remained on Marissa's lips as she finished the arrangement and placed it in the refrigerated showcase. She'd just finished cleaning up her work area when the bell rang to announce another customer. She looked up with a welcoming smile that instantly fell from her face.

Johnny.

His presence filled the shop, seeming to make the interior shrink. He brought the smell of the outdoors with him, the scent of sunshine and fresh spring air coupled with the subtle evocative scent of maleness.

Odd that she would smell him when she never noticed any scent other than the greenery and floral odors that pervaded the store.

Panic clawed up her throat, clogged her pores. What was he doing here? In her shop? She was vaguely aware of the sounds of Benjamin working in the backroom…the whisper of stiff broom against the tiled floor, the clang of the metal dustpan against the trash bin.

Please stay in the back, Benjamin. She hoped…prayed her son would remain where he was until Johnny left.

"Hello, Johnny," she said, grateful that her voice didn't reveal her utter panic. "What are you doing here?"

He walked around the confines of the shop, not speaking for a moment. He wore a pair of jeans that looked new, and a short-sleeved navy T-shirt that emphasized his biceps and the broadness of his shoulders.

She remembered how those shoulders felt, how his muscles moved and bunched beneath his sun-bronzed skin. Heat swept through her, heat ignited by unwanted memories. How was it possible that her body could remember so vividly what her mind wanted to forget?

Anxiety once again reared up inside her as he walked around, touching vases, smelling flowers, acting as if he had all the time in the world.

Maybe every man who got out of prison acted as if he had all the time in the world, but Marissa didn't want this man in her shop. Benjamin might come out of the backroom at any moment and Marissa wasn't ready to face the consequences of opening that particular Pandora's box.

"Flowers By Marissa. So you actually achieved your dream of owning a flower shop." He finally spoke, his voice low and deep. "What happened to old Mrs. Grady?" he asked, referring to the previous owner of the flower shop.

"She passed away four years ago. I bought the store from her son." Marissa heard the sound of water running in the sink in the backroom. She knew Benjamin would be cleaning the sink, and when he finished he'd come out. "What can I do for you, Johnny?" she asked, desperate to get him out of the shop.

"I want a wreath."

"A wreath?"

His eyes flickered darkly. "For my mother's grave."

Of course. His mother had died four months ago. He'd been in prison and hadn't had a chance to grieve for her, to say any kind of a goodbye. She nodded. "What kind of flowers would you like?"

"It doesn't matter. Whatever you have in stock."

"If you'd like to leave and come back in about a half an hour, I'll have it ready for you then." Marissa forced a smile and stepped out from the counter, eager to walk him to the door.

"I'll wait. I've got nothing better to do."

"Hey, Mom, I'm all done. Can I go to Billy's now?" Benjamin asked as he walked out of the backroom. He smiled a polite hello to Johnny.

"That's fine, Benjy," Marissa said, resignation taking the place of anxiety. She studiously kept her gaze away from Johnny and instead focused solely on her son. "Be home by six and don't go anyplace else."

As Benjamin flew out the door, Marissa turned to look at Johnny. He stood unmoving...as still as a statue. And in the stillness Marissa sensed the storm to come.

He knew.

It had taken only a single look at Benjamin's face, and he knew that the dark-haired, blue-eyed boy was his son.

"Johnny..." she began, unsure exactly what she intended to say.

He held up a hand, as if to warn her to be quiet. And for the space of an endless eternity, he said nothing. He drew in a deep breath and expelled it.

Once. Twice. As if in marshalling his breathing rhythm he was getting control of his anger.

And he was angry. She could see it in the flames of

his eyes, feel it radiating out from him with the force of a giant palm pressing harshly against her chest.

"He's mine." He said the words with challenge, as if expecting her to deny it.

She hesitated and averted her gaze from him. She didn't want to answer, wished she could lie. She wished she could give him a logical reason that Benjamin was his spitting image, a reason that had nothing to do with paternity.

"Tell me," Johnny thundered.

Marissa looked at him once again, then nodded, knowing there was no point in any kind of denial. "Yes." The secret she had guarded from everyone in Mustang, even from her own family, was now in his hands.

He turned away from her and stared out the front window. His back was stiff. His shoulders appeared to grow broader, muscles more pronounced as moments of silence stretched endlessly. "Damn you." He whirled around to face her once again.

She flinched beneath the venom of his curse, but didn't avert her gaze from his. She wasn't ashamed of her choices, she'd made them with the instincts of a mother bear. She'd done what she needed to do in order to assure Benjamin a childhood without scorn, without ridicule.

"How could you keep this from me? My God, how could you not tell me about him through all these years?" He raked a hand through his hair, obviously stunned. Again he drew in a series of deep breaths, releasing them with studied control. "What does he know about me?"

"Nothing."

One of Johnny's dark eyebrows raised in disbelief. "Nothing? Mustang's always been a town where everyone knows everyone else's business. Surely things haven't changed around here that much. Somebody had to have told him something about me."

Marissa shook her head. "Nobody knows that you're Benjamin's father."

"What did you do? Tell everyone it was an immaculate conception?"

She flushed beneath his derisive tone. "Everyone believes Benjamin is Brian Theron's son, and I've never contradicted that belief."

Brian was the young man she'd been dating just before she started seeing Johnny. Brian and his family had moved from Mustang before Benjamin's birth and the rumor had circulated that he'd run away from his paternal responsibilities.

"All Benjamin knows is that his father went away and never came back," she added.

"That's about to change. You have to tell him the truth." Again challenge lit his eyes, a challenge Marissa met.

"Johnny, you can't just show up here and start making demands," she said, pleading with him.

He stared at her in disbelief. "You can't honestly expect me to just leave things as they are," he said. "I'm home now, and I want to be a father to my son." He clenched and unclenched his hands at his sides. "How could you keep this from me for all these years?" he repeated.

"I did what I thought I had to do," she answered softly.

"Well, now you can undo it. Tell him the truth about me. He should hear it from you, but if you don't tell him, I will."

Marissa's heart beat frantically. "Okay…I'll tell him, but give me a little time…a few days."

His eyes glittered darkly. "You've had plenty of time. Ten years to be exact. I've lost ten years that you've had with him. I don't intend to lose another day of Benjamin's life."

He walked to the front door of the shop, then turned back to her once again. "I'll be back later for the wreath, and tonight I'll drop by your place to get acquainted with my son." With these final words, he slammed the door of the shop behind him.

Marissa opened her mouth, wanting to protest.

Things were spinning too fast, flying out of control. But her protests refused to be voiced. She knew there was little she could do to halt the changes that were about to occur in her life.

She leaned against the counter and closed her eyes, wondering how on earth she would tell Benjy that the man who was his father had just returned home after spending ten years in prison for murder.

On the first day of Johnny's incarceration, he'd been attacked by four fellow inmates who intended to show him the social structure of prison life.

As a young, new inmate, Johnny knew the attack was a test that would determine how he lived the rest of his time. He'd suffered a broken rib and nose, and bruises and contusions. The four men had also gone to the hospital with a variety of injuries that marked Johnny as a man to avoid.

The beating he'd taken that day had hurt like hell, but it didn't even come close to the utter gut-wrenching he'd felt the moment he'd seen Benjamin. Marissa's son.

His son.

He got behind the wheel of his pickup and slammed the door, anger still burning and twisting inside him.

Marissa had lied to everyone. No wonder she'd shown up at the prison three weeks earlier to talk him out of returning here. She'd been guarding her secrets.

Marissa hadn't wanted anyone to know that the boy was his. She was ashamed. Ashamed of him. Ashamed of the love they had once shared.

She'd never really believed in his innocence, she'd never really believed in him.

Damn her. Perhaps the knowledge of his son's existence might have made the ten years he'd served different...better. At least he would have had something to keep him going, something to look forward to when he got out of prison.

Marissa had betrayed him by believing he'd committed the crime, by refusing to stand beside him, and turning her back on him when hours before his arrest she had professed undying love for him.

Marissa.

When she'd shown up at the prison, he'd been shocked by how little time had changed her. She was still tall and slender and carried herself with the stride of self-confidence. Her eyes were the same color of rich caramels, her hair a frothy fall of variegated blond strands. She still looked like a golden girl, the mayor's daughter, unattainable to the likes of Johnny. And yet, she'd been his girl for a little while...before life decided to kick the hell out of him.

During the first few months in prison, Marissa had haunted him with memories of the silken softness of her skin, the sweet honey of her mouth, her whispered sighs of passion that warmed his neck as he possessed her.

The moment he'd seen her again, that old desire had flared hot and needy. He hated her for making him remember. He hated her for making him want her once again.

But, more than anything, he hated her for the lies and deceptions that had kept his son a secret.

He slammed the truck into gear and pulled away from the curb. Maybe he was a fool. After all, what did he have to offer a son? A ten-year-old pickup, a ranch that had fallen apart, and a father who'd lost his ability to dream.

Maybe the best thing he could do for Benjamin was stay out of his life. The boy had survived just fine without him so far. Maybe having no father at all was better than having a father who was an ex-con…a man who was believed to have killed a seventeen-year-old young woman, the daughter of one of the most prominent families in town.

"No." The protest bubbled out of him and he slammed the palm of his hand against the steering wheel. No, he could be a good addition to Benjamin's life. Johnny knew all about the void having no father could leave in a boy's life.

The pickup, despite being ten years old, was like new, and with hard work and sweat the ranch could become a prosperous home. He'd gone to jail for a crime he hadn't committed and he would teach his son that sometimes injustice prevailed.

And what did it matter that he had no dreams for himself? From this day forward his dreams would be for his son.

Chapter 2

Johnny couldn't remember the last time he'd been so nervous. He pulled his truck against the curb in front of the attractive white two-story house. Three-twenty-two Oak. Marissa's home.

He turned off the engine but remained in the car, summoning the courage to go inside and talk to his nine-year-old son.

He'd faced many killers and crazies in prison and still, his stomach hadn't clenched like it did now; his nerves hadn't felt frayed and ragged as they did at this moment.

What if Benjamin hated him? What if he and his son never managed to bridge the gap of Johnny's absence in the important growing years of his son's life? How deep the heartache if Benjamin wouldn't allow his father to love him, if he didn't love Johnny?

Johnny stared at the house. It was attractive, with spring flowers bordering the sidewalk. Brick planters of

flowers sat on each side of the porch, as if welcoming
visitors with colorful bouquets.

From all the houses on the block, he would have been
able to pick this one as Marissa's. She'd always loved
flowers. He found it oddly comforting that at least that
one thing hadn't changed.

He thought of all he'd missed already in Benjamin's
life. His first step, his first tooth, the first time he said a
word. He'd missed his first day of school, and a hundred
other firsts. So many special moments that would never
be repeated.

He opened his truck door and stepped out, suddenly
eager not to waste another moment, afraid of missing
another minute of his son's life.

Marissa answered his knock, opening the door but not
smiling a welcome. A worried frown etched across the
center of her forehead, and Johnny felt an instantaneous
desire to reach out and smooth it away. And that desire
summoned anew the anger he'd fought all day to control.

"Come in," she said with all the warmth of a woman
inviting in a dreadful disease.

He stepped into the living room and looked around
curiously. After his years of gray existence in a jail cell,
he had become more aware of colors and details, soaking
them in like an arid sponge.

The room radiated with her personality. A floral pattern sofa filled the room with bursts of color. The rich
burgundy tones were deepened by accent pillows and
matching draperies. Greenery was everywhere, trailing
vines on shelves and potted plants by the windows, giving the appearance of a living room in the middle of a
flower garden.

It was also obvious that in this garden was a child. A
baseball mitt sat on the top of the television, ready for

Benjamin to grab whenever he headed out the door. A pair of small athletic shoes, socks stuffed inside, rested by the end of the sofa, and an array of baseball cards was fanned out on top of the coffee table.

"You didn't come back this afternoon for the wreath," Marissa said, taking his attention away from the room. "If you still want it, I brought it home from the shop this evening. You can take it with you when you go."

Johnny nodded absently. "Where is he?"

"I sent him next door for a little while. His friend Billy lives there and they were going to work on homework together. I'll call him home in just a minute." She motioned him toward the sofa.

"Did you tell him? About me?" Johnny eased down on the couch, surprised to find it not only attractive, but comfortable as well.

She nodded and perched on the edge of the nearby chair. Again the wrinkle was back, deepening as she frowned. "I told him."

"And?" Johnny sat forward, trying not to notice how great she looked in the deep blue blouse and tight-fitting jeans.

"And he's confused, and happy and upset and a hundred different emotions all at once," she said. "He doesn't understand why, if you were innocent, you went to prison."

"Yeah, that's confused me, too," he said dryly.

Marissa sighed and settled deeper into the high-back chair, looking smaller and tired, and achingly vulnerable.

"And he doesn't understand why I didn't tell him about you a long time ago."

He nodded, a knot of anger expanding into a ball in his stomach. "That question crossed my mind as well."

"Johnny, I didn't keep this secret to hurt you." She

paused a moment to draw a deep breath, then continued. "I did it to protect Benjamin. As his father, for the last ten years what could you have offered him? Weekend visits in that hellhole? Is that what you would have wanted for your son?"

She leaned forward, her eyes ablaze with the conviction of the rightness of her choices. "You know the people in this town, Johnny. You know how judgmental and small-minded they can be at times. I could live with the stigma of being single and pregnant, but I didn't want him to live with the stigma of a convicted killer for a father. Whether you were innocent or not, the jury found you guilty, and people don't forget that. You of all people know how cruel kids can be."

Although logically, Johnny knew she was right, emotionally it hurt like hell. And beyond the fact that she'd kept Benjamin's paternity a secret was the fact that she'd so effectively turned her back on him.

Had it been because of her pregnancy or simply because her professed love had been nothing but a shallow, empty emotion?

Maybe he'd simply been some sort of teenage rebellion for her? The poor cowboy least likely to date the mayor's gorgeous daughter. Maybe she'd been trying to prove something to herself, to her parents. It didn't matter. None of it did.

"There's no going back in time to make things different," he said. "We're stuck with the way things are here and now. I can't stop people from talking about me, but I can help Benjamin deal with it. I'm not going away, Marissa. I'm going to be here for a long time, and I intend to be a real father to that boy."

With a weary nod, Marissa stood. "I'll call him home." She picked up the phone on the end table and punched a speed-dial number. "Hi, Alice, it's me. Can you tell Benjy to come home? Thanks." She hung up the phone and turned to Johnny. "Please don't hurt him."

Her words once again stirred his anger. What did she think he intended to do? Before he could reply, the front door burst open and Benjamin ran in. He stopped short at the sight of Johnny, his expression instantly wary.

"Hi, Benjamin," Johnny said, as he drank in the boy's features. So like his own. The dark hair, the blue eyes… the cleft in his chin. A swell of deep, rich love welled up inside Johnny…love as he'd never known it before.

"Hi," Benjamin replied and sat in the chair Marissa had vacated moments earlier.

"You know who I am?"

Benjamin nodded, and looked at his mother for reassurance. "You're Johnny Crockett, and Mom says you're my father."

"That's right," Johnny replied. "How do you feel about that?"

Benjamin shrugged and averted his gaze from Johnny's once again. "I don't know."

It was a good answer. An honest one. It would take time for a connection to grow, time before the boy trusted Johnny. Johnny respected that. He knew he would have to prove himself to Benjamin. Saying he was a father and truly being one were two different things.

"I see you like baseball," Johnny said, pointing to the sports cards scattered on the coffee table. "You play on a team?"

"Yeah. The Mustang Mavericks." Benjamin's eyes lit up and he leaned forward. "I'm the pitcher. Coach says I've got a real good arm."

"How about I get us all something to drink?" Marissa asked. "Iced tea?"

Both Johnny and Benjamin nodded, and Marissa left the room. For a moment an awkward silence grew between father and son.

"You were in prison." Benjamin looked at Johnny curiously. "Mom said it was 'cause a girl got killed."

Johnny nodded, oddly satisfied that Marissa hadn't told Benjamin that he'd killed a girl, but only that a girl got killed. Did that mean she believed his innocence?

He sighed and looked at Benjamin, knowing the conversation he was about to have would decide if Benjamin trusted him or not, liked him or not. "That's right. Her name was Sydney Emery and somebody killed her."

"How come they thought it was you?"

How many times had Johnny asked himself that same question? He thought about it a long moment before answering. "Sydney and I were good friends, but her family didn't like me, so we were secret friends. We'd meet in an old shed between her house and my house. One night she had called me to meet her later that night, and when I got there she was dead."

Johnny shoved away the memories of finding Sydney with the mottled ring of bruises around her neck, her eyes opened and forever staring in terror. He'd barely had time to take it all in before the sheriff had arrived. "Because we'd met so many times prior to that night, my fingerprints were all over the shed. The sheriff figured the two of us had a fight, and I killed her."

"But it was somebody else, right?" There was a quiet intensity in Benjamin's voice.

"Right."

Benjamin held Johnny's gaze with the candor of an adult. His nod was barely perceptible, but it spoke volumes to Johnny. It was a nod of acceptance, a gesture of belief.

"Did you love that Sydney girl?"

"Yes, I did. I loved her like she was my sister."

"Did you love my mom?"

Just as Benjamin asked the question, Marissa appeared in the doorway, carrying a tray of drinks and cookies. She froze and looked at Johnny, obviously having overheard her son.

Johnny hesitated a moment. "Yes. I loved your mother," he said softly and saw the flush of color that swept over Marissa's face. "But that was a long time ago."

"And now things are different," Benjamin said in a grownup voice.

"Yes. Now things are different," Johnny agreed.

"Here we go…iced tea for everyone," Marissa said as she walked over and set the tray on the coffee table.

Benjamin leaned forward and grabbed a cookie, then looked first at Johnny, than at his mother. "So, you guys don't love each other anymore, right?"

She never loved me, Johnny wanted to say. *She lied all the times she told me she did. She didn't stand by her man, she ran and lied and was ashamed to admit there was ever anything between us.*

"You know how Sammy Walters's parents are divorced? They don't live together, but they both love Sammy very much," Marissa explained. "It's kind of like that."

Benjamin thought for a moment, then nodded. "Okay, so does this mean on the weekends you'll play ball with me and stuff?" he asked Johnny.

Divorced parents. Weekend fathers. Shared custody. That was a reality in Benjamin's generation.

"Yes, I'll play catch and stuff with you whenever you want me to…not just on the weekends, but any day, any time of the week," Johnny answered. He didn't intend to be a weekend father. He was going to be an everyday father.

"Any time?" Benjamin repeated, with a shy smile. "You'd play catch with me right now?"

Johnny didn't hesitate. "Right now…if it's all right with your mom."

"Ah, she won't care. She tries to play catch with me, but she throws like a girl!" Benjamin exclaimed as he jumped off the chair. "We'll share the glove, okay?"

"Okay," Johnny said, warmth suffusing him. He knew the importance of a baseball glove, and Benjamin's generous offer to share his with him touched him.

He looked at Marissa, wanting her to know it appeared she'd done a fine job raising Benjamin. He appeared to be a well-mannered, well-adjusted young man.

She nodded, as if she'd read his mind. "Go on, then…before it gets too late," she said as she shooed them out the front door.

As Johnny stepped outside into the cool, evening twilight, Benjamin held his glove out to him.

A shy smile once again curved the boy's mouth. "You can use the glove first…Dad." Although the word fell rather awkwardly from Benjamin's mouth, Johnny's heart soared at the sound of it.

Dad.

For the first time in ten years, Johnny smiled, a smile that not only curved his lips, but warmed his heart as well.

Marissa stood at the window and watched the two males, bonding in the most traditional way men bonded, through sports. The late evening sun cast the front yard in hues of gold, painting father and son with the same warm tones.

The thing she'd most feared for the past ten years had just happened, and she knew it was much too soon to determine what changes would now occur in her life. One thing was certain, there would be changes and not all of them would be pleasant.

But, it was difficult to think about unpleasantness as she saw the utter joy on her son's face as he tossed the ball back and forth with Johnny.

Benjamin had been starving for male companionship. Although Marissa's own father, Jeffrey, tried to do what he could with the boy, between his duties as mayor and running the hardware store he owned, very little time was left for a needy grandson.

Marissa frowned, realizing she was going to have to talk to her parents. She was going to have to tell them that Johnny was Benjamin's father before they heard it through town gossip.

She knew her parents wouldn't be pleased with the news, but she felt confident they would support her and Benjamin no matter what. Their support had been one of the few things Marissa had been able to count on through the last ten years.

She watched Johnny as he caught a series of Benjy's super-duper pitches. The tension that had lined his face was gone and without that tautness he looked just like he had during the month they had shared years ago.

The jeans he wore were worn, and fit him like they'd been tailor-made to hug his firm thighs, ride his slender hips and mold perfectly to his tight buttocks. His T-shirt exposed biceps that bulged, and strong, tanned forearms.

The clothes must have been at his house, part of his

past. Since he'd been away, he hadn't changed much physically, so his clothes from years ago would still fit…except perhaps his shirts would be snug around his arm muscles…muscles that looked far more formidable than she remembered from the past.

She turned away from the window, uncomfortable with the heat that surged through her as she watched Johnny. She picked up the glasses from the coffee table and carried them into the kitchen.

Johnny had told Benjamin he'd loved her once, but she knew they had been words spoken to soothe a little boy, words that had little to do with truth.

Johnny had never loved her. He'd wanted her. She couldn't deny his passion, his desire for her. But, even though she'd once believed differently, love had never entered into it.

If he'd loved her, he would have told her about Sydney. If he'd loved her, he wouldn't have been leaving her arms to meet Sydney in the shed where she was ultimately murdered.

She shook her head and focused on rinsing the glasses and placing them in the dishwasher. It doesn't matter anymore, she told herself firmly.

Her love for Johnny had died the day a jury convicted him for Sydney's murder.

She wandered back into the living room, her gaze seeking the dainty bud vase that sat on one of the shelves in the built-in bookcases. The vase held a single flower, a dried pink bitterroot. Johnny had given it to her the night they'd first made love.

She wasn't sure why she'd kept it all these years. Perhaps as a marker defining the leap from girlhood to womanhood. Maybe she'd kept it to remind herself of the unreliability of love professed in the middle of lovemaking.

Sighing heavily, she moved back to the window. She didn't believe Johnny had murdered Sydney: if she did there was no way she'd allow him to have anything to do with Benjamin. No, she knew he wasn't guilty of murder, but as far as she was concerned he was guilty of deceit, guilty of breaking her heart, and ten years in prison hadn't absolved him of that particular crime.

Johnny and Benjamin played catch until the sun dipped below the horizon and darkness crept across the sky. It was Marissa who called them in, reminding Benjamin that it was a school night and he needed to take a bath and get ready for bed.

"Can Dad tuck me in?" Benjamin asked.

"Benjy, maybe Johnny has other things—"

"No, I'd like to stick around and tuck him in," Johnny replied. The tension was back on his face, as if whatever peace he'd found playing ball with Benjy had shattered the moment he'd walked back into the front door and faced her once again.

Marissa nodded and turned to her son. "Bath time."

"Okay," Benjamin agreed. He smiled at Johnny. "I'll be back down in just a minute."

"Not a minute," Marissa protested. "I want a full scrubbing and that takes longer than a minute."

"Then two minutes." Benjamin giggled as he raced up the stairs, leaving Marissa and Johnny alone in the living room.

"He's a good kid," Johnny said. "You've done a fine job of raising him." He sank down on the sofa. "I know things are going to get tough as the news gets out that I'm home and taking an active role in Benjamin's life. I know my presence here in Mustang is not only going to make things more difficult on Benjamin, but on you as well.''

''We'll deal with it,'' Marissa said tightly.

''And I have a feeling things are going to get much more difficult as I start turning over stones looking for the person who killed Sydney.''

''Oh Johnny, why don't you just let it go? Get on with your life? The sheriff couldn't find the real killer ten years ago, what makes you think you can solve it now?''

''Let it go?'' He stared at her incredulously. ''I spent ten years behind bars for a murder I didn't commit and you just want me to get on with my life as though nothing happened?''

He rose from the chair, eyes flaming with the anger that she'd realized had become so much a part of him. ''For ten years all I've thought about was getting back here to find out what really happened that night.''

''Johnny, nothing—and nobody—can ever give you back the time you've lost,'' she said.

He stepped around the coffee table and moved directly in front of her. He stood so close she could feel his body heat, feel his breath fanning her face with evocative warmth. His eyes were dark, as if reflecting the darkness that now resided within him. ''It wasn't just time I lost, Marissa,'' he said softly.

She wanted to move away, needed some distance from him. His nearness made it difficult for her to breathe, yet she couldn't move away…felt hypnotized by the intensity of his gaze.

''It took me nearly half an hour to get dressed to come over here tonight. You know why? Because I couldn't decide what to wear. For the last ten years I haven't had to make a decision about anything. I was told what time to get up, what to wear, what to eat and when to sleep.

Personal choice is only part of what I lost for the last ten years.''

"Johnny, I..." She started to take a step backward, but he stopped her by grabbing her forearm. Her response was instantaneous. Sparks of heat flowed from her arm and spread throughout her body.

"You know what was worse than the loss of all freedom?" Johnny asked softly, his voice a warm caress on her neck. He released her arm and instead touched her cheek gently with the pad of his index finger. "The loss of touching another person, of having somebody touching me. That was the worst of all. Ten years of no touching, no kisses, no making love. You can't imagine what that's like."

"Yes, I can," Marissa replied breathlessly. "I know exactly what it's like."

He stepped back in obvious surprise, his hand falling away from her face. "You don't honestly expect me to believe that in all this time, you haven't been with anyone."

"What's so hard to believe about that?" For some reason, the disbelief in his voice stirred anger inside Marissa, as did her shocking response to his touch. "I know I can't relate to your years in prison, but the last ten years of my life haven't been particularly easy. Raising a child alone takes time and energy, so does running a business. Benjamin and the flower shop have been my priorities, and there's been little time for anything else."

"Hey, Dad, I'm ready to be tucked in." Benjamin's voice preceded him down the stairs. Clad in an oversized T-shirt and a pair of striped pajama bottoms, Benjamin said a quick good-night to his mom, then he and Johnny disappeared up the stairs.

While they were gone, Marissa paced the living room

floor, trying to forget the fact that her cheek still burned with the fever of Johnny's touch. He'd always managed to stir her with a simple touch, a certain smile, by his mere nearness.

She'd been eighteen when they started seeing each other, and it hadn't taken long for him to awaken a passion in her she'd never felt before…or since…until now.

She hadn't been able to tell Johnny that one of the reasons there had been nobody else in her life was because he had been such a powerful, all-consuming lover. And when he was sentenced to prison, it had taken years for her heart to stop aching at the mention of his name or the fleeting memory that crossed her mind.

"He's all tucked in," Johnny said as he came back down the stairs. "Although he told me that he's outgrown good-night kisses."

She forced a smile, still tense from her thoughts. "That happened about a month ago. All of a sudden he decided good-night kisses are for babies."

Johnny moved to the window and gazed out into the darkness of the night. "I still can't believe I have a son." His voice was thick with emotion and when he turned to look at her, his eyes were glazed with a hint of moisture. "I'm going to be a good father, Marissa. I swear it."

"I know that, Johnny," she replied. "But things are going to be difficult, and you're just going to make things worse by digging up Sydney's murder."

"Right now the only thing I have to give to my son is my word that I didn't kill Sydney Emery. That's not good enough. I have to find the real killer, absolve myself not only with Benjamin, but with everyone here in Mustang."

"Johnny, it's been so long…how would you even begin to investigate the murder after all this time? How in the world do you expect to find the real murderer—especially if he or she has left town?''

''I don't know how this will shake down. All I do know is the first thing I'm going to do is get copies of all the reports, the medical and physical evidence. Everything that was used to convict me can also be used to bring me closer to the real killer.''

''The Emerys aren't going to like you reopening this case,'' she said.

Johnny laughed, a bitter, harsh sound. ''What are they going to do to me? Put me in jail? Ruin my ranch? They can't do anything to me that hasn't already been done.'' He sighed wearily and raked a hand through his hair. ''I guess I'd better get home.''

''I'll get the wreath for you.'' Marissa hurried to the mudroom, where a spare refrigerator held various cut flowers. On the second shelf was the wreath she had prepared for Johnny, a stunning effusion of white carnations. She returned to the living room where she handed it to him.

Together they walked to the door and stepped out on the front porch. ''I told Benjamin maybe he could come out to the ranch and spend some time with me on Saturday, if it's all right with you?''

She nodded. ''I could bring him out on my way to work Saturday morning, then pick him up around lunchtime.''

''Whatever works best for you,'' he agreed.

Once again Marissa realized he stood too close to her, invading her personal space with his heat, his overwhelming masculinity. ''Ten years is a long time for a man to go without a woman or a woman to go without a man.'' His voice was low and husky and created a swirl of heat in Marissa's stomach.

His lips were so close to hers, achingly close, and she fought the desire to lean her head forward, press her mouth against his.

"It's still there, isn't it, Marissa?" he said softly.

"What?" she asked, knowing exactly what he was talking about.

He touched her cheek, trailing a river of heat in the wake of his caressing fingers. The scent of the carnations was overpowering, adding to the sensual nature of the moment.

"Passion. Desire. Physical want," he whispered, his lips still achingly close to hers. "Despite the time that has passed, despite all that has happened, it's still there simmering between us."

"It doesn't matter if it is or not." With enormous effort, she stepped back from him, her voice shaky with suppressed emotion. "There's no going back, Johnny. At least not for us."

"Not even once…for old time's sake?" His eyes glittered darkly in the glow from her porch light. His gaze beckoned…promised. "We were good together, Marissa." He touched her cheek gently, rolled a finger across her bottom lip. "It doesn't have to mean anything, Marissa. It didn't before."

Her breath caught at his words. "I never make the same mistake twice," she finally said. She backed away, putting the screen door between herself and him. "Good night, Johnny."

He nodded, turned and walked to his truck without a backward glance. Marissa slipped into the house, closed the front door and leaned heavily against it, surprised that after all this time, her heart was still capable of being hurt by Johnny.

Chapter 3

It had become customary for Marissa's mother to pick up Benjamin from school on Friday and take him home with her.

At seven in the evening, Marissa closed the flower shop and her father closed his hardware store and Marissa drove her father home to the family ranch and picked up Benjamin. Most evenings they all ate dinner together before Marissa and Benjamin headed back to their house in town.

For most of the afternoon, Marissa had prayed that Benjamin would heed her wishes and not mention his father to her parents. She'd explained to him that it was important that her parents hear the news directly from her.

By the time she reached her parents house, she instantly knew Benjamin hadn't said anything. Dinner was pleasant, with small talk and harmless town gossip accompanying the roast and potatoes.

After the pleasant meal, Benjamin went outside to play, and Marissa remained at the table with her parents, knowing she had to tell them the secret that she'd shared with only one other person.

Eugenia Sawyer poured her daughter another cup of coffee, then returned to her chair next to Marissa. "It's obvious there's something on your mind, dear," she said as she exchanged a glance with her husband.

Marissa looked at her mom and dad and smiled. "You two know me too well." Her smile faded and she took a sip of her coffee, unsure where to begin to unravel her lies of omission, lies that had begun ten years before. "We've never really talked about Benjamin's father," she finally said. "I know you both believe Brian Theron is his father, but he's not."

Jeffrey Sawyer frowned at his daughter. "What do you mean, he's not? You were dating Brian...who else could it be?"

"Brian and I were never intimate, and after we broke up, I started seeing somebody else," Marissa explained.

"Who? I don't remember you dating anyone else," Jeffrey said.

Marissa drew a deep breath, knowing the shock waves her confession would generate. "Johnny. Johnny Crockett," she said softly. Jeffrey's eyes widened and he fell back in his chair in stunned silence.

"We met the night of the Spring Festival and spent hours in his truck, talking and getting to know each other. Then we saw each other every night for the next month... until the morning he was arrested for Sydney Emery's murder."

Jeffrey still appeared shocked, but Eugenia nodded, seemingly unsurprised by Marissa's confession. "I knew there was somebody and I knew it wasn't Brian," she said as she reached across the table to take Marissa's hand in hers. "I suspected it might be Johnny. Millie Creighton called me one evening to tell me she thought she'd seen you with Johnny down by Miller's Pond."

"Then why in the hell didn't you tell me?" Jeffrey sputtered, looking first at his wife, then at Marissa. "Johnny Crockett—" he shook his head "—dear God. Does Benjamin know?"

Marissa nodded. "I told him yesterday, and last night Johnny came by to see him."

"Is Benjamin okay with this?" Eugenia asked.

"Yes. He's probably doing better than anyone else right now," Marissa said.

Jeff stood and paced the floor next to the table. "Johnny Crockett," he repeated the name with a shake of his head. He stopped his pacing and eyed Marissa with indignation. "Well, it's obvious the man took advantage of you ten years ago. You were nothing but a kid."

"Johnny is only a year older than me. He was just a kid, too, Dad."

"He was man enough to be romancing two women and get himself convicted of killing one of them!" Jeffrey exclaimed, the words sending an arrow of pain through Marissa's heart.

"Jeffrey, that's enough," Eugenia said and squeezed Marissa's hand.

"That's not enough," Marissa's father sputtered. "My God, the man is a convicted felon. He was not only having sex with Marissa, but he was arrested for murder and spent ten years in prison. There are folks in this town who never did like Johnny, people who believe he killed that girl and wish he'd never come back here."

"You're talking about the Emerys," Marissa said. "I

can't blame them for hating Johnny. They truly believe he killed Sydney, but he didn't.''

"You know he's innocent for a fact?" Jeffrey asked.

"No, but I know it in my heart," Marissa stated emphatically.

"It doesn't much matter what you know or feel. As far as the Emerys are concerned, Johnny Crockett is the devil incarnate and they're going to use their money and influence for a major exorcism.''

"They can't hurt him any more than he's already been hurt," Marissa replied.

"Don't be too sure," her father countered. "The Emerys wield a lot of power in Mustang, and Rachel Emery isn't a woman to cross.''

"Johnny served time for the crime he was convicted of. There's nothing the Emerys can do to make him leave here," Marissa said.

Again Eugenia squeezed Marissa's hand. "Your father and I don't want to see you or Benjy in the middle of a feud with the Emerys.''

"That's right," Jeffrey agreed. "I have a feeling things are going to get ugly around here. The only reason why there hasn't been any problems so far is because Brad Emery is out of town.''

"Surely Jesse will make certain there are no real problems," Marissa said, indicating the present sheriff of Mustang.

"The problems the Emerys can make might be bigger than what the sheriff can handle," Jeffrey said. He studied Marissa for a long moment. "You know we'll help you fight if you want to have Johnny's parental rights taken away. It might be the best thing for Benjamin.''

Marissa shook her head, knowing her father meant well, but not in the least interested in that particular solution. "What good will that do? Then Benjamin can grow up blaming me because he doesn't have a relationship with his father." She shook her head again. "No, that isn't the answer. I won't keep Johnny out of Benjamin's life."

Eugenia's eyes were knowing as she gazed at Marissa. "I know how difficult it must be for you to see Johnny again."

"I think I'll go outside and find my grandson," Jeffrey said, apparently assuming the two might need some time alone for woman talk. He left through the back door, leaving Marissa and her mother alone.

"He broke your heart, didn't he?" Eugenia asked softly.

Marissa nodded and forced a small laugh. "I thought he loved me." She sighed, remembering the first night she'd met Johnny. "He started out as my hero."

Eugenia looked at her daughter curiously. "How so?"

Marissa leaned back in her chair, allowing her memory to take flight, carry her back to that time so long ago. "It was the night of the Spring Festival Dance. You probably remember, I went with Brian to the dance. We'd been bickering on and off for weeks. Brian had rented a motel room for the night of the dance, and I wasn't interested in what he had in mind." A blush warmed her cheeks.

"I never did like Brian," Eugenia admitted. "The fact that he was the best quarterback in the county and was a relatively handsome young man didn't impress me. And although he had good manners, I had the feeling it was just slick polish hiding a mean spirit."

Marissa smiled, surprised at her mother's astuteness. "Brian wasn't really mean until he drank. And the night of the dance, he'd been drinking most of the evening."

Marissa's smile faded as she remembered Brian becoming more surly and demanding as the night progressed.

"Around eleven, Brian decided it was time for us to go to the motel. I told him I didn't want to, that he could just take me home." She paused a moment to sip her coffee. "Brian had decided it was time for us to become intimate. He insisted that I was the only girl he knew who refused to go all the way. I stormed outside and he followed me. He backed me up against the building and was bullying and belittling me."

She frowned, remembering Brian's hot, boozy breath in her face, his hands pawing at her. He'd been like a man possessed, his single goal to force her to bend to his will.

"Johnny stepped out of the shadows." She smiled. "So tall and strong. He was like an avenging angel come to save me." For a moment she allowed herself to fully fall back into the memory of that night.

"Brian, stop!" she exclaimed, trying to push him away. His legs were splayed and his hips pinned hers against the rough wood of the community building.

In all the months she'd been dating Brian, he'd never really frightened her. But he scared her now. His eyes gleamed with a wildness she'd never seen before and his attempt at seduction was not only clumsy, but simmered with suppressed brutality. His hands clenched her upper arms painfully tight as he kissed her neck, his boozy breath making her half-nauseous. "Brian, please stop!"

"Brian, please stop," he mimicked, his lips a snarl of unpleasantness. "That's what you always say. Stop. No. Don't do that. I swear, Marissa, you're the last virgin left in Mustang. Come to the motel with me, baby."

"I told you I just want you to take me home," she said, tears springing to her eyes as he tightened his hold on

her arms. She should have never come out here with him. She'd known he was drunk. She should have protested when he led her to the back of the building. "You're hurting me," she said.

"Don't you know you hurt me every time you tell me no?" Brian released her arm and instead grabbed her breast, his fingers squeezing. "You're a tease, Marissa. You promise, but never deliver. It's time now for you to pay the piper." His hips ground into hers.

"Let her go, Theron," the deep voice thundered and both Brian and Marissa sought the source.

He stood nearby, his face half-hidden by shadows cast from the cowboy hat he wore. He wasn't dressed for the dance. Instead of formal wear, he wore worn, tight jeans and a T-shirt that displayed his athletic build.

"Go away, Crockett. This isn't any of your business," Brian snarled.

Johnny Crockett. Marissa knew he was a year older than her. She'd seen him around town but had never spoken to him. She had always found him sinfully handsome but they ran in different social circles so their paths rarely crossed. She knew little about him other than he was poor and at the area rodeos he was a bull rider starting to make a name for himself.

"I'm making it my business," Johnny said, his voice calm and controlled. "I've only been standing here a few minutes but I believe in that time the lady told you no several times."

Brian released Marissa and turned to face Johnny.

"You want to make it your business? I'll whip the hell out of you." Brian took a step forward, threw a wild punch and fell to the ground in an alcohol stupor.

Johnny stepped over him to reach Marissa. "Are you all right?" he asked.

*Marissa nodded and to her horror, tears sprang to her
eyes. Now that the threat was gone, she realized she'd
been terrified. Her tears came fast and furious, uncontrollable in their release.*

*"Hey, you're okay," Johnny said softly and brushed
the tears gently from her cheeks.*

Looking back, Marissa thought perhaps that was the
moment she'd fallen in love with Johnny Crockett. She
shook her head, pulling herself back from the past and
to the present. "Johnny offered to drive me home. We
left Brian lying on the ground, snoring in an alcoholic
stupor. When we got in Johnny's truck, I realized I
wasn't ready to come home yet. We ended up driving
around for the next three hours, just talking and getting
to know each other. Johnny and I saw each other every
night after that. By the third or fourth time we went out,
I felt like I'd known him forever. It's hard to explain, but
there was a connection between us."

Eugenia smiled. "That's not so hard to understand. I
felt the same kind of thing the first time I went out with
your father. I knew he was the one I wanted to spend the
rest of my life with."

Marissa nodded. "That's what I felt for Johnny. And
I thought he felt the same for me. We shared dreams,
hopes, made plans for the future. We had almost six
weeks of dreams and hopes. He told me he loved me and
I believed him. I believed him until the morning after the
senior prom, when he was arrested, and I heard that Sydney Emery was dead and that Johnny had been seeing
her, too."

"So he was dating Sydney at the same time he was
seeing you?"

"I guess so," Marissa replied. Even after all these
years, the knowledge sent a shaft of pain through her

heart. "I never saw Johnny again after the morning of his arrest. By the time his trial was over, I realized I was pregnant and knowing he was probably going to prison, I thought the best thing I could do was put him behind me." Marissa laughed without humor. "In all these years, I never thought about what I would do when Johnny finally got out of prison and came home."

Eugenia smiled. "We rarely allow ourselves to consider the consequences of our actions." She tilted her head and looked at her daughter curiously. "Do you still love him?"

"No," Marissa replied quickly, vehemently. "I'm not even sure I like him." She took a sip of her coffee, unwilling to tell her mother that although she was certain she didn't love Johnny, there was still a physical attraction between them, a chemistry that was volatile.

She set her cup back in the saucer and returned her mother's gaze. "He's changed. He's not the same man I knew before. He's so angry and bitter."

"If what you say is true, he served a lot of time for a crime he didn't commit. That would make anyone angry," Eugenia said. "Maybe Benjamin will help heal the scars Johnny now carries. Perhaps Benjamin can make Johnny remember who and what he was before Sydney Emery was found dead. I have a feeling Johnny needs Benjamin much more than Benjamin needs Johnny."

The next morning her mother's words echoed in Marissa's head as she and Benjamin drove toward the Crockett ranch. Marissa couldn't imagine the Johnny who had returned from prison needing anyone. He appeared hardened, his anger creating a shell around him that would keep him alone.

Johnny had been back in town for two days, and, as

Marissa had expected, as news had gotten out about his return, the town buzzed with gossip and rumors.

All day yesterday, customers and friends had stopped by the store, serving up speculation about Johnny and what would happen when Brad Emery came back to town and heard his stepsister's killer had returned to Mustang.

While Marissa drove slowly by the huge colonial mansion on the hill south of town, she thought of the family who lived within. The Emerys were the most prominent, wealthy people in half the state of Montana.

Although Sydney had only been a year younger than Marissa, the two had never officially met. Sydney, along with her younger sister, Gillian, had been homeschooled. Their mother, Rachel, had allowed the girls little freedom to interact with the other young people in town. The only Emery who was highly visible in Mustang was Bradley Emery, Rachel's stepson and Sydney and Gillian's half brother.

It was Bradley who collected the rent on the businesses his family owned in town, Bradley who made frequent appearances at charity functions and town meetings.

In the years since Sydney's death, now seventeen-year-old Gillian and her mother had simply become more reclusive than ever before. Bradley, now thirty-five, also spent more time at the family ranch and less time in town.

Marissa tightened her hands on the steering wheel as she passed an old, rusty shed. She was surprised to find the structure still standing. As the scene of Sydney's murder, she would have assumed the Emerys had torn it down long ago.

The shed was halfway between the Emery mansion and Johnny's one-story ranch house. It was a lot more than the old shed that made the distinction between the two properties.

The Emery pasture was emerald green and covered with grazing cattle. The fields closer to the house were green with spring wheat and barley.

Crossing into Crockett territory, the landscape was less attractive. The fields lay barren and in the pastures where there was a good stand of grass, there was no livestock.

Johnny's father had walked out on Johnny and his mom when Johnny was six, leaving his wife and son nothing but the ranch to sustain them. Johnny's mother had done what she could to keep things going, but by the time Johnny was in high school, the Crocketts were Mustang's poor.

At eighteen, Marissa hadn't cared whether Johnny had a dollar in his pocket or a million dollar bills, she'd fallen head over heels in love with him from the moment he'd saved her from Brian's lascivious advances.

"Mom?"

Benjamin's voice pulled Marissa from her thoughts. "What, honey?" she asked as she turned down the lane that would take her to Johnny's place.

"Do you think Dad was scared while he was in prison?"

"I don't know, Benjy. You'll have to ask him," Marissa replied. She tried to imagine what prison time would be like for a man like Johnny, but it was impossible.

The young man Marissa had known was truly a cowboy at heart. Johnny had loved the outdoors, loved working the land. What little money he made riding bulls went directly back into the ranch.

How difficult it must have been for him, not to see the stars at night, feel the warmth of the sun on his face. How difficult to spend each waking hour in a tiny cell, never feeling the kiss of the wind, or smelling the scent of newly bloomed wildflowers.

All she really knew was that in his time of imprisonment, a daunting rage had been born, and there were times she felt that anger was pointed directly at her.

She frowned as she drove past a copse of trees and Johnny's house came into view. She hadn't been out here in years, but the condition of the house and outbuildings shocked her.

She'd heard the place had fallen into ruins, but hearing and actually seeing were two different things.

Weathered gray with two broken windows and a sagging front porch, the house radiated crushed spirits and bitter failure.

The outbuildings all cried out for new lumber and roofing, and fresh paint. However, the corral sported fresh lumber and a shining new gate.

As Marissa pulled the car to a stop, Johnny stepped out of the house. Marissa felt her breath catch at the sight of him. He was shirtless, with worn, faded jeans riding low on his hips.

"I see you have your priorities straight," Marissa said as she got out of the car. She gestured to the newly repaired corral, then to the house. "Looks like you've still got a lot of work ahead of you."

Johnny knocked the black hat he wore back on his head and followed her gaze. He nodded. "Yeah, but hard work never scared me. Besides, structurally everything is sound, the place just needs some cosmetic surgery. I'm replacing the broken windows this afternoon, the beginning of the face-lift."

"I can help you," Benjamin offered, standing close to Marissa.

"That would be great. I could use an extra pair of hands," Johnny replied, his gaze warm as it lingered on his son. "If you want to, you can go on inside and explore. Pick out the bedroom you'd like to be yours if you ever spend the night here."

"I can pick any of the rooms I want?" Benjamin asked. "Even the biggest one?"

Johnny laughed, a deep, pleasant rumble. "Yes, even the biggest. And in one of those rooms, you'll find a little surprise."

"Oh boy." Benjamin gave Marissa a quick hug. "I'll see you later, Mom." He tore off running and disappeared into the house.

"I got him a couple packages of baseball cards," Johnny explained. "I can't do much for him right now," he continued, his gaze not meeting hers. "You've had the sole financial responsibility for him for too long. It might take me a couple of months to get on my feet, but eventually I want to contribute to his support."

"We're doing all right, Johnny," Marissa replied. "He doesn't lack for anything."

His gaze met hers, dark and intense. "This isn't about his needs or wants. It's about me being his father, taking the responsibility of a father."

Marissa didn't protest again, realizing it was pride that shone from his eyes. He needed to do for Benjamin and in doing so perhaps he could salvage his self-esteem.

"Tell me about him," Johnny said suddenly. "Tell me everything there is to know about Benjamin."

Marissa remembered what her mother had said...that Johnny needed Benjamin far more than Benjamin needed Johnny. She looked at Johnny, saw the hunger on his face. "His favorite food is pizza, and he loves the color blue. He dislikes cruelty of any kind, and he has a wonderful sense of responsibility. He has a quirky sense of humor and likes practical jokes."

"How much did he weigh at birth? What was his first

word?'' Johnny looked at her, his yearning to know his son apparent in the shining depths of his eyes.

Marissa closed her eyes, remembering that night nine years and three months ago. Despite the fact that her parents had been at her side, she'd felt lonely and frightened.

Her labor pains had not only hurt her physically, but mentally as well, reminding her that the baby she gave birth to would not have a father. Single parenthood terrified her, and her heart ached for the little boy who wouldn't know his father's love. ''He weighed seven pounds, ten ounces, and he was born with a full head of dark hair. When the doctor placed him in my arms, I thought he was the most beautiful, perfect baby that had ever been born.''

''I wish I could have been there.'' His voice was filled with a yearning so deep, so profound, Marissa felt it in her own heart.

She didn't want to feel his pain, didn't want to shoulder the burden of his grief over time lost and never regained.

He sighed, and in the depth of his sigh, Marissa heard all his loss, the loss not only of time, but of hope. She didn't know for sure what he'd felt for her years before, but she knew they were not the same people they had been.

She never again wanted to feel the all-consuming, crazy depth of love she'd once felt for him, because when that love fled, or was withdrawn, it left a hole too big in the heart.

Despite her intentions otherwise, his grief over missing so much of Benjy's life reached inside her and clutched her heart.

She placed her hand on his forearm. ''Johnny, Benjamin still has a lot of life to live. He's going to want you, need you to be a part of that life.''

He nodded, then looked down to where her hand still clutched his arm. "I always did like your hands, Marissa," he said, his smooth, deep voice slicing through her in a wave of heat.

She started to pull her hand away, but he stopped her, placing his on top of hers and guiding it to his bare chest. "So soft...so small and dainty, yet I can remember how magical they feel against my chest, across my stomach...."

"Johnny, stop," she said, attempting to pull her hand from his. The feel of his sun-warmed chest, and the dark wiry hair that tickled her palm, made her heart pound faster, her legs grow weak.

He released her hand, his eyes dark and hooded. "I need to have you one more time, Marissa. It's what I thought about each night in prison. It's what kept me going. We had no closure, and I need to make love to you one last time for that closure to happen."

"You're talking nonsense," she said, stepping backward, needing physical distance from him. "We've had ten years to resolve anything that might have been between us at one time."

"If you've resolved it so well, then why is your heart pounding so fast? Why do you tremble at my touch?" His eyes were knowing and the smile he gave her held a touch of arrogance.

She hated him for being able to affect her on such a primal level. She hated him for the fact that she wished he would make love to her just one more time.

"I've got to get to work," she said, refusing to answer his questions. "I'll be back to pick up Benjy around noon."

"Why don't I bring him home after supper this evening?"

"I'm not sure he'll want to stay that long," Marissa replied. After all, this was the first day Benjamin would be spending with his father...but that father was in fact a stranger.

"Then I'll bring him home whenever he's ready," Johnny countered. "And if he wants to go home early and you aren't home from the flower shop yet, then I'll bring him by there."

"Okay," Marissa agreed, needing to be away from him, feeling as if somehow his touch had disturbed her equilibrium.

She started toward her car, but paused as she heard the sound of horse hooves, saw a cloud of dust stirred in the distance. Within seconds a horse came into view, a man riding hell-bent for leather toward the Crockett ranch.

Johnny moved to stand next to her.

"It's Brad Emery," Marissa said. Tension rippled through her as she realized not only was Brad riding hard and fast, but coiled in his hand was his infamous bullwhip.

Fear shot through Marissa. She'd seen Brad use that bullwhip. Each year at the fair, he showed his prowess at a demonstration of talent. He could flick the flame off a candle, flip out the eye of a plastic doll. But it wasn't a candle or a doll he was after now.

As he drew closer, she saw rage in his eyes...eyes that were directed intently at Johnny.

Chapter 4

As Brad Emery came closer, Marissa could see the horse's rolling eyes, the flaring nostrils. It was as if the rage of the man astride struck terror in the heart of the beast.

"Johnny," she said, her voice a warning as Brad reined in, dismounted and faced Johnny, bullwhip in hand.

"If you've come to whip my butt, I hope you didn't come alone," Johnny said, standing tall and seemingly unafraid as he faced the equally tall, broad-shouldered man.

"I don't need help fighting my battles," Brad exclaimed, blood rage darkening the hue of his brown eyes. "You've got some nerve, Crockett, coming back here where you've caused nothing but pain and heartache."

"We've been through this before, Emery. I had nothing to do with Sydney's death." Johnny's voice was cool, calm, but Marissa felt the tension that shimmered in the air between the two men.

"You're a liar. You killed her. You squeezed her neck until she was dead. And now you get to continue your life, but Sydney is dead to us forever." Brad's face was red with fury, the redness extending across his scalp, showing beneath his pale blond hair.

"Brad," Marissa said as she stepped toward him, wanting to stop the madness before it went any further. "Brad, please..."

Johnny grabbed her arm and pulled her back, a protective gesture that seemed to further enrage Brad. The whip uncoiled, hanging loose, but with the tension of a snake getting ready to strike.

"Oh, that's right," he said, his handsome features twisted into something mean, and unbecoming. "You can come back here and find some other poor innocent woman to bed. How about it, Marissa? Do you like sleeping with a murderer?"

Marissa gasped with shock at the ugliness of his words.

Brad smirked knowingly. "I guess if you can't get an Emery, the next best thing is the mayor's daughter," he said.

"That's enough," The words snapped from Johnny with the sharpness of gunfire. "You're trespassing, Emery. Get the hell off my land."

"You bastard, your presence in Mustang is going to kill Rachel and Gillian. Knowing you're here, living just fine and dandy, it's breaking their hearts. Rachel lost a daughter, and Gillian a big sister. You lost nothing but a little time."

Without warning, Brad cracked the whip. It licked precariously close to Johnny's cheek. Johnny didn't flinch. A small scream of fear erupted from Marissa. She knew that a kiss from the whip could lay open a wicked wound or take out an eye.

"Mom?" Benjamin called from the porch, his voice reedy thin with fear.

"Marissa, go with Benjamin into the house," Johnny said, his voice cool and deadly controlled.

Marissa hesitated, afraid that without her presence the two men would kill each other. But, one look at her son spurred her to do what Johnny had said.

Benjamin stood on the porch, frozen like a statue, his eyes widened in fear.

Marissa ran to the porch. The two men continued to face each other as she hurried Benjamin into the house.

Once inside, Marissa moved to the front window, afraid to watch…afraid not to watch the confrontation taking place outside.

She couldn't hear what was being said, and from her new vantage point she could only see Brad's face and Johnny's back.

"Mom?" Benjamin's voice was small, subdued with fear as he touched her arm.

Although she felt the need to continue to watch the drama between the two men, her son's need was greater. She turned away from the window and pulled him toward the sofa, where they sat side by side.

She drew him close to her, felt the tension that stiffened his slender shoulders. "He thinks Dad killed his sister, doesn't he?" he asked.

"Yes, honey, he does. He's sad about his sister's death, and sometimes sadness turns to anger." She hugged Benjamin close, knowing this was just the first taste of what Johnny might expect by returning home.

"Didn't Dad tell him he *didn't* kill that girl?" Benjamin asked.

"Yes, but Brad doesn't believe your father."

"Do you believe Dad?" Benjamin gazed at her with trusting eyes.

"Absolutely," Marissa answered without hesitation. "Your dad is a good man who got caught up in things outside his control."

"Yeah, that's what I think," Benjamin said.

At that moment Johnny walked through the front door. Both Benjamin and Marissa jumped up to meet him. Benjamin hugged him around the waist.

"Everything okay?" Marissa asked worriedly.

Johnny nodded as he patted Benjamin's back. "Brad just needed to blow off some steam. Basically he told me to get out of town."

"Are you leaving?" Benjamin asked. He pulled away from Johnny and looked up at him with unabashed anxiety. Marissa knew what her son feared…that he'd only just discovered his father three days before and already there was the threat of his father going away.

"No, son. I'm not going anywhere," Johnny said firmly. "This is my home and I have every right to be here. Nobody is going to drive me away." His gaze met Marissa's and in the blue depths Marissa saw his fierce determination, coupled with a hint of hurt vulnerability.

"You knew it was going to be tough," she said softly, affected by the trace of pain in his eyes.

He nodded, then looked at his son. "Benjamin, did you find the baseball cards?" Benjamin nodded. "Why don't you go into one of the bedrooms and sort them out? I'll walk your mom out to her car so she can get to work."

"Okay," Benjamin agreed and he dashed off down the hallway.

"Yeah, I knew settling here wouldn't be easy," Johnny said as he and Marissa stepped out of the house and onto the front porch. "I guess I thought ten years passing might dull the Emerys' hatred of me, that their pain might be lessened by the passing of time."

"Maybe you should call Jesse. Maybe there should be an official report of this confrontation," Marissa suggested.

"Nah, there's no reason to bother the sheriff. Brad just needed to vent. I imagine I won't be bothered by him again."

They reached Marissa's car and she leaned her back against the driver door. "But what if you are?" Worry coursed through her as she remembered Brad's rage, the sharp snap of his bullwhip. "Brad has a bad temper, and he's more than proficient with that whip. He could hurt you before you even see it coming."

"Worried about me, Marissa? Be careful. You wouldn't want the townspeople to get wind of that." Johnny leaned forward, placing an arm on either side of her, effectively trapping her against the car.

"Of course not!" she snapped, angered by how quickly her body reacted to his nearness. She could feel the heat of his bare chest radiating toward her, felt her nipples tighten in response. Her legs felt wobbly and her heart pounded an unsteady rhythm. "I'm sure you can take care of yourself," she replied.

"In some things perhaps, but not in all things." He smiled, letting her know he wasn't talking about standing up to Brad, but something far more intimate.

He touched her cheek softly, his thumb caressing down her skin to trace her jawline. "Did you think of me, Marissa? In the darkness of night for the last ten years, did you think of me...my touch...my kiss?"

She wanted to lie. She didn't want to give him the satisfaction of knowing how often she'd thought of him, how deeply she'd yearned to be in his arms one last time. But, the lie refused to be verbalized.

"Yes." The word whispered from her as if torn from the depths of her soul. "Yes, I thought about you. I thought about your kisses, I thought about our lovemaking." She batted his hand away from her face, and he took a step backward. "But that doesn't matter anymore. I don't know you, Johnny. Ten years have passed. I'm not that vulnerable, innocent young woman anymore, and I'm not willing to have a cheap affair with you because your hormones are raging from ten years of imprisonment."

She opened her car door and slid behind the steering wheel. "You are part of my past, Johnny. And the only role you have in my future is as Benjamin's father, nothing more. We'll share his life, but that's all we'll share." She slammed her car door to emphasize her statement.

As she pulled away, she looked in her rearview mirror and saw him standing where she'd left him, a smile curving his lips. And in the smile, she read the knowledge that he intended to be something more to her than Benjamin's father.

Johnny watched her drive away, wondering why he felt the need to torment her. To torment himself? He wasn't sure if he wanted to punish her, or if he was somehow testing himself.

He could still smell the sweet fragrance of her, feel the silken softness of her skin and still maintain control, but for how long?

Ten years was a long time for a man to go without making love to a woman, to go without intimacy of any kind. Although his body ached with the need for physical release, there was a touch of fear there as well. Celibacy had become a way of life, not only celibacy of the body, but deprivation of the soul as well.

During his prison time he'd lived in a self-imposed bubble of isolation, inviting no friendships, trusting only in himself. At the moment he didn't trust in anything or anyone else…except Benjamin. A relationship with his son was the only kind he wanted. So, he was back to the same question…why did he feel the need to torment either of them? It was a question with no answer.

"Dad, can the bedroom with the blue wallpaper be mine?" Benjamin called from the front door.

Johnny nodded, unsurprised that his son had chosen that room. It had the best view of the corral and was the only bedroom adjoining the bathroom. "Sure," he said as he walked toward the porch.

"And sometimes I could spend the night with you and sleep in that room?"

"Anytime you want and your mom says it's okay."

"Cool!" Benjamin disappeared down the hallway as Johnny entered the house. Johnny smiled and shook his head, wishing the dilemmas he knew he would face in the coming days were as easy as choosing a bedroom.

He and Benjamin had a good day together. They worked side by side as they replaced the broken windows, then began the bigger job of painting the outside of the house. As they worked, Benjamin kept up a steady stream of chatter, telling Johnny about school, his baseball buddies and all the things that were important to a nine-year-old.

At lunchtime they stopped and made bologna sandwiches, then sat on the porch and ate them with chips and sodas. "I like it out here," Benjamin said as he finished the last of his sandwich. "I wish we could all live here. You and me and Mom."

"Benjamin," Johnny began, knowing he needed to stop that particular dream from taking root in his son's head. "You know that isn't going to happen."

"I know." Benjamin sighed heavily. He popped a chip into his mouth and chewed thoughtfully. "Did you live here when you were a boy?"

"Yes, and my dad lived here when he was a boy," Johnny explained.

Benjamin looked at him curiously. "Where's your dad now?"

Johnny hesitated, as always a black void yawning inside him at thoughts of his father. "I don't know. He left my mom and me when I was six."

Amazing that after all the years, Johnny could still remember so vividly sitting on this very porch, waiting for his father to return. He'd sat there from sunup to sundown for three days before his mother finally told him his dad was never coming home.

"He left and never came back?"

"Nope. He never came back."

Benjamin's hand reached out and curled around Johnny's. So small in comparison, yet containing a wealth of compassion. At that moment Johnny wished it were in his power to give his son the earth, moon and stars.

Later that evening, when he took Benjamin home, he didn't get out of the truck. Instead he watched as Marissa opened the door to welcome her son. "Want to come in?" she called from the porch.

He shook his head, waved goodbye and drove off. After spending the entire day with Benjamin, he felt oddly vulnerable, too vulnerable to spend any time with Marissa.

The next morning, Johnny stood on the porch, watching the sun rising over his land, remembering how difficult life had been for his mother. She worked the ranch day in and day out. Unable to afford the kind of help they needed, she worked herself to death trying to make the ranch profitable.

When Johnny was a young teenager, he begged his mother to sell the ranch. He knew they could get a good price for the land, and she could live the rest of her life comfortably in a smaller house in town. She was appalled at the very suggestion.

"This is all I have to give you, Johnny. The ranch is your legacy. Your grandpa gave it to your father, and one day it will be yours," she'd said.

And now it was his inheritance to pass on to Benjamin. But at the moment, in its current condition, it was an empty bequest. A ranch with no livestock, land with no crops.

Initially, when Johnny had thought of coming back home to Mustang, it had been with the sole purpose of finding Sydney's killer and clearing his name. Now he had a dual challenge, to find a killer and create a dream ranch to pass on to his son.

Over the next couple of days, Johnny kept busy, repairing and painting the old house, cleaning out the barn and mowing the areas of lawn and pasture that had grown into weeds. At night, he studied the files he'd found among his mother's things, files that chronicled the murder of Sydney Emery and the ensuing investigation.

He spoke to Benjamin on the phone every day after school, although he didn't speak to Marissa. He consciously stayed away from her, needing to focus all his energies on work. He knew that when he was around Marissa, his mind tended to wander to other kinds of activities.

But he also knew that he needed to give Marissa some space. He knew how difficult it was for her to have him suddenly back in her life, in her son's life.

By the weekend, Johnny had done as much as he could with the funds he had available. The house sported a new coat of paint, the surrounding lawn was neat, and he'd carted off dead tree limbs, broken machinery and other trash that had accumulated in his absence.

His mother had left behind a small life insurance policy, but the amount wouldn't accomplish what he needed.

Johnny needed seed money, he needed capital to build his ranch. With this thought in mind, Saturday afternoon, he took off for a one o'clock appointment with Gary Feeney, the loan officer at the Mustang First National Bank.

As he drove by Flowers By Marissa, a pang of unexpected pride filled him.

She'd done it.

Owning a flower shop had been Marissa's dream when she'd been eighteen. On those nights they'd shared, she'd talked of her dream, imagining a chic little shop where everyone would order special arrangements for special occasions.

She'd accomplished her dream, despite the burden of being a single parent. She'd gone after what she wanted and gotten it, while he was just starting to think about what he wanted.

He parked in front of the bank and drew a deep breath. Johnny had never liked to ask anyone for anything, but he knew it took money to make money. He raked a hand through his hair, wondering if perhaps he should have gotten a haircut before meeting with Feeney.

"To hell with it," he muttered. Short hair or shaggy. it wouldn't matter when it came to a loan.

He walked into the hushed, cool interior of the bank and instantly felt the stares of half a dozen people. He'd almost gotten accustomed to it, but not quite. In the past week of being home, he knew he'd been the latest subject of speculation and gossip.

Approaching the woman at the teller window, he was grateful he didn't recognize her. "Hi. May I help you?" Her friendly, almost flirtatious smile indicated she had no idea who he was or the crime he'd been convicted of.

"I have a one o'clock appointment with Gary Feeney," he explained.

"If you'll wait just a moment, I'll see if Mr. Feeney is ready for you." She disappeared from the counter and returned moments later, the smile and the flirting twinkle in her eyes now absent. Apparently in the moments she'd been gone, somebody had filled her in on his sins of the past. Anonymity lasted only so long in a town the size of Mustang.

"Mr. Feeney is waiting." She pointed to a doorway nearby. "If you go through that door, Mr. Feeney's office is the second on the right."

"Thank you." Johnny left the counter and walked toward the doorway, his back tingling with the strength of the stares that followed him.

Feeney's office door was closed. Johnny knocked on the hard wood, the sound echoing in the long hall.

"Come in," Gary Feeney's voice drifted through the door to Johnny.

Johnny opened the door and walked into a small, windowless office. Gary sat behind a large, walnut desk. Johnny approached, a hand held out in greeting.

"Have a seat, Johnny," Gary said, ignoring the outstretched hand.

Johnny sat in one of the two chairs facing the desk, a

sinking sensation in the pit of his stomach. It didn't bode well that the short, balding man hadn't shaken his hand.

"What can I do for you today?" Gary focused back on the paperwork laid out in front of him, as if Johnny didn't warrant his full attention.

Anger was bubbling over in Johnny, but he swallowed it, not wanting to ruin his chances of obtaining a loan because he couldn't control his emotions from breaking loose. "Generally when one comes to talk to a loan officer, it's because he is seeking a loan."

"Generally when a man comes to see me concerning a loan, he either has a job or something substantial to offer as collateral," Gary replied, still not bothering to look up.

"I have collateral. I have my land."

Johnny's comment now garnered Gary's full attention. He laughed, a low, unpleasant sound. "Everyone knows the Crockett land isn't worth anything. Hell, your old man deeded it to your mama because he knew it was worthless."

"That's not true," Johnny returned, still feeling anger swelling in his chest. "The land is as good as any in the state of Montana." He leaned forward, needing to connect with this man who held the key to his future…his son's future. "I can turn that land into a prosperous ranch, all I need is a chance and a little capital."

"We don't give chances or loans to murderers." The words were said slowly, distinctively, as if Gary thought perhaps Johnny suffered some sort of brain damage.

The words sliced through Johnny, leaving an open, gaping wound that momentarily left him speechless. Gary's negative attitude wasn't about how good or poor the Crockett land was, it was about the Emerys, and the power they wielded in Mustang.

Johnny stood, knowing his business here was finished. "Say hello to the Emerys for me," he said as he started toward the door.

Gary smiled. "I will. Rachel, Brad and Gillian are three of our most valued customers here at Mustang First National Bank."

Johnny held the vision of Gary's self-satisfied smirk inside as he stormed out of the bank. On the sidewalk, he paused, trying to think past the anger, past the emptiness of failure.

He had a feeling there was little point in trying to establish accounts at the feed store or any of the other businesses in town.

The Emerys would be "valued customers" every place in Mustang, and Johnny had a feeling no proprietor would be willing to buck the Emerys to aid him in any way.

So he was finished before he got started, beaten before any fight had begun. He'd grown up with nothing, and it looked as if he'd die with nothing.

An inner voice railed against the hopelessness that tried so desperately to crush him in its grip. If it were just himself he had to worry about, it would be easy to give up, roll over and play dead. But it wasn't just *his* future at risk…it was *Benjamin's* as well.

Johnny climbed into his truck and leaned his head against the backrest. He didn't want to go home, but he didn't have any other place to go. There was no place in Mustang he would be welcomed.

It wasn't until he was headed back to his ranch that he remembered there was at least one place in town where he could go and nobody would give him a second glance.

The Roundup invited the kind of anonymity Johnny

hadn't enjoyed since coming back to Mustang. The bar, housed in a flat wooden building with a neon cowboy flashing from the roof, was just as Johnny remembered it.

Although he'd been too young before prison to spend any time in the dive, he, along with his peers, had known the Roundup was a place where the men on the fringes of society relaxed. Just as a temple beckoned the God-fearing, the Roundup encouraged the heathens.

Despite the early hour, there were several trucks parked in the gravel lot. Johnny parked his own truck and got out. The anger, coupled with the despair that had stirred in him earlier, still beat inside his stomach as he walked into the dim, smoky confines of the bar.

He sat at a table by himself, one where he could sit with his back against the wall and see everyone who came in. In the past ten years, he didn't know what might have changed. For all he knew the Emerys might own the place now and some hulking, bruising bouncer would attempt to eject him.

Instead of a bouncer, an attractive blond waitress approached his table. "What can I get for you, cowboy?" she asked.

"A bottle of beer, it doesn't matter what kind."

She nodded and drifted away. A beer and a plan, that's what he needed. The waitress returned with an ice-cold, inviting bottle of beer, and Johnny took a long, deep draw. Leaning back in the chair, he relaxed and mused over the morning's events.

Intellectually, he couldn't blame the Emerys for hating him, for trying to make his life as difficult as possible. They truly believed he'd killed Sydney.

Emotionally, their hatred of him, their desire to see him destroyed was difficult to take. He'd never really gotten an opportunity to grieve for Sydney, who had been a beautiful, troubled young woman. Johnny had loved Sydney like a sister. The horror of finding his best friend's body still haunted his nights.

But his grief for her had gotten all tangled up with his arrest and the death of his personal freedom. Her loss had become his as well, and it was difficult to separate the two in his mind.

He took another drink of beer, overwhelmed by the fact that he had no idea where to begin to find out the truth about who killed Sydney. He'd read and reread the newspaper articles and reports his mother had saved, but they contained nothing that pointed a finger to anyone but him.

Even if he never discovered Sydney's murderer, he had to figure out some way to get some money for the ranch. It was impossible for him to build anything for Benjy without some funds.

"Refill?" The waitress appeared, breaking into Johnny's thoughts.

"No, thanks. But maybe you can give me some information. You know anyone who's looking for help on any of the ranches in the area?"

She shrugged her slender shoulders. "I wouldn't have a clue. But you might ask Cameron." She pointed to a man sitting at the bar. "He might know somebody."

"Thanks." Johnny finished his beer before he approached Cameron. "Excuse me, I was wondering if I might talk to you," Johnny said to the dark-haired, somber-looking man.

The man's gaze darted to the stool next to him, inviting Johnny to sit. "Okay."

Johnny slid onto the empty stool and held out his hand. "I'm Johnny Crockett." He waited for his hand to be avoided, for an expression of revulsion to twist the man's features.

"Cameron Gallagher," the man replied, shaking Johnny's hand with a firm grip.

"Can I buy you another drink?" Johnny gestured to the nearly empty glass in front of Cameron.

"No, thanks." Cameron offered Johnny a friendly smile. "You see, my wife is at home preparing for a surprise party she's throwing me for my birthday. I told her I had a couple errands to run so she'd have some time alone to get things ready. I don't think she'd appreciate me returning home three sheets to the wind."

Johnny smiled, a tinge of envy winging through him as he saw the warmth that lit Cameron's eyes at the mention of his wife. "Happy birthday," he offered.

"Thanks. So, what can I do for you?"

"The waitress mentioned you might know someone who might be looking for some part-time help." It was the most difficult thing Johnny had ever asked. Men who owned their own ranches didn't work for others.

Cameron eyed him for a long moment. It was an intense, searching gaze, and Johnny met it unflinchingly. "I could use a pair of extra hands on my place a couple days a week."

"I'm a hard worker," Johnny replied.

Cameron nodded, a frown wrinkling across his brow. "Johnny Crockett…why is that name familiar?"

Resignation speared through Johnny, the sharp sword of opportunity found, then lost. "I recently got out of prison," Johnny said flatly.

Cameron waved his hand dismissively. "I knew that…this is something else." He snapped his fingers. "You used to be quite a bull rider, right?"

Relief soared through Johnny. He nodded.

"Yeah, a couple of my ranch hands were talking about the upcoming rodeo, and one of them was wondering if you would enter the bull-riding contest."

"Upcoming rodeo?"

Cameron nodded. "Mustang County Rodeo will take place here in town in two weeks. I hear there's going to be a pretty decent purse for the bull-riding event. In the meantime, if you're serious about looking for work, be at my place next Monday morning at six."

For the first time all day, hope rose up inside Johnny. Finally, a chance, a real chance.

"Thanks," he exclaimed as he stood. "I appreciate the opportunity. I'll see you first thing Monday morning."

Johnny left the Roundup, his heart pounding with the promise of the future. Emerys be damned. He'd build something for Benjamin despite them.

It wasn't until he was halfway back to town that he realized he had impulsively headed for the flower shop.

Funny, that instead of going back to his ranch, he couldn't wait to share his plan for success with Marissa. He decided not to analyze the impulse and instead just followed it.

Chapter 5

"I'm back for the next load," David Graham said as he flew into the flower shop.

"Terrific, I've got five more arrangements ready for delivery," Marissa exclaimed.

The Saturday before Mother's Day was one of the biggest days of the year for Marissa. Usually she handled all the deliveries from the flower shop herself, but twice a year, on Valentine's Day and this day, Marissa hired David to help her out.

When she finished loading the teenager's van with the arrangements to be delivered, she checked her watch. Almost three and she was already exhausted. Two more hours and she'd close up the store, change her clothes and get over to the school where the end-of-the-year school program began at six.

She sank down on a chair, enjoying the momentary peace and quiet of the store with no customers. The morning had been a deluge of people in and out, ordering last-minute flowers and plants for their mothers.

Marissa remembered a Mother's Day ten years ago when she'd sat in a field and watched while Johnny gathered wildflowers for his mother.

She closed her eyes and tilted her head back, remembering the warmth of the sun on her face on that day, the sweet scent of the flowers that had surrounded her. After Johnny had picked enough of the flowers for a large bouquet, he and Marissa had made love in the cool, lush grass beneath a shady tall tree.

Oh, how she'd loved him. He was unlike anyone she'd ever known. It didn't matter to her that he had nothing tangible…he had dreams and ambition, and she'd wanted to be there to share his life with him.

Suddenly the jangle of the bell above the door sounded, and she looked up, wondering if her thoughts had somehow managed to conjure him up.

Johnny walked through the door with the confident stride and the jaunty smile she remembered from years ago.

"You look like the cat who swallowed the canary," she said, trying to ignore the quickening of her pulse at the sight of him. Surely her response was due to the bittersweet memories she'd just been indulging.

"Ha, more like the canary who got bit by the cat." Johnny swept his dark hat from his head. "I had an appointment earlier with Gary Feeney at the bank. I was hoping to get a loan." He leaned a hip against the counter, handsome as sin and with a new light of assurance shining from his eyes.

"And you got it?" she asked.

"Not hardly." He laughed derisively. "For a moment I forgot just how small Mustang was. Apparently the

Emerys' power reaches into all corners. But it doesn't matter. I've got a better plan than a loan.''

His eyes sparked with the same light they'd had when he was nineteen. The light was warm, filled with hope, and hypnotically beckoned Marissa in. ''And what's this plan of yours?'' she asked, trying to still the erratic pounding of her heart.

''Starting Monday, I've got a part-time job working at the Gallagher ranch,'' he said, a touch of defiance in his tone.

''Cameron Gallagher? He's a nice guy. He's got the cutest stepdaughter you ever saw.'' She kept her voice carefully neutral, knowing the enormous step he'd taken in deciding to work for another rancher.

Ranchers rarely worked any place but their own land, and if they did, it was usually the last step before complete bankruptcy. But, for Johnny, she knew it was his first step toward his own redemption.

''And I'm entering the bull-riding event at the rodeo next month.''

''You're crazy,'' Marissa said, calmly. She stared at him to see if perhaps he was joking.

''What's crazy about it?'' he demanded. He shoved away from the counter and paced the floor of the flower store like a caged animal, his fingers dancing around the brim of the hat he held. ''Working for Cameron part-time is the only way I can stay afloat for the time being.''

Marissa frowned, knowing he was being obtuse by choice. ''You know that's not what I'm talking about.''

He grinned, like a mischievous boy. ''Guess that means you're talking about my plans to enter the bull-riding event.''

''Of course that's what I'm talking about,'' she said, sarcastically. ''Johnny, you know how dangerous bull riding can be. You might have been good at it at one time, but that was years ago.''

"Actually, it's been less than a year since I rode a bull." Johnny picked up a heart-shaped glass vase, the object looking exceptionally small and dainty in his grasp. He turned it over and looked at the price tag. He winced. "My God, do people actually pay that kind of money for a vase?"

Marissa walked around the counter and snatched the vase out of his hands. "What do you mean, you rode bulls less than a year ago?" She set the vase back where it belonged.

"In prison. A couple of times a year, some of the towns surrounding the prison would hold a rodeo. The prisoners with good behavior records were given the opportunity to participate. For the past five years, I've ridden the bulls in various rodeos. Three out of the five years, I was the reigning champion."

"And what do you win?" She couldn't imagine what prizes prisoners would receive for winning any contest in prison.

"Privileges. Extra time in the yard for exercise, getting to see an approved movie." He shrugged. "Different things that people who aren't in prison take for granted."

"What happened the other two years?" she asked, remembering he'd said he'd been champion three out of five years.

Johnny stopped pacing and instead leaned against the plate glass window, his eyes lit with the distance of memory and the fever of challenge. "The first year I drew a devil Brahman bull named Black Heart, and I wasn't on his back for two seconds before he sent me skyward." He shook his head with a chuckle. "But Black Heart was easy compared to the bull I drew the next year. Tornado.'' He said the name as if that told the whole story.

"What happened?'' Marissa asked, caught between natural curiosity and a reluctance to encourage him.

He began pacing once again, moving back and forth directly in front of Marissa. Each time he drew near, she smelled his scent, the evocative fragrance of musky aftershave and a fresh spring breeze.

"Tornado had a set of horns as sharp as twin knives and a furious left spin that usually unseated most riders. I almost rode him to the buzzer. Had I been stronger, better prepared, I would have had him. Unfortunately, Tornado unexpectedly twisted right instead of left and I flew off. I landed on the ground and before I could get up, Tornado expressed his displeasure with me.''

Marissa's heart was in her throat. "You were hurt?''

Johnny smiled. "Let's just say I spent a little time in the prison infirmary following the rodeo. Want to see the memento Tornado left me with?''

"Okay,'' Marissa said. "Wait!'' she exclaimed as he began to unbuckle his belt.

"I thought you wanted to see my scar,'' he said innocently. But his gaze was anything but innocent.

"Not if it requires you to drop your pants,'' Marissa replied, heat rising to her face.

He shrugged with another mischievous grin. "Your loss,'' he said. "I've been told the scar looks just like a heart.''

"I know exactly what you're doing, Johnny Crockett,'' Marissa said in an accusing tone. "You're trying to get me all flustered so I'll forget to tell you how crazy you are.''

Johnny laughed. "Ah, Marissa, you've always been difficult to detour from your goals.''

"Johnny, please reconsider entering the rodeo, or at least enter another event." She placed her hand on his forearm, desperate to change his mind.

"I can't enter any other event," he scoffed. "Bull riding is my talent, it's what I do."

"That's not true," Marissa protested. "You're a rancher, Johnny."

He shook off her hand, a flash of anger firing in his eyes. "I was a rancher. Now I'm a convicted murderer. I can't ranch without money, Marissa. And nobody in this town is going to give me half a chance."

"Cameron Gallagher is giving you a chance," she said. "Work for him, put that money back into your place."

"You know I'll never get ahead by doing that. I need that prize money. I need to win the bull-riding event. It's the only way I'll be able to build something to pass on to my son."

"All your son needs is his father." Again Marissa grasped his arm. "Benjamin needs you alive and well. Why risk being badly hurt…or worse?"

He looked down at her hand, then covered it with his own. When he looked at her again, his expression was one of deep yearning. "Marissa, I need to be more than what I am right now for Benjamin. I want more to offer our son."

"Having you in his life is enough," she replied softly.

"No, it's not enough." He stepped away from her and raked a hand through his hair. "If I win that prize money I can start a college fund for Benjamin and use some of the money to restore and update the ranch so that one day he'll have something worthwhile from me."

He stepped toward her once again and placed his hands on the sides of her face. "It's all or nothing for me,

Marissa. If I don't at least try by entering the rodeo, then I don't deserve him calling me dad. For Benjy, I'll take my chances on a bull.''

He dropped his hands and forced a light laugh. ''Hell, I survived ten years of prison, I can survive eight seconds on the back of a bull.''

Marissa wanted to change his mind. Her fear for his safety ran deep and heavy. She'd been to too many rodeos, seen too many men forever crippled or maimed by the bulls. However, before she could say another word, Benjamin flew through the door.

''Hi, Dad,'' he said, his delight in seeing his father obvious on his miniature features. ''Hi, Mom, I made you a card today in art class.'' He handed Marissa a colorful card that read ''Happy Mother's Day'' on the front, and ''I love you'' on the inside.

''Thanks, honey,'' Marissa said and grabbed him long enough to kiss him on the cheek.

''Ah, Mom,'' he replied, swiping at his cheek as if in distaste. He smiled at Johnny. ''Are you coming to my play tonight?''

''Play? What play?'' Johnny asked and cast a sideways look to Marissa.

Instantly guilt swept through Marissa. She should have told Johnny about the school play.

''There's a play at Benjamin's school this evening,'' she explained.

''And I'm gonna sing a solo,'' Benjamin said.

''A solo? I don't see how I can miss it,'' Johnny replied. ''How about we all ride together to the school? What time does the play begin?''

''Six,'' Benjamin said, ''but I have to be there at five-thirty.''

"Then why don't I pick up you and your mom at around five-fifteen?"

"Super!" Benjamin exclaimed. "I'm gonna go sweep up the backroom. I'll see you tonight, Dad." With these words, he disappeared into the backroom.

"You might have asked me before talking to him about us all riding together," Marissa said, feeling as if she'd somehow been manipulated.

"You might have told me about the program," he returned evenly.

She nodded, knowing he was right. "You're right, I should have told you about it. But, you have to understand, I've parented Benjamin alone for nine years. It's going to take me some time to remember to share."

"Fair enough. Is there a reason you might not want me to go to the program? If that's the case, I can think of something to tell Benjy." His gaze was dark as he waited for her reply. "Are your parents going to be there?"

"No, they can't make it this evening. Dad has some sort of a meeting. And of course there's no reason I wouldn't want you to come. But we aren't going home. You can pick us up here. We'll be ready for you at five-fifteen."

The bell jangled and two young girls walked in, their boisterous voices filling the small confines.

"I'll see you later," Johnny mouthed, then strode out the door.

It wasn't until after Marissa had taken care of her customers and hung the Closed sign on the door that she had time to reflect on Johnny's visit.

His plan to enter the rodeo worried her. The price he might possibly pay seemed far too high for the reward offered.

Benjamin didn't care what kind of tangible things his father had to offer him. All Benjamin cared about was having his father as an emotional, loving support in his life.

But Marissa knew Johnny wouldn't be deterred from his plans. He would enter the rodeo. Marissa didn't care if he won or not. She knew all she could do was pray for his safety.

She also knew why Johnny had asked if she had a problem with the three of them attending the school play together.

If Johnny went with Benjamin and her, then by tomorrow morning the entire town would know that Johnny was Benjamin's father.

It had been a mistake inviting himself along with Marissa and Benjamin to the school play. Johnny knew it was a mistake the moment Benjy and Marissa got into his truck and Marissa's scent filled the interior.

Flowers, with a hint of mysterious spice, it was the same fragrance she'd worn years ago. The memory of that fragrance had tormented him for ten long years.

Not only did she smell good enough to eat, she looked gorgeous enough to ravish. She wore a navy dress, cinched with a belt at her slender waist. The dress draped becomingly down her hips, ending just above her shapely knees. The dark material emphasized her blond hair and the square neckline exposed her delicate collarbones.

Johnny clenched his hands on the steering wheel, fighting against his physical response to her utter attractiveness.

Instead he tried to focus on his son, sitting next to him. "You nervous about your solo?" he asked.

"Nah. I like to sing, and it doesn't bother me to do it

in front of people. I sang a solo in church last year and everyone told me I sounded like an angel.''

"You must take after your grandma Crockett," Johnny said. "She had a voice like an angel, too." He was surprised by his memory of his mother's voice.

"I didn't know your mother sang," Marissa said.

Johnny loosened his grip on the wheel, relaxing somewhat as he thought of his mother. "She sang all the time when I was little. She sang while she washed dishes, sang while she vacuumed or picked tomatoes."

He frowned. "She stopped singing after my father left. I missed it." He swallowed the emotion that had suddenly crept into his throat. "Anyway, I can't wait to hear you sing," he said to his son.

"I like to sing. It makes me happy," Benjy said.

Johnny smiled. "Have you ever heard your mother sing?"

Benjamin nodded and winced. "No offense, Mom, but it's bad."

"I can't help it that I'm a little tone-deaf," Marissa said, defensively.

"A little? One time your mom and I were walking in the pasture and she started singing and the cows all bawled and ran away," Johnny said.

Benjamin cupped a hand over his mouth and giggled, the sound musical and sweet.

"And another time she was singing and a neighbor called 911 because she thought somebody was hurt," Johnny fabricated, rewarded with another of Benjamin's giggles. His laughter was music to Johnny's ears, but Marissa's laughter was like succor for his soul.

"Your father is telling whoppers," Marissa said to her son, but her eyes were lit with merriment. "I might not be able to sing, but your father can't dance. He has two left feet. The one time I danced with him, I had to go to the hospital and have little casts put on all the toes he stepped on.''

Johnny laughed aloud at her story. ''And you accuse me of telling whoppers?''

Benjamin placed a hand on Johnny's knee and his other hand on Marissa's. ''This is fun,'' he said.

Fun. He'd forgotten how much fun Marissa could be. Not only had they shared a passion he'd never felt before or since, they'd shared lots of laughter as well. He'd missed having that in his life.

All too soon, Johnny pulled into the elementary school parking lot. There were already a number of cars and trucks parked there because of families coming to the yearly show, and mothers and fathers coming to see their children perform.

Johnny, Benjamin and Marissa all got out of Johnny's truck. Before they started walking toward the school's front door, Benjamin stopped his parents. ''I sort of lied before,'' he said in a small voice.

Marissa bent down to eye level with her son. ''Lied about what, Benjy?''

''I *am* kinda nervous,'' he confessed.

Johnny squatted down so he too, was at eye level with his son. ''You'll do fine,'' he said, his heart softening as Benjamin leaned against him with the trusting innocence of childhood.

''Your mom and I are going to sit as close to the front as we can. If you get too nervous, you just look at us and know how proud we are of you. In fact, why don't we make up a secret signal. If you get nervous, you look at me and I'll pull on my ear…like this.'' Johnny pulled his lobe in an exaggerated gesture.

Benjamin giggled. ''I feel better,'' he said.

Both Johnny and Marissa straightened. "Good, then we'd better get inside," Marissa said, her gaze lingering for a long moment on Johnny.

The look she gave him was sweet and soft, and tension instantly built inside him. He wanted to yell at her to stop it, warn her that it was dangerous to look at him as if she cared about him, as if she wanted him.

She had cared about him long ago, had wanted him physically, but her feelings for him had been shallow, not strong enough to stand up to the tribulations life had thrown at him.

He knew now that he'd been her walk on the wild side, her taste of forbidden fruit. The mayor's daughter and the town's poor, bad boy…the relationship had been destined to fail from the very beginning. And he truly believed had it not been for Benjamin, she would have written him out of her life long ago. But, even knowing all this didn't stop him from wanting her.

As they approached the schoolhouse door, Johnny shoved these thoughts aside. Anxiety took the place of anger as he anticipated walking into an auditorium of his fellow townsmen.

Mustang wasn't just a town, it was a close-knit community that functioned much like a dysfunctional family. Privacy was difficult to attain and most secrets were known to all. However, Johnny knew that Marissa's secret of Benjamin's biological father had remained undisclosed until tonight. With Johnny at her side watching Benjamin's performance, the secret would be no more. He only hoped that neither Benjamin nor Marissa paid in any negative way because of his relationship to them.

Entering the doors of the school, Johnny was instantly hit with the scent of childhood, of chalk and papers, of floor wax and crayons. "Smells the same as it did twenty years ago," he said.

Marissa smiled. "It's one of the universal scents that everyone recognizes."

Johnny's tension grew as they approached the double doors that led into the auditorium. The sounds of the crowd within drifted out. Johnny had kept a low profile since getting out of prison. Most of his trips into town had been directly to Marissa's shop or to the grocery store. This would be the first time he'd be seeing so many of the townspeople together in one place…and he wondered how his presence would be met.

Just before they reached the doors to the auditorium, Benjamin grabbed Johnny's hand. "I'm glad you came, Dad," he said. And in that impulsive, innocent statement, Johnny's nerves subsided and he found the courage to face whatever might lie ahead.

As the three of them entered the back of the auditorium, the people talking nearest them stopped. Like a wave effect, the quiet grew until there was a complete and utter silence. It lasted only a moment, then the chatter of people resumed, making Johnny wonder if he'd only imagined the silence.

One look at Marissa and he knew he hadn't imagined anything. Twin spots of redness rode her cheeks and her back was stiffened as if in defense.

"I've got to go backstage," Benjamin said and with a nod from his mother, he raced ahead of them down the wide aisle toward the stage.

"I feel like I'm facing a firing squad," Johnny said softly as he and Marissa started up the aisle. With each step forward, Johnny could hear the whispers that followed their progress.

He focused on nobody, instead eyeing the empty seats

on the first row in front of the stage. He breathed a sigh of relief as he and Marissa sat down, the only two people on the first row.

Marissa offered him a small, nervous smile. "I suddenly feel like breaking out into a rendition of 'Let's Give Them Something to Talk About,'" she said.

Johnny grinned back. "At this point the song would be redundant."

"It would have been easier to slide into a seat in the back," she admitted.

"Yeah, but we told Benjy we'd be right up front."

Again she gave him that soft look, the one that twisted his insides and stoked desire into his veins. "You're good with Benjamin," she said.

He shrugged and stared at the red velvet curtain that covered the stage. "It's easy to be good with Benjamin. He's a fantastic boy."

Marissa laughed. "Spoken like a true father."

He looked back at her, wondering if she had any idea how beautiful she looked, if she regretted agreeing to attend this function with him? The last thing he'd want would be for Marissa and Benjamin to somehow pay for him being a part of their lives.

"You wouldn't think he's so fantastic if you experienced one of his stubborn fits." She tilted her head with another smile. "Or perhaps you would still find him fantastic because I suspect he gets that stubborn streak from you."

"I think it's possible he got that particular trait from both of us," he returned. "By the way...when I stopped into the shop earlier, I didn't realize it was Mother's Day. Happy Mother's Day, Marissa."

"Thank you," she murmured, looking down at her hands clasped together in her lap.

"Marissa, I thought I'd find you here somewhere." A slightly overweight perky blonde approached, her blue eyes dancing with liveliness and a friendly smile curving her lips.

"Lucy, what are you doing here?" Marissa said, then turned to Johnny. "Johnny, this is my dearest friend, Lucy Allen. Lucy…Johnny Crockett."

"Hi, Johnny. We met years ago, but it's nice to see you again."

Johnny was surprised by the friendliness that remained in her clear blue eyes. No hint of fear or revulsion. "Nice to see you again, too," he replied.

"So what are you doing here?" Marissa repeated as Lucy perched on the edge of the chair next to her.

"There are going to be refreshments after the show, and I promised Mom I'd help serve," Lucy replied.

"Lucy's mom is the sixth-grade teacher," Marissa explained to Johnny.

"And if you'll excuse us for just a moment, I really need to talk with Marissa." Lucy grabbed Marissa's arm and tugged her to the end of the aisle where they could speak together in some semblance of privacy.

As the two women spoke, Johnny shifted positions in the chair. The auditorium was quickly filling with people, although nobody joined him and Marissa on the front row.

It appeared there was little forgiveness in the hearts of his fellow townsmen. Unsurprising, he thought with an edge of bitterness. Not that it mattered to him.

He didn't need anyone in his life except his son. There had been a time when he'd believed he needed somebody. His gaze went to Marissa. He'd believed he needed her. He hadn't been able to imagine living his life without her, living his future without her by his side.

Even though she'd professed the same kind of emotions to him, she'd run at the first sign of trouble, turned her back on him as if he'd never meant anything at all to her. He'd never make the same mistake again. He'd never need her again. He might want her, he might entertain enormous desire for her, but he'd never give her his heart again.

However, he had to admit she'd shown courage coming here with him tonight, a courage that had surprised him. But, he was certain that valor had been bred strictly for Benjamin's sake.

The lights overhead flickered on and off, indicating the program about to begin. Marissa hurried back to her seat next to Johnny.

"Sorry about that," Marissa said as she flashed a smile his way. "It took longer than I expected for Lucy to express her displeasure with me."

"Displeasure?"

Marissa nodded. "Best friends don't keep secrets from each other, and she can't believe I didn't tell her about you."

He didn't ask her why she'd never told anyone about him. They'd been through that already. She'd said it was for Benjamin's sake, but that didn't explain the fact that she'd never told anyone about him while they were dating, before he'd been arrested and she'd discovered her pregnancy.

Their dates had always been secret trysts in places where nobody would see them together. At the time he'd been touched, thought it was because she didn't want to share him with anyone else. At the time he hadn't cared…he'd have met her at the garbage dump if that's what she'd wanted.

He knew different now. Shame. There had been no

other reason for her to keep his presence in her life a secret. He'd been the poor, fatherless Crockett kid, and she'd been the golden daughter of the mayor. She hadn't wanted any of her friends to know she was dating him. She'd been ashamed to be seen with him.

Yet, it was hard to work up any real anger. That time was so distant, and as she'd said before, they were now two different people.

"Johnny?" Her voice was a soft whisper.

He turned and looked at her.

"Are you all right?" The disarming wrinkle appeared across her brow, letting him know she had sensed his tension.

"Sure, I'm fine considering I'm the town pariah." He gestured to the empty seats surrounding them.

Marissa took his hand in hers, her grasp warm, her skin soft. "Give them time, Johnny. They're good people who don't understand the truth about you, the truth about your innocence. You frighten them, and many of them owe too much money to the Emerys to show any support for you."

Johnny nodded and released her hand, finding the softness, the warmth far too pleasant. "It doesn't matter whether anyone accepts me or not. I've had ten years to grow accustomed to being alone. I'm good alone. I don't need anybody in my life."

"But there's somebody who desperately needs you," Marissa said softly. "Benjy."

At that moment the lights overhead dimmed and the velvet curtain drew open to display the stage. Johnny's gaze sought his son, who stood stage left. Yes, Benjamin needed him…and he needed Benjamin. What he couldn't understand was the slight disappointment that had shot through him at her words. Disappointment in the fact that she hadn't said she needed him, too.

Chapter 6

Marissa had been to dozens of school plays before, but none of them had felt quite so special as this one. She knew the reason why this one was different. Johnny sat next to her, filling her senses with his nearness.

The heat from his body warmed her, the scent of his cologne teased her with myriad unwanted memories. His hands rested on his thighs, capable hands with a sprinkling of dark hair across the back of each one.

He'd told her he loved the smallness, the daintiness of her hands. And she loved the size of his, big enough to perfectly cup her breast, but not so big as to be clumsy. She felt the warmth of her thoughts sweeping through her.

Despite the pain he'd caused her, the betrayal she'd once felt, she'd held the memories of those days and nights they'd shared close to her heart, unable to bear shoving them aside.

She wondered if that's why there had never been an-

other man in her life. She'd used the excuse of her business and her son, pretending those were the reasons she
didn't have any relationships with men. The truth was
that Johnny had branded her heart, left scars that nobody
else had ever been able to heal.

She stirred in the chair, leaning forward as Benjamin
stepped out of the crowd and to the center of the stage.
Nobody had ever questioned the identity of Benjamin's
father. With Johnny gone for so long, and nobody knowing he and Marissa had dated, everyone had easily ac-
cepted that Benjamin was Brian Theron's child.

With Johnny back in town, it was impossible not to
recognize Benjamin as his. Marissa had heard the whispers that followed them as they'd walked to the front
row, knew that her friends and neighbors were seeing the
resemblance between father and son for the first time.
Johnny's eyes...his chin...the way his hair grew...they
all were there on Benjamin, the mark of the father on the
child.

As the intro music to Benjamin's song began, he
squinted to see beyond the footlights, his eyes twinkling
as he saw his parents on the front row. Johnny tugged
his ear, just as he'd promised he would, and Benjamin's
smile widened broadly.

Warmth flooded Marissa. She didn't care what kind of
censure she suffered because of Johnny's relationship to
Benjamin. Nothing the people of Mustang could do to
her would make her sever the growing love between father and son. Nothing would force her to deprive Benjamin of Johnny's love. They needed each other.

With a smile still lighting his features, Benjamin began
to sing, his voice achingly clear and sweet. She felt
Johnny's pride as he leaned forward, his mouth opened
in utter awe. Unconsciously his hand reached for hers,

and in that moment of parental pride, they were united as one.

She'd watched Benjamin perform so many times before, almost always alone in her pride. Sharing with Johnny the talent of their son filled her heart with joy.

All too quickly Benjamin's performance was over and Johnny removed his hand from hers. Marissa didn't understand the dichotomy of her own feelings where he was concerned.

He'd hurt her badly before. If she were smart she would have absolutely nothing whatsoever to do with him. She would allow him liberal visitations with Benjamin and nothing more.

But, there was a part of her that still yearned for his smiles, dreamed of his touch, wished somehow that history could be rewritten where the two of them were concerned. However, there would always be the spectral vision of a murdered girl between them.

Sydney. Other than speaking of the circumstances that had seen Johnny imprisoned, he and Marissa had never spoken of what Sydney had meant to Johnny. Marissa didn't want to know. She didn't want to know how much of Johnny's heart had been shared between herself and Sydney.

Marissa pulled her thoughts away from the past and focused on the grand finale taking place on stage. At the end of the cowboy song medley, everyone rose to their feet, giving the smiling children a standing ovation.

The curtain closed for the final time and the auditorium lights went on, bathing the audience in their fluorescent glare. "What happens now?" Johnny asked as he and Marissa stood.

"We stand around and visit, drink too-sweet punch and eat bad cookies. It's a tradition at these school functions," Marissa explained. At that moment the kids came pouring out of the door from the backstage area.

Benjamin came running toward them, a huge grin on his face. "Did you like it?" he asked, looking first at Marissa, then at Johnny.

"Like it? We loved it!" Marissa leaned down and gave him a kiss on the cheek.

"Ah, Mom," he exclaimed, wiping his cheek as if to swipe away the kiss.

"I'm so proud of you, son," Johnny said as he clapped a hand on Benjamin's shoulder.

"Are we gonna get some cookies?" Benjamin asked.

"I've got an alternative idea," Johnny offered. "I bought a gallon of Rocky Road ice cream this afternoon. We could go back to my place and celebrate Benjamin's talent with a big bowl." He looked at Marissa. "I thought maybe you'd like to see some of the work I've done around the place in the last week."

Marissa's first impulse was to say a resounding no. This was exactly what she didn't want, a personal relationship with Johnny. But the look on Benjamin's face stilled her initial rejection.

"Rocky Road is my favorite," Benjamin said.

"I know." Johnny tousled his son's hair. "You told me that last time we were together." He looked at Marissa. "So, what do you think?" He held her gaze for only a moment, then he looked toward the crowd gathering around the refreshment table.

Marissa suddenly realized how difficult it had been for him to come here this evening, to be put on public display so to speak. He'd done it for the love of Benjamin. But she knew standing around trying to visit with people who believed him to be a murderer would be sheer torture.

"What do you think, Benjy? Are you up for some Rocky Road?" she asked.

"Sure," he agreed enthusiastically. "I'd rather have ice cream than the crummy cookies they always have here."

"Then let's go," Johnny said.

It took them only minutes to leave the school and head out to Johnny's place. The sun was drifting low in the sky, as if reluctant to give way to night. As they drove with the windows down, the smell of sweet pastures, rich earth and wildflowers flowed through the windows. Marissa couldn't imagine living anywhere else in the world but here.

"Beautiful, isn't it?" Johnny said, as if he had read her thoughts. "I missed it so much…the smell of home."

Benjamin shrugged. "It smells like air to me."

Johnny laughed, a deep rumble that echoed warmly through Marissa. "That's Montana air, son. The best kind there is."

"I've never been anywhere else, so I don't know if it's the best or not," Benjamin replied.

For the next few minutes of the drive, they discussed the show. While Benjamin filled them in on the backstage antics of his classmates, Marissa tried to keep her gaze focused away from Johnny. But it was difficult.

He looked so handsome in his crisp white shirt and navy slacks. Although his hair was long and rather shaggy, like Benjamin's, it suited his features. But it wasn't just his physical appearance that touched her, it was his laughter as he responded to Benjamin's stories, the warmth that lit his eyes each time he gazed at his son.

He was more open when Benjamin was around, the anger she always sensed in him seemed to dissipate when

Benjy was near. It was as if the rage of injustice couldn't be sustained beneath the power of his love for his son.

She turned her head to peer out the side window, afraid that it would be all too easy for him to take her in again, make her care about him when he'd already told her their time together in the past meant nothing to him.

Maybe she should start dating. Jesse Wilder, the handsome sheriff of Mustang, had indicated on more than one occasion that he'd like to get to know her better. She frowned, knowing that although Jesse was handsome and witty, he didn't have what it took to erase Johnny from her memory, from the place where he'd burrowed into her heart.

"Hey, Mom, look at the horses." Benjamin drew her attention, pointing to the Emery pasture, where a dozen horses frolicked and danced in the evening air.

"The Emerys always did have nice horses," Johnny said, his voice carefully neutral in tone.

"Some day I want a horse of my own. Bobby Willis has a horse and I get to ride when I go to visit him, but that's not like having your very own," Benjamin said. "Grandpa lets me ride old Tandy, but she's no better than riding the metal kiddie horse in front of the grocery store."

"Tandy is still alive?" Johnny asked with surprise. "I thought she was older than dirt ten years ago."

Marissa laughed. "Yes, surprisingly enough, Tandy is still alive."

She knew he was remembering how often she'd ridden the old brown horse from her parents' ranch to his. Her parents had rarely allowed her to use the car, so the old nag had become an unknowing third party to Johnny and Marissa's secret trysts.

The sun was just kissing the day goodbye as they

turned onto the lane that led to Johnny's house. Almost immediately Marissa could see the results of his work over the last week. Dead brush and tree limbs had been removed and the lawn leading up to the house had been neatly cut.

"Hey, Dad, it looks great," Benjamin said.

"It certainly does," Marissa replied. Deep twilight added a pale golden glow to the newly painted house, giving it a warmth and sense of welcome that had been lacking before.

As Johnny drove closer, Marissa frowned, squinting against the approaching darkness of night as she realized something wasn't right. The paint across the front of the house was splotched...or streaked.

Johnny cursed beneath his breath and as the truck came to a halt directly before his home, Marissa could see exactly what the streaks were...letters in red spray paint. The message was clear, vivid against the pristine new white paint.

Murderer. Get out of Mustang.

The ugly vandalism shouldn't have surprised Johnny, but it did. He wanted to reach over and cover Benjamin's eyes, wished Benjamin was young enough that he couldn't yet read. But of course that wasn't so.

He heard Benjamin's swift intake of breath at the same time he heard Marissa's, even as shock and anger rippled through him. He turned off the truck engine but kept the lights on, their beams pointing to the front of the house where the message had been sprayed.

He said nothing. Words refused to form in the mire of hopelessness that filled him. Nobody was ever going to let him forget. He would never be able to find any kind of peace here, never be able to build anything substantial in the face of such hatred.

"We can paint over it."

Benjamin's voice was low and innocent as he offered a simplistic solution to the problem.

"We could have a painting party right now," Marissa added. "It's not quite dark yet and with the lights from the truck, we can see just fine to do a little cleanup work."

Their solid support drove away Johnny's hopelessness and replaced it with determination. Their faith in his ability to continue on shamed him. It would be easy to give up, pick up and move on to someplace where he had no history, no baggage following behind him. But, where there was no history, there was no Benjamin, and that simply wasn't an option.

"A painting party might be fun," he agreed not looking at either Benjamin or Marissa, but instead imagining having to face the graffiti in the glare of the sun the next morning. He had a feeling it would look much worse in bright daylight than in the lavender shades of deep evening.

"And our reward when we get done can be a big bowl of Rocky Road," Marissa said.

Johnny turned and looked at her and for a moment their gazes held. In hers, he saw no pity, no compassion. Any hint of those emotions would have angered him.

What he saw instead was empathy, and strength shining in the chocolate-brown depths of her eyes. Oh, how he'd wanted to see those emotions from her years before. He remembered vividly sitting in the stinking, filthy jail cell waiting to see what happened next. He knew no matter how bad things looked for him, as long as Marissa believed in him, as long as she loved him, he'd get through whatever fate threw at him.

But, she hadn't come to the jail. She hadn't sent him a note or passed along a message, and in her silence, he'd known the truth.

"Johnny?" She looked at him quizzically.

He mentally pushed at the anger his thoughts had summoned. He knew the fury he'd once entertained toward her had no place in his life now, but he was unable to completely liberate himself from its grip. It had been with him too long, had come to feel almost comfortable.

"Let's get to it," he finally said and opened his truck door. As Benjamin climbed out behind him, he looked at Marissa in her pretty blue dress. "You can't paint in that," he said.

Marissa got out of the truck and looked down at her dress as if just realizing it wasn't appropriate paintwear. "Do you have an old shirt and sweatpants I could throw on to work in? And maybe an old shirt for Benjy?"

"Yeah, I'll find something. While you're both changing, I can get the paint ready to go."

It took Johnny only minutes to rummage up one of his old shirts for Benjamin. He got another of his shirts and a pair of his mother's jogging pants for Marissa. While Marissa changed clothes, Benjamin and Johnny went out to the shed to get what was needed to do the job.

"Dad?"

Johnny grabbed a gallon of paint and handed his son several brushes. "Yes?"

"You aren't gonna let them run you off, are you?" Benjamin's voice was slightly shaky with uncertainty.

Johnny set the paint can down and crouched in front of his son, his hands on the boy's slim shoulders. "Nobody is going to run me off."

Johnny saw the doubts in Benjamin's eyes...recognized the need to believe coupled with the reality of trust unearned. There was not enough concrete relationship between them for Benjamin to unconditionally believe his father's words. Johnny knew there was nothing that could take those doubts from Benjamin, nothing but time.

"Benjamin, I've already missed nine years of your life. I promise you that nothing and nobody is going to make me miss another minute." It was the best Johnny could give his son at the moment...and for the moment it seemed to be enough.

Johnny stood and picked up the paint can, then he and Benjamin left the shed.

Night was falling fast, reaching out with dark fingers to grasp the last of the day, The grass held the faint sparkle of the evening dew and the air smelled sweet and clean.

Johnny and Benjamin made their way to the front porch. Marissa was still inside changing her clothes. Johnny popped the lid off the paint can and stirred the thick liquid.

"Dad?" Benjamin sat on the top stair of the porch, next to where Johnny worked. "I think Mom made a mistake."

Johnny looked at Benjamin in surprise. The boy's features were starkly lit by the lights of the truck and the glow of the porch lamp. "What do you mean? She made a mistake about what?"

"About you and me." Benjamin frowned thoughtfully. "She should have told me about you a long time ago."

"She did what she thought was best," Johnny replied, trying to keep all emotion from his voice.

"Yeah, but if I'd known about you before, I could

have written you letters and sent you pictures and stuff like that,'' Benjamin continued.

Johnny focused on stirring the paint once again, desperately trying to rein in the emotions that swirled inside him.

Would it have made a difference to know about Benjamin? Would letters and pictures from his son have eased the time served? Kept his hope alive? Nurtured the dreams that instead had died?

Through the myriad emotions that raged through him, one fought for and won dominance…anger. It swept through him, hot and thick, comforting in its simplicity.

''Okay, the master painter is ready to go,'' Marissa said as she stepped out of the front door.

''Great, let's get started,'' Johnny said, still fighting against the anger of years lost, precious moments not shared.

Within minutes all three of them worked side by side, dabbing pristine white paint across the slashing red of the large letters.

Again and again, despite his desire to the contrary, his gaze shot to Marissa. She'd looked lovely early in the evening in her tasteful navy dress, but there was something particularly alluring about a woman clad in a man's shirt and a pair of jogging pants that didn't quite fit right.

His mother had been shorter than Marissa, and the soft cotton fleece clung to Marissa's curves as they never had to his mother's. The shirt he'd loaned her, an old white dress shirt he'd outgrown, appeared to mold to the thrust of her breasts. Through the thin material he could see the lace of her bra.

He tightened his grip on his paintbrush, needing to cling to his anger. Surely if he remained angry with her the desire that flowed through his veins would dissipate.

Surely if he reminded herself that she was here with him now only because of Benjamin, he could maintain the ire that kept passion at bay.

It took them about half an hour to finish the painting. While Johnny and Benjamin put the paint away and cleaned up the brushes, Marissa went inside to make a pot of coffee and dip up three bowls of ice cream.

Benjamin ate his ice cream in no time, then stretched out on the sofa in front of the television. Marissa and Johnny remained at the table, finishing their ice cream, and sipping coffee as a strained silence grew between them.

"The play was fun, wasn't it?" Marissa said, a forced smile curving her lips.

"Sure, it was fun," Johnny agreed.

He knew she sensed the tension in him, knew it by the way she shifted positions in her chair, how her fingers drummed an uneasy rhythm on the table, and her gaze kept darting around the room as if seeking an escape route.

"Do you think it was Brad Emery?" she asked, her gaze finally settling on him.

He shrugged, knowing she was talking about the ugly graffiti that had decorated his home. "Probably, although it could have been anyone who believes I killed Sydney." He paused a moment and took a sip of his coffee.

Marissa took advantage of the pause by spooning a dollop of her ice cream into her mouth. Johnny took another sip of coffee. If he kissed her now, she would taste of sweet ice cream and nuts. Her mouth would be cool, but would warm quickly beneath the heat of his own.

His body reacted to his wayward thoughts and he fought against it, seeking his anger to use as a shield against his desire. Dammit, he didn't want to want her.

"You realize you might feel some negative feedback after tonight," he said, grateful when she pushed her ice cream bowl aside.

"Negative feedback? You mean because of my past relationship with you?" She shook her head, and waved a hand as if to dismiss the very idea. "These people are my friends, my neighbors. I'm a respected business-woman, and I can't imagine anyone in Mustang giving me a hard time."

"Such naiveté," Johnny said, and smiled sardonically. He leaned forward in his chair and didn't attempt to hide the bitterness that roiled inside him. "Ten years ago I thought I had friends here, people who knew me and knew what kind of a man I was. When trouble found me, I thought those friends would rally around me. They didn't, and don't think those friends and neighbors of yours won't be the first to cast stones at you." He leaned back.

Marissa was silent for a moment, her cheeks wearing stains of color. "You've grown hard, Johnny."

He snorted, "Yeah, well, prison tends to do that to a person."

She took a sip of her coffee, her eyes not reflecting any of her thoughts. He had no idea what she was think-ing…feeling, and that bothered him.

"What progress have you made in clearing your name and finding out the real killer?" she asked.

Johnny's bitterness momentarily seeped away beneath the weight of weariness. "Not much." He raked a hand through his hair. "I've studied all the reports, files and news clippings. The police files list five other men as possible suspects. All five of the men worked on the Em-ery ranch."

"But that's good!" Marissa exclaimed. "So, what did the investigation show about these men?"

"What investigation?" The bitterness returned, eating at his insides with insidious claws of despair. "According to the files there was no real investigation, a few cursory questions to each of the men and that was it." He drew a deep breath. "The way I see it, the authorities already believed they had the guilty party...me." He cast her a taut smile. "I believe it's called a rush to justice. I was poor, without social power and I had a reputation as a brawler. I was a perfect fall guy."

Again Marissa was silent, her brown eyes deep pools of contemplation that offered nothing. "So, what's your next move?"

"To see what I can find out about the five men that were originally listed as potential suspects." Johnny stood abruptly. "Look, I don't want to go into this right now," he said. He didn't want to think about all the work ahead of him in attempting to clear his name. Right now the truth seemed as elusive as happiness and his need to pursue it was like a deep, gnawing hunger inside him.

"We should get home," Marissa said. She stood and quickly cleared the table of their bowls and cups. Then together she and Johnny left the kitchen and walked into the living room to find Benjamin sound asleep on the sofa.

Marissa started to rouse the boy, calling his name softly.

"Don't," Johnny said. "I'll carry him to the truck." He scooped up Benjamin into his arms. Benjamin stirred, turning toward the warmth of Johnny's body, but didn't awaken.

The ride to Marissa's home was accomplished in silence. Benjamin slept, Johnny drove and Marissa stared out the passenger window as if seeking elusive answers in the darkness.

When they got to Marissa's house, Johnny carried the still sleeping Benjamin upstairs to the bedroom decorated in rearing wild stallions and spurred cowboy boots. Gently, he placed Benjamin on the bed, then removed the dress shoes the boy had been wearing. He still wore the paint-splattered, cast-off shirt of Johnny's. Seeing his son in the too-big shirt he had once worn caused Johnny's heart to squeeze tight in his chest.

Half-grown. At nine, Benjamin was halfway to being an adult. Johnny had missed almost all of his childhood. He'd never see Benjamin as a toddler, running toward him as he babbled da-da. He would never experience the joy of holding Benjamin as a tiny newborn, or smell the scent of sweet infancy.

As he left Benjamin's bedroom, his anger once again grew hard and cold in his chest. Marissa had come to the prison to talk him out of returning to Mustang. She'd never intended to tell him about his son if he hadn't returned to his hometown. His return had forced her hand. The thought expanded his core of anger and it pressed suffocatingly tight inside him.

Marissa stood at the bottom of the stairs waiting for him. She smiled as he approached, the smile wavering slightly as he drew nearer. "Everything all right?" she asked, the hesitancy in her question letting him know she felt the tension that rolled from him.

"Fine," he returned evenly as he walked past her and to the front door. He knew he should leave the house, get out, get away from her before the anger took complete possession of him.

At the door he turned back to her, wishing she didn't look so damned alluring, wishing his anger was strong enough to suppress the desire that just looking at her pulled forth.

He ached with the need to hate her, but found it impossible to hate that which he so desired.

"Good night, Johnny," she said as he opened the door.

He started to reply, but instead stopped fighting his need. He released the door, took one step toward her and without warning wrapped her in his arms and pulled her tight against him.

She opened her mouth as if to protest, but he didn't give her a chance. He covered her mouth with his own, somehow wanting to punish her for not loving him enough years before.

She pushed her hands against his chest in protest, but it was a protest that lasted only a moment. What had begun as punishment on his part quickly turned into deep, ravenous hunger, and what had started as a protest on her part transformed into eager, hot surrender.

Her mouth tasted of the lingering flavor of the ice cream she'd eaten earlier. He held her so tight he could feel the thrust of her breasts against him, feel the frantic beating of her heart mirroring the rhythm of his own.

Her surrender was total and acquiescence complete as her body melded against his, her soft curves molding to the angles and planes of his body as if made to do just that.

Her tongue touched his, and sizzling flames streaked through his veins. The taste of her, the scent of her, the feel of her so close to him evoked emotions he'd tried to forget, sentiments he'd tried to suppress.

He'd thought he could kiss her, then walk away, but as his body responded to the nearness of hers, he realized a kiss wasn't enough. It hadn't been years ago and it wasn't now.

He ran his hands down the length of her slender back, remembering how perfectly their bodies had once fit together. Even as an inexperienced teenager, Marissa had displayed a natural, healthy passion, a greediness that had driven him wild. It was the memory of their past love-making that now stoked a wildness inside him. He didn't want to think anymore…he just wanted to fall into the pleasure of tasting Marissa.

Cupping her buttocks, he pulled her more tightly against him, knowing she would be able to feel the extent of his arousal. The intimate contact made her gasp, stiffen and pull her mouth from his.

Instantly he released his hold on her, damning himself, damning her. He'd meant to remain in control, but had come precariously close to losing it.

He took a step backward, desire not abated, but rather simmering dangerously. Her lips were red and slightly swollen from the deep, long kiss they had shared. As he watched her, she took a finger and touched her lips, as if stunned by what they had just shared.

"Why…why did you do that?" she asked, slightly breathless.

He shrugged and stuffed his hands into his jeans pockets, afraid that if he didn't confine them they would pull her into another embrace. "I remember you were pretty good at kissing years ago…I wanted to see if you've improved with age."

Marissa's cheeks pinkened. "And have I?"

Johnny paused a moment, drawing in air to steady himself, refusing to allow her to see that she affected him in any way. He'd intended the kiss to punish her, and the need to do so remained stronger than ever. "Hell, Marissa. I've spent the last ten years in prison. At this point in my life kissing most any woman would feel good."

Her eyes darkened at the hurtful words and his harsh tone. He waited for a sense of satisfaction to sweep through him, but it didn't happen. He drew a deep breath, suddenly weary. "Good night, Marissa," he said and without another word, without looking at her again, he left the house.

He drove too fast going home, carefully keeping his mind as blank as possible. Gravel spewed beneath his tires and the rear end of the truck fishtailed as he turned onto the road that led to his ranch.

The taste of Marissa still filled his mouth, her scent still eddied in his head. It had been a mistake to kiss her. He would never, could never forgive her for not standing beside him so long ago. He couldn't, wouldn't forgive her for stealing so much of his son's life, for all the lies she'd engendered in the last ten years.

However, what he couldn't understand was why, if he intended his kiss to be a punishment to her, he was the one who felt most punished?

Chapter 7

"Get out of bed, you lazy bum. We've got some talking to do," Lucy's voice pulled Marissa from a deep sleep. She cracked an eyelid to see Lucy pulling open her curtains, allowing into the room the brilliant morning sunshine.

"Go away," Marissa grumbled and closed her eye once again. She didn't want to get up. She didn't want to awaken enough to think.

If she woke up, she knew that she would think about the kiss that had rocked her to her toes. Besides, she knew what Lucy wanted to talk about...Johnny. And Marissa didn't want to think or talk about him. "Come back in two hours," she said. "It's still the crack of dawn."

"I'm not leaving, and it's the crack of ten o'clock," Lucy countered. She grabbed hold of the bottom of the blankets and yanked, pulling them off Marissa and onto the floor. "Get up, girlfriend. You've got some explaining to do."

Marissa rolled over on her back and glared at her friend. "How did you get in here?"

"Benjy let me in. He's in the living room watching some movie on the VCR."

"As soon as I'm fully awake, remind me to kill him," Marissa replied.

Lucy laughed. "I'll go put on some coffee and you get dressed. I'll meet you in the kitchen in ten minutes. If you don't show, I'll come back and drag your butt out of that bed." With this warning, she disappeared from the room.

Marissa remained on her back for a long moment, staring up at the bedroom ceiling. It had been late when they'd returned from Johnny's place, but despite her tiredness and the lateness of the hour, sleep had refused to rescue her from troubling thoughts.

She'd tossed and turned, playing and replaying that kiss in her mind, wondering how a simple meeting of their lips had been so disturbing. It had been dawn when she'd finally fallen into a troubled sleep, a sleep haunted by dreams of Johnny...and of Sydney.

With a resigned sigh, she pulled herself out of bed and padded into the bathroom. It took her only minutes to comb her hair and brush her teeth, wash her face, then pull on a robe over her nightgown.

As she belted the robe, she walked down the hallway and into the living room, where Benjy was stretched out on the sofa, engrossed in his favorite movie. As she passed him on her way to the kitchen, she kissed his forehead. "Good morning."

"Morning, Mom," he said absently, frowning momentarily as she walked between him and the television.

"Ah, perfect timing," Lucy said as Marissa went into the kitchen and sank down at the table. She poured two cups of the fresh-brewed coffee, then joined Marissa, sitting across from her.

"Okay...spill your guts," she demanded.

Marissa blew on her coffee, then took a sip, enjoying Lucy's sigh of impatience. "Spill my guts about what?" she asked, although she knew perfectly well what Lucy wanted to hear.

Lucy rolled her eyes. "You show up last night at the school play with the most notorious man in town. Suddenly everyone realizes your son looks just like him and you can't think of anything I might want to talk about?"

Lucy's cupid lips turned downward in a frown of hurt. "We've been best friends since fifth grade. I thought we told each other everything. But obviously I was the one doing all the telling and you were the one keeping secrets."

Marissa recognized her friend's hurt and she reached out and covered Lucy's hand with hers. "Lucy, nobody knew about Johnny, not my parents, not you...I didn't tell a soul that I was seeing him."

It was difficult for her to explain why she'd kept her relationship with Johnny a secret. "I was so crazy about him. I felt as if what we had was so special...I wasn't ready to share those feelings with anyone else at the time. I loved him so much, I was afraid talking about it might somehow jinx it."

She released her hold on Lucy's hand. "Besides, my relationship with Johnny was over almost as soon as it began. He was arrested and I realized while he was romancing me, he was apparently also romancing Sydney."

Even now, after all the years that had passed, the pain

of Johnny's betrayal created a gnawing emptiness in her heart. She wondered if it was a hurt that would ever heal.

"So, what about last night? The two of you together? Everyone was buzzing about it when you left. Even Millie Creighton was running around trying to find out the scoop on you and Mustang's sexiest ex-con."

"Oh terrific," Marissa moaned. Millie Creighton... Mustang's zealous social reporter. The woman was like a tenacious tick, burrowing into a story and sucking it for all the drama she could. The last thing Marissa wanted to see was a column in the *Mustang Monitor* about herself and Johnny.

"So?" Lucy repeated. "Come clean...are you and Johnny back together?"

"Absolutely not," Marissa replied, more impassioned than she'd intended. She paused a moment to take another drink of her coffee, then continued. "Johnny went with us last night to the school play because Benjamin invited him. As Benjamin's father, Johnny and I have to remain in close contact."

Lucy shook her head. "I can't believe Johnny is Benjy's father. Like everyone else in town, I really thought Brian Theron got you pregnant, then dumped you and moved out of town."

"I didn't think it was in my best interest, or Benjamin's for anyone to know any different. Johnny was in prison. I didn't know if he'd ever get out. What good could come from me telling anyone he was Benjy's father? I didn't think about him eventually returning to settle here." She smiled ruefully. "Stupid, huh?"

"Women are rarely logical when it comes to matters of the heart," Lucy replied. She eyed Marissa curiously. "It must have been strange seeing Johnny after all these years. Any sparks left between the two of you?"

"None." Marissa's reply came a second too late to ring true. Lucy grinned knowingly and a blush warmed Marissa's cheeks. "Okay…maybe a few sparks are still simmering, but I don't intend to allow them to flare any hotter."

"Why not?" Lucy asked. "You've always said you believed he was innocent of Sydney's murder."

"I do believe he's innocent," Marissa agreed. "Nobody will ever make me believe that Johnny had anything to do with Sydney's death."

"Then why not let those sparks explode into something exciting? Lord knows, I don't know how you manage to stay celibate and sane at the same time."

Marissa laughed. "Contrary to what you think, sex isn't the be-all and end-all of life."

"But it was good with Johnny, right?" Marissa's cheeks flamed hot again. "You don't even have to answer that…the answer is written all over your face." Lucy leaned forward. "Why not enjoy yourself, Marissa? You've spent the last ten years working and raising Benjamin. Why not indulge yourself in a torrid affair with Johnny?"

"Because I don't do affairs," Marissa retorted, uncomfortable with the entire conversation. She ran her fingers around the rim of her mug. "Besides, one round with Johnny Crockett is all my heart can take." She stared reflectively at the last of the coffee in her mug. "He broke my heart, Lucy. Every time he made love to me, he told me I was the only one in the world for him…and every time he said that, he lied. He told me just a few nights ago that all we had in the past really didn't mean anything to him. It would be impossible for me to get past that."

She looked at her friend again. "Besides, he's not the

same man he was ten years ago. He's not the man I fell in love with. He's grown hard and bitter. I don't think there's room in Johnny's heart for love except maybe love for Benjamin.''

"That's so sad," Lucy said. "It's too bad you two couldn't rediscover the love you lost. I mean, it would be so romantic if after everything that has happened and after all the years that have passed, you two got together again.''

Marissa shook her head. "You can't rediscover what you never really had. I loved Johnny, but he didn't love me. We can't rewrite history and make it something it wasn't.''

She stood, tired of the topic of the conversation. She'd gone over the same territory in her mind all night, reminding herself that no matter how deeply his kiss had stirred her, it meant nothing to him. He'd told her as much when he'd said they should sleep together, that it didn't have to mean anything…it never had.

She hadn't believed her heart was still capable of aching, but his words had caused an enormous, breath-stealing pain.

His kiss had confirmed one thing—she needed to guard her heart where Johnny Crockett was concerned.

She'd thought her heartache of years before would be strong enough to immunize her from his charms, but the kiss had told her differently. She was still vulnerable to Johnny, and intended to guard her heart accordingly.

"More coffee?" she asked Lucy as she added fresh brew to her own cup.

"No, thanks, I'm fine," Lucy replied.

"That's enough about me. Tell me what's going on in your life," Marissa said as she rejoined her friend at the table.

Lucy took the not-so-subtle hint and changed the subject. "I've been seeing quite a bit of Derrick Masters lately."

"Derrick Masters? As in Dr. Derrick?" Derrick was the local veterinarian, a handsome thirty-something who had moved to Mustang some months before.

Lucy grinned. "Yup. In fact, I'm seeing him tonight. I think he just might be Mr. Right."

"Oh, Lucy, that's wonderful," Marissa exclaimed, fighting down a small surge of envy as she saw the way Lucy's eyes sparkled, the smile that lit her from within as she spoke of Derrick. Someday, Marissa thought. Someday she wanted that for herself.

"Are you handling all the floral decorations for the prom?" Lucy asked after she had extolled on all the virtues of Dr. Derrick.

"I haven't heard officially, but I assume so. I've done the floral arrangements for the past four years." The high-school prom was held in the gymnasium, and usually the decorations were a combination of real flowers and painted backdrops. Next to Valentine's Day and Mother's Day, the prom was the biggest profit maker for Marissa's shop. "I expect to hear from Mrs. Emery sometime this week about what kinds of flowers they want this year."

Lucy nodded, then frowned. "Don't you find it odd that Mrs. Emery is on the school board but both her daughters were tutored at home and didn't go to school?"

"I've always found the Emerys odd," Marissa replied, thinking of Sydney's mother, stepbrother and sister. "Even though Rachel works on the school board and Bradley is on the town council, they keep to themselves."

"Every time I see poor Gillian in town, my heart goes

out to her. She looks so lonely and so terribly sad." Lucy leaned forward. "You know she's just the same age Sydney was when Sydney was killed. Seventeen." Lucy shook her head. "So young…and Sydney used to have the same look as Gillian does…a haunted look. Even though she was from the richest family in town, something about the way she looked always made me feel sorry for her."

Marissa didn't want to think about Sydney. Although her heart ached for the girl who'd lost her life at the hands of a killer, she couldn't forget that Sydney had been the girl who'd shared Johnny's heart. Her death would always remain between Marissa and Johnny.

If Johnny decided he wanted a relationship with Marissa once again, Marissa would never know if she'd won Johnny's heart through default. She'd never know if Sydney had been his one true love and she was nothing more than a second choice.

Of course, it didn't matter now. She was never going to give Johnny another chance, nor did she believe he would want another chance with her. There was too much water under the bridge, too many heartaches piled on top of one another. They could never go back, she could never gain back the utter innocence and trust she'd brought to Johnny, an innocence and trust he'd destroyed.

"I can't believe prom is only a couple weeks away." Lucy leaned back in the chair, her smile wistful with memories. "God, I loved my senior-year prom. I went with Jason Hewlett and he bought me my very first orchid corsage. I thought he was the most handsome, debonair, sexy guy in the entire school." She wrapped her arms around herself and sighed. "Good memories." Lucy looked at Marissa curiously. "You didn't go to our senior-year prom, did you?"

Marissa smiled, remembering that night so long ago. "Yes and no. That was the time period that I was dating Johnny. I knew he didn't have money to go to the prom, so I told my parents I was going alone. I got all dressed up and met Johnny behind the high school."

Her memories burst forth inside her, warming her as she hadn't been warmed in a long time. Johnny had been dressed in a pair of jeans and a crisp, white dress shirt. His boots had been polished to a high gloss and his cowboy hat had sat on his head at a rakish angle. He'd taken Marissa's breath away.

"We could hear the music from the band spilling out through the open back doors of the gym. We danced for hours, just the two of us in the wooded area behind the school," Marissa said. She didn't tell Lucy that after they'd danced, they'd made love...slow, beautiful love in the sweet-smelling grass with the moon and the stars overhead. It had been a night of dreams...and she'd awakened the next morning to news of a nightmare. Sydney's body had been found, and the sheriff was on his way to Johnny's house to arrest him.

Marissa had climbed astride old Tandy and for the first time in years, the old nag had run like the wind. Marissa had arrived at Johnny's house just in time to see him being placed in handcuffs and shoved into the back of the sheriff's vehicle.

"Look, there's no way there's ever going to be anything between Johnny and me. He's Benjamin's father and that's the only role he'll play in my life," Marissa said, then frowned, realizing her outburst had come out of nowhere.

Lucy looked at her in surprise. "Okay," she said slowly. "So, who are you trying to convince? Me or yourself?"

The ringing of the telephone saved Marissa from having to reply.

"I'll get it," Benjamin called from the living room.

Marissa stood, feigning nonchalance but too agitated by their conversation to sit still. She grabbed a sponge and swiped the top of the counter.

"Mom...Dad wants to talk to you," Benjamin called from the living room.

Marissa smiled a quick apology to Lucy, then picked up the kitchen phone handset. "I've got it, Benjy," she said and heard the audible click of her son hanging up his receiver.

"Good morning." Johnny's deep voice glided across the line.

"Hello, Johnny, what can I do for you?" Marissa consciously kept her voice cool and controlled despite the warmth his voice evoked in her. She couldn't remember ever having a phone conversation with him before, and found his voice impossibly sexy.

"I thought maybe you and Benjy might like to go out for some pizza with me this evening."

"I'm sure Benjy would love to get some pizza with you tonight," Marissa replied.

"And what about you?"

Marissa clutched the receiver more tightly against her ear. This was exactly what she knew she couldn't allow to happen.

Johnny had to realize what his role in her life was going to be...and she knew her appeal to him at the moment was due to the fact that no other woman in town would have anything to do with him.

"I couldn't possibly go with you this evening. I have a date." Her words were met with silence. Lucy's eyebrows shot up in surprise and Marissa instantly regretted the impulsive lie.

"A date?" Johnny finally spoke, saying the words as if they were foreign to his vocabulary.

"Yes…you know…where a man and a woman go out, have dinner together, perhaps see a movie."

"And who is this date with?"

"A friend of Lucy's. It's all arranged." Marissa shot a frantic look to her friend. "We're double-dating this evening." If Lucy's eyebrows shot any higher, they would be completely off her head, Marissa thought as she stifled a flurry of hysteria. "I was going to get a sitter for Benjy, so this works out perfectly."

Marissa was aware that her voice was almost a full octave higher than normal. She drew a deep breath to steady herself. "My date should be here around six-thirty. Why don't you pick Benjy up around six, and we'll talk then about what time you can bring him home."

"Fine, I'll see you this evening."

It took Marissa a moment to realize he'd hung up. She hung her receiver back in the cradle then looked at Lucy. "I certainly hope your Dr. Derrick has a friend, because somehow in the next couple of hours you have to find me a date for this evening."

Chapter 8

A date. She had a date. Johnny stared at the phone receiver long after he'd hung it up, shocked not only by the fact that she had a date, but by his own reaction to her announcement.

Who was her date with? Was it the first time she'd gone out with him or the fifth...or the twentieth? Was it casual or serious? Question after question filled his head.

She'd told him she hadn't slept with anyone since their time together so long ago and he believed her. But, at the same time she'd told him that, he'd gotten it into his head that she also hadn't dated.

He stepped out of the house and onto the front porch, where he sank into on old patio chair. Somehow it had comforted him to believe that she'd kept herself just as isolated, just as alone as he had been during his time behind bars. But of course it had been foolish to think that a woman as beautiful as Marissa wouldn't have had plenty of dates over the past ten years.

Eventually she'd probably marry one of the most eligible bachelors in Mustang. Benjamin would have a stepfather, a man who would probably be successful and able to give the boy all the things that Johnny couldn't.

A rope of despair tied itself into a knot in Johnny's gut. Had he been wrong to force Marissa to tell Benjamin that he was Benjy's father? Had he only been thinking of himself and not his son?

He thought back to the night before, when Benjamin and Marissa had helped him paint the graffiti that covered the front of his house. What ugliness was he bringing into their life? Perhaps Marissa had been right all along in keeping his fatherhood of Benjamin a secret.

Still, it was too late to go back now. He couldn't imagine playing any other role in Benjamin's life than that of father. That particular relationship was easy...the emotions involved were clean and simple. He loved Benjamin with all his heart.

Much more complicated were his feelings where Marissa was concerned. He wanted to hate her, and hated wanting her. It was a curious dichotomy, one that had kept him up most of the night before.

He'd kissed her in an effort to somehow punish her, but it hadn't worked. The only thing the kiss had achieved was to make him want her more.

He'd gone to bed with the taste of her lips still on his mouth, the scent of her perfume filling his head. And in sleep, he'd gone back in time. He'd dreamed of holding her in his arms, remembering the warmth of her skin against his, the press of her full breasts against his chest.

In his dream he'd made love to her. Slowly...sweetly he'd possessed her, their bodies moving in perfect rhythm as they reached the pinnacle of pleasure together.

He'd awakened feeling bereft, as if he'd lost something

precious. Not only was he not sure what he'd lost, but he also wasn't sure exactly what he had done to lose it.

He stood, a wild recklessness coursing through him. He had several hours to spare before it would be time to pick up Benjamin. There were no pressing chores to be done, no livestock to tend, but he knew exactly how he wanted to spend the extra hours.

For the past couple of days, he'd been asking around about the men who the police had originally written up as potential suspects in Sydney's murder. Johnny had discovered one of the men had died, two of them still worked on the Emery ranch, and the two left had taken other jobs in town.

He also knew that on Sundays, while many townspeople attended church and enjoyed potluck lunches, many of the ranch hands spend their day off at the Roundup.

Johnny had no idea whether any of the men would talk to him or not, but he recognized it was a case of nothing ventured, nothing gained. Maybe, just maybe he'd get lucky and one of them would remember something that would point a finger of accusation toward somebody other than Johnny.

Besides, the anonymous call that had come into the sheriff's office the night of Sydney's murder telling the sheriff something was amiss at the old abandoned shed had come from the pay phone on the building outside of the Roundup. There was only one person who could have made that call...the killer.

It was Johnny's misfortune and the ill-timing of fate that when the sheriff arrived, Johnny was standing over Sydney's dead body. Even after all this time, there were still nights when Johnny suffered nightmares of Sydney's death, nights when her dead eyes haunted him and cried out for justice.

With justice in mind, Johnny arrived at the Roundup just after noon. The place was jumping with activity. The jukebox blared, glasses clinked and the sound of masculine voices filled the air.

Johnny eased onto an empty stool at the bar and ordered a burger, fries and a beer. The beer arrived first, cold and frothy. He took a sip of the brew as he spun around on the stool so he could observe the other patrons.

Two of the names that had been on the list Johnny had recognized. Scott Beamon and Clint Mayfield. Johnny had a vague picture of both men in his mind, although he was aware that his mental picture was ten years out-of-date. Still, he thought he would be able to identify either man if he saw him.

Surreptitiously he eyed each cowboy, careful to keep his eye contact minimal. In a place like this, eye contact could be perceived as a challenge and Johnny knew how quickly tempers could explode when macho posturing was mixed with booze.

When his hamburger and fries arrived, he turned back around and ate. The food was surprisingly good. The burger was oversized and charbroiled to perfection. The fries were greasy, but thick and golden brown with seasoned salt.

For a few minutes Johnny focused his entire attention on the pleasure of the food. For ten years he'd eaten the adequate, but relatively tasteless prison fare. Since his freedom, he'd taken to enjoying his meals as he never remembered doing in the distant past.

As he ate, the door opened and closed, admitting more cowhands as others left. Johnny had just finished his burger when the door opened and Clint Mayfield walked in.

Although the face of Johnny's memory was less wrin-

kled, the hair two shades darker than the gray that
streaked through it, Johnny was certain of the man's identity. He was even more sure when Clint's gaze fell on
him, and Johnny saw Clint's eyes darken with enmity.

Clint walked to the opposite end of the bar from where
Johnny sat. He sat on one of the stools and ordered a
drink, his gaze refusing to meet Johnny's.

Johnny finished his meal, then slid off his stool and
walked around the bar to where Clint sat. "Buy you a
drink?" he offered the older man.

"Nope. I can buy my own," Clint replied, still not
looking at Johnny.

"Could I talk to you for just a few minutes?"

Clint finally looked at him, his dark eyes filled with
dislike. "Now why in the hell would I want to talk to
you?"

"I'm hoping you're a man with a code of ethics, that
truth means something to you."

"Depends on whose truth we're talking about...yours
or the Emerys'?"

"It should be one and the same," Johnny replied.

Clint didn't respond for a long moment. He took a
deep drink of his whiskey, then rubbed his grizzled chin
thoughtfully. "I'll tell you right now, the Emerys pay
better than any other ranches in the state. I'm not going
to say or do anything that jeopardizes my position with
them."

"Did you know you were listed as one of the suspects
in Sydney's murder case?"

Clint nodded. "I figured as much. The sheriff questioned most of the hands on the ranch and there was a
bunch of us without alibis." Clint's eyes narrowed.
"However, the sheriff seemed pretty certain they already
had the killer in custody...you."

"Did you know Sydney?" Johnny asked, pushing forward despite Clint's obvious reluctance.

"Not personally. Her and her little sister didn't leave the house much." Clint frowned down into his drink. "I'd see Sydney sometimes, standing at her bedroom window staring outside. It wasn't natural…the way those girls were kept inside like prisoners." Clint clamped his mouth tightly closed, as if sorry he'd said as much as he had.

"Was Sydney seeing anyone that you know of? Dating one of the ranch hands? Did you hear any talk about her and anyone else?"

"No way," Clint replied. "Bradley would have killed any of the hands that looked twice at her." Clint downed the last of his drink and stood. "And that's all I got to say to you."

Johnny didn't try to stop Clint as he walked away from the bar. He knew he'd gotten as much as he could from the man. Unfortunately, it wasn't enough. It wasn't much of anything.

Surely somebody had to have seen something that night, heard something. He went back to his stool and sat down. He ordered another beer and as he sipped it, he thought back to all the nights he'd spent time with Sydney, all the conversations they'd had, seeking a clue as to why anyone would want to kill her.

He and Sydney had often sat in that old shed and talked. At the time their conversations hadn't seemed all that momentous, they'd just been passing time…sharing loneliness. Now it seemed imminently important that he remember every word of those conversations.

Sydney had talked about her love for her little sister, Gillian. She'd spoken of her intense desire to eventually get away from Mustang. She'd spoken little of her mother and her stepbrother, but Johnny had guessed that she resented them for their strictness with her.

He frowned into the last of his beer, feeling as if he was forgetting something, overlooking something important. But what? What had Sydney said or not said, done or not done that might lead him to her murderer?

He motioned the bartender over with a wave of his hand.

"Another beer?" the bartender asked.

"No. How about a little information?"

The bartender shrugged. "Information about what?"

"How long you been working here?" Johnny asked.

"Two years. Why?" The short man eyed Johnny with a hint of belligerence. "You got a problem with me?"

"No. I'd like to talk to somebody who was working here ten years ago," Johnny explained.

"Ten years ago?" The bartender frowned and swiped a wet towel across the countertop. "I wouldn't know who worked here that long ago. You might ask Gus Winstead over there…I think he's been coming in here since the beginning of time."

Johnny looked at the man the bartender indicated. Gus sat alone at a table in the corner, his wispy gray hair barely covering the shine of his scalp. He leaned back in his chair, his gaze focused intently on the whiskey bottle just in front of him.

"From what I hear, he was once a decent ranch hand…that was before the accident that crippled his right leg. Since then, he's mostly drunk all the time."

"Thanks," Johnny said to the bartender. He paid his tab, then walked toward Gus, fairly certain there was no way the old man would be able to help him.

"Mind if I join you?" he asked the old man.

Rheumy blue eyes peered up at him, then gestured

grandly to the seat across from him. "Last I heard, it was a free country."

Johnny nodded and sat across from him. "Heard you're a regular around here."

Gus snorted. "I get any more regular they'll be changing the name of this place to my name."

"Been coming here long?"

"Long enough." Gus eyed Johnny suspiciously. "You taking a survey?"

"Just looking for somebody who might have been around ten years ago," Johnny replied, realizing the old man was sharper than he'd initially suspected.

"What's so special about ten years ago?" Gus asked.

"A girl died…she was murdered."

Gus took a long drink directly from the bottle of booze. He belched, then nodded. "The Emery girl."

"You remember the night she died? Were you here that night?" Johnny leaned forward, mentally willing the old man's memory to work.

"I was here. Sitting right here at the table when I heard the news. And at the time I thought it was a damned shame that the wrong Emery got murdered."

Johnny sat back, stunned by the bitterness that radiated in Gus's voice. "Who would have been the right Emery?" he asked softly.

"That black-hearted, whip-snapping Bradley Emery…the devil take his soul." Gus threw back another long drink of the whiskey then stared at some indefinable spot above Johnny's head. "I worked for the Emerys for seven years. I was a damn good hand to have around. The little Emery girl…" he frowned.

"Gillian," Johnny supplied the name.

Gus nodded. "Gillian. She was about four when I saw her last. She had a broken arm and was wearing a cast.

She was standing on the porch and looked so sad…I gave her a piece of gum. I didn't think nothing about it and I went back to working a new horse in the corral.'' His gaze lowered and met Johnny's, and in the depths of his bloodshot blue eyes, Johnny saw hatred.

"Wasn't but a few minutes later that Bradley came looking for me. He wasn't nothing but a snot-nosed kid at that time, but he carried that whip everywhere he went. He hollered at me, told me if his stepsister needs gum, he'll get it for her, that Emerys don't mix with cowhands and I was to keep my distance. Then that boy cracked that whip. Scared the bejesus out of the horse I was on. He reared up and I fell off. The horse came crashing down atop of me…crushed my leg like a toothpick in a lawn mower.''

Gus drew a deep breath and raked a hand over his grizzly whiskered chin. "Damn boy ruined my life in the snap of a whip. He left me laying there on the ground, screaming for help. The other hands came running to help me, but Brad didn't even look back.''

Johnny drew a deep breath of his own, stunned by the story of brutality he'd just heard. He'd always known Brad was a man with a short fuse, but he hadn't realized just how merciless Brad could be.

"So you were here when you heard about Sydney's murder?'' Johnny asked after a moment of silence.

Gus looked at him with confusion. "Yes. Yes, I'm pretty sure I was here…either that night or the next one. I don't rightly remember.''

Suddenly Gus's pale blue eyes clouded over. "I hope her death broke his heart. I hope his heart bled tears of sorrow. He had it coming. Damned boy…damned Emerys…they all had it coming.'' He grabbed the bottle and held it close to his chest, and Johnny knew he'd lost him to whatever inner demons plagued his soul.

Johnny left the Roundup, questions still boiling in his head. Eventually, he would catch up to the other men listed as potential suspects, but for now he had enough food for thought.

It was odd that Gus Winstead hadn't been on the list of suspects. He obviously nursed a deep, abiding grudge against the Emerys. Was it a grudge strong enough to murder an innocent young woman? He doubted it; the old man seemed to care for Sydney and Gillian.

It was difficult to imagine the drunken old man being capable of physically harming someone anyway. However, ten years ago he wasn't so old. A man didn't need two strong legs to strangle a woman to death…all he needed was two powerful hands, and Gus Winstead had those.

As he drove toward his ranch, he tried to tamp down the feeling of hopelessness that pervaded him. Maybe Marissa had been right. How did he expect to solve a murder ten years after the fact when the authorities hadn't solved it at the time it had taken place? Maybe he was just spinning his wheels, wasting time that could be better spent in the present rather than digging into the distant past.

A mental picture of his son blossomed in his head. For Benjamin, he wanted to clear his name. Forever, there would be a seed of doubt, a question of Johnny's ultimate innocence unless Johnny found the true perpetrator of the crime. He couldn't stop digging. He had to make himself remember those nights when he and Sydney had spent so many hours talking. It was important that he search his memory for any clues as to why she was killed.

Eventually he would find the four other men on the

list of suspects and he would talk to each one. If one of them was the real killer, then if nothing else, by questioning them he might force the killer to show his hand.

In the meantime all he could do was try to remember the past. As he climbed into his truck, he smiled thoughtfully. He had to try to remember his past with Sydney, and desperately wished he could forget his past with Marissa. He didn't seem to be accomplishing either very well.

"Frank Lambino."

Marissa gripped the phone receiver more tightly against her ear. "Pardon me?"

"Frank Lambino. He's a good friend of Derek's, and he's your date for the night," Lucy explained. "Derek says he's a good-looking Italian who is looking for Ms. Right."

Nerves fluttered in Marissa's stomach. The thought of a real date was frightening...the idea of a blind date was terrifying. "Maybe you should call Derek and—"

"Don't even say it," Lucy jumped in before Marissa could finish the sentence. "I'm not about to cancel for you. You asked me to find you a date, and I did. You told me there's no way you and Johnny have anything going on, Benjamin isn't a baby anymore and it's high time you enjoyed an adult evening in the company of a handsome male."

"Okay, you're right." Marissa drew a deep breath, hoping to still her fluttering tummy.

"Of course I'm right. We'll be there to pick you up around six-thirty, okay?"

"Okay," Marissa agreed, feeling as if she'd just conceded to oral surgery.

"And, Marissa…try to work up some enthusiasm between now and then." With those words Lucy hung up.

Enthusiasm. It was difficult to fit any in around the dread that coursed through Marissa's mind. It wasn't until late in the afternoon, as she took a long, liberating bubble bath, that the dread began to ebb and a hint of anticipation appeared.

She lay back in soothingly warm water, the scent of exotic flowers drifting upward from the bubbles that surrounded her. Lucy was right. It was high time she indulged herself in an evening where her male companion didn't call her "mom."

She was almost twenty-nine years old, and there were nights she ached to be held in strong arms, days when she wanted a man who would share her laughter, dry her tears.

It was time she admitted she was a healthy, normal woman who was lonely, a woman who had put her own personal needs on hold for too long.

Closing her eyes, she tried to conjure up a picture of what Frank Lambino might look like. Lucy had said he was a handsome Italian. He'd probably have dark, almost black hair and skin a deep, rich hue. And his eyes would be the intense blue of a gas flame. She frowned, realizing that her mental picture was not of a man she might meet, but rather one of a man she knew intimately. Johnny.

Dammit, why couldn't she get him out of her head? Why did it seem that he invaded all parts of her? He found his way into her dreams, crept into her fantasies at unguarded moments, and stole into her thoughts no matter how she tried to keep him out.

It was time to cast him away. She knew there was no way he would ever really belong to her. It was time for her to put the memories of her first love aside, to make room for a lasting love in her heart.

Tonight was a perfect time to begin looking for what so many other women her age had found…lasting love. With this thought in mind, she finished her bath and dressed with extra care.

By five forty-five, she was ready. She stood in front of her dresser mirror and surveyed her reflection critically. The short-sleeved red dress she'd chosen to wear had never been worn before. It had been an impulse buy, far too expensive to wear to work at the shop, but far too pretty to pass up.

The silk material felt luscious against her skin. The scoop neck displayed a hint of swelling breast, the cinched waist complemented her slenderness and the swirling full skirt felt deliciously sinful against her hose-clad legs. She wore a tad more makeup than usual and her hair had been blown and curled to fall to her shoulders in soft curls.

"This is as good as it gets," she murmured as she picked up the small handbag that matched the dress and left her bedroom.

"Wow, Mom, you look pretty," Benjamin said as she walked into the living room.

"Thank you, Benjy." She sat down on the sofa next to him. "You're sure it's okay with you…this dating stuff?" It seemed odd to be talking about dating with her nine-year-old son, but she wanted him to be all right with the idea.

He gave her a look of studied patience. "Mom, I'm not a little kid anymore. I know about people dating. Sammy Walters's mom goes out on dates all the time. Sammy says it isn't so bad 'cause the guys she dates always try to get on his good side by buying him stuff and taking him places.''

Marissa laughed and shook her head. "Sounds to me like Sammy is a little operator."

"No, Mom, he's just a fourth-grader," Benjamin replied.

Again Marissa laughed and gave her son a hug. At that moment the doorbell rang. Marissa opened the door to admit Johnny.

His gaze moved slowly down the length of her, pausing to linger at the scoop neck before moving languidly down the length of her legs. Marissa felt the heat of his gaze as tangible as an actual touch and the heat of a blush leapt to her cheeks.

"Hi, Dad," Benjamin jumped off the sofa and greeted Johnny with a wide grin. "Doesn't Mom look pretty?"

"Indeed, she does," he said, his gaze dark and shuttered.

"Well, I'm sure you guys have a fun night planned. Pizza, right?" Marissa said, eager to hurry them along before her date arrived.

"Right," Johnny agreed. "What time do you want me to have him home?"

Marissa frowned, unsure how to work the situation. "He has school tomorrow. His usual bedtime is nine."

"Then I'll have him back here and in bed by nine, and I'll just hang around until you get home."

Marissa breathed a sigh of relief. "That would be great. I promise I won't be late." She grabbed her purse from the sofa. "I'll give you my house key." She hurriedly pulled the key from the ring of keys she carried, then handed it to him. "Then I guess I'll see you later," she said. She leaned down and kissed Benjy on the cheek. "And I'll see you in the morning."

"Hey, Benjy, why don't you grab your ball and glove? Maybe after dinner we can play catch in the park before coming home."

"Okay!" Benjamin disappeared down the hallway and into his bedroom.

Marissa checked her watch, getting more and more nervous. She didn't want Johnny here when her date showed up. It didn't feel right. "You coming, Benjy?" she called down the hall.

"Yeah," he said, running out of his room, glove and ball in hand. "Okay, let's go," he said to Johnny.

"I could use something cold to drink before we take off," Johnny said.

Marissa eyed him narrowly, suspecting that he was lingering on purpose. She strode into the kitchen and had just begun to pour a glass of cold lemonade when the doorbell rang. She finished pouring, then closed her eyes as she heard Johnny greet her date for the evening.

Terrific. Nothing like an old lover meeting a potential new one.

When she returned to the living room, a handsome, dark-haired man stood beside Johnny. "Ah, here she is now," Johnny said.

Marissa thrust the glass of lemonade into his hand, then smiled at the other man. "Hi, Frank, I'm all ready."

"Great. Shall we?" Frank placed a hand in the small of her back and led her through the door and into the pleasant evening air. "You look terrific," he said as they walked toward the car where she could see Lucy and Dr. Derrick in the back seat. "I rarely do the blind date scene, but I think I'm going to have to thank Derrick and Lucy for talking me into this one." His smile was warm and filled with interest.

Pleasure swept through Marissa. She'd forgotten just

how good masculine attention could feel. It had been for-ever since she'd last basked in the glow of knowing somebody found her attractive and wanted to know her better. She consciously shoved thoughts of Johnny out of her head and instead focused on giving herself entirely to the evening and the man who was her date.

They decided to eat dinner at the only Italian restaurant in town. Within minutes they were seated at a private table in the corner of A Taste of Italy. As they waited for the waitress to take their orders, Frank and Marissa performed the courtship dance of becoming better ac-quainted.

When the waitress appeared at their table, Marissa or-dered ravioli and a glass of red wine.

"Why don't you have a glass of soda instead," Frank replied. He smiled, his brown eyes warm and friendly. "That's what I'm having."

Marissa shrugged. "Okay," she agreed, although she thought it odd he would want her to change her drink order.

The meal was pleasant, the conversation quick and filled with laughter, but it didn't take Marissa long to realize that despite the fact that Frank was handsome and seemed to be a genuinely nice guy, there were no sparks for her…none whatsoever.

When they were finished with the meal, Derrick and Lucy ordered after-dinner drinks, and Frank ordered a soda refill. Marissa followed Frank's lead, wondering if perhaps he had an alcohol problem.

As they left the restaurant Lucy and Derrick walked ahead and Marissa decided to broach the subject with Frank. "I guess you aren't much of a drinker," she be-gan.

"Oh, I enjoy a drink now and again," he replied. He

looked at her curiously. "Your ex-husband told me that you were having a little problem with the bottle."

Marissa stopped dead in her tracks and stared at Frank in astonishment. "What?"

Frank shrugged. "It's not a problem with me, Marissa. I have several friends who are recovering alcoholics."

"But I'm not a recovering alcoholic," Marissa sputtered. "I mean...I'm not an alcoholic at all." Damn Johnny. He'd tried to sabotage her date before it had even begun. "And he's not my ex-husband," she added.

"Oh, I thought..." Frank broke off with a frown. "Then what is his relationship to you?"

"At this moment he's nothing but a baby-sitter." She drew a deep breath in an attempt to control her anger. How dare he! How dare he involve himself in any way in her personal life. He might be Benjamin's father, but that was the only role he had claim to.

She smiled at Frank. "Forget him," she said, "and anything he said to you. He's nothing but an arrogant, conceited pain, and when I see him again, I'm going to kill him."

Frank laughed and grabbed her hand in his. "And I promise if you do, I'll post bail."

Chapter 9

Benjamin and Johnny were the only two people enjoying the last light of day at Mustang's town park. They had eaten dinner at The Pizza Palace, seemingly the "in" place for kids to take mothers for Mother's Day dinner.

Conversation was nearly impossible between the two because the noise level in the restaurant was thunderous. Eating pizza with Benjamin had given Johnny an opportunity to obsess about Marissa.

Obsess. He knew that's exactly what he was doing, and for the life of him he couldn't figure out why. Granted, she'd looked like a million bucks when she'd opened the door to greet him.

Seeing her in that sexy red dress with her hair a tumble of curls had momentarily made his head swim and his senses reel. He'd wanted to run his hands down the cool silk, feel the heat of her flesh beneath. He'd wanted to tangle his hands in the soft fall of curls, pull her against him so he could lose himself in her.

He'd taken a certain perverse pleasure in the fact that Frank whatever-his-name, had been shorter than himself, and had a nose that arrived into a room a full minute before he did.

"Okay, sport, time to head home," Johnny said as he looked at his watch.

"Ah, come on, Dad. Just a little bit longer," Benjamin replied.

"No way. I promised your mom I'd have you home and in bed by nine." He jogged over to his son and placed a hand on his shoulder. "I need to go by your mom's rules so she lets me spend time with you whenever we can."

"All right." Together they walked to Johnny's pickup. Moments later, they were in the truck and headed back to Marissa's house.

"Does your mom date pretty often?" Johnny asked, instantly cursing himself for his need to know. It's just natural curiosity, he tried to tell himself, although he knew a liar when he heard one.

"Nah…this is the first time I ever saw her go out on a date," Benjamin replied.

Johnny felt a rush of satisfaction flood through him. So, this wasn't a fifth or a tenth date with Frank, but rather a first.

"Where did your mom meet this Frank guy?"

"She didn't know him until tonight. He's a friend of the guy Lucy is dating," Benjamin explained.

Not only a first date, but a blind date. Johnny's satisfaction grew by leaps and bounds. It wasn't until later when he had Benjamin tucked into bed and he wandered into her living room that he once again found himself obsessing about her.

What if she and the Italian Stallion hit it off? What if

after a single date Marissa realized she was head over heels in love with the man? Johnny made himself comfortable on the sofa and looked at his watch.

Eleven. Surely she would be home anytime. After all, she'd said she wouldn't be late. And what did he care if she came in starry-eyed and singing the praises of Frank?

He sure as hell didn't want her in love with him. In fact, he wasn't even certain Marissa was capable of true love. After all, in the last ten years she apparently hadn't made a love match.

Maybe she was a woman who never really gave her all to any man, a woman who held a piece of herself back, making absolute love impossible.

He'd once believed her capable of love, had thought she loved him heart and soul. Ten years ago when they'd been lovers, he'd had no hint of her holding back. She'd appeared to come to him fully, with no pieces in reserve. And he'd come to her the same way, vulnerable, open, believing their love was sanctioned by God and as durable as the land beneath their feet.

He'd been a stupid fool, and he would never again be a fool for any woman…especially for Marissa Sawyer. He never again wanted to feel the yawning emptiness he'd felt when he realized Marissa wasn't coming to the jail to see him. Marissa hadn't loved him enough to believe in him.

It was almost midnight when he heard the sound of a car pull into her driveway. He moved to the front window and peered out, watching as Frank and Marissa got out of the car and approached the house.

They stood in the glow of the porch light for a moment, then Frank kissed her cheek, turned and walked back to the car. Johnny moved away from the window as he heard the front door creak open.

"That wasn't much of a good-night kiss," he said sarcastically. "He must not have been overwhelmed by you."

She glared at him, her brown eyes sparking with barely controlled emotion. "Is Benjamin in bed?" she asked as she tossed her purse onto the sofa.

"Sound asleep," he replied.

"How dare you!" she began, moving so close to him he could see the golden flecks in the center of her eyes. "How dare you imply to Frank that I have a drinking problem. The *only* problem I have in my life at the moment is *you.*" She poked a finger into his chest to emphasize her statement.

He grabbed her wrist and pulled her tight against him. "And I'm a problem that won't go away in twelve steps," he said. He felt the quickening of her pulse, the sweet shudder of desire that swept through her.

Without warning, driven by a need bigger than reason, he crushed his mouth to hers, his hunger for her hot and fluid in his veins. She opened her mouth to him and her arms wrapped around his shoulders, as if she felt his need and responded with a need of her own.

The back of her dress was cool beneath his touch, but he could feel the heat of her skin radiating from within. The erotic sensation of the warring temperatures heightened his tactile pleasure and he caressed his hands up and down her back.

"I'm mad at you," she said as the kiss ended, but she didn't move from his embrace.

"I know," he replied and pressed his lips against the skin just behind her earlobe. Her breath accelerated and she dropped her head back, allowing him access to the sweet-scented column of her throat.

"I really want to hate you," she confessed, her voice a breathless whisper against his neck.

"The feeling is mutual," he replied, then his mouth covered hers again, making any further conversation impossible.

He didn't want to talk. He didn't even want to think. He just wanted to be with her. The fears that had assailed him initially upon his release from prison, fear of being an inadequate lover, fear of being intimate, were momentarily silent, overwhelmed by desire, mute beneath his screaming need for her.

"Marissa?" He broke the kiss and placed his palms on either side of her face. With the single utterance of her name, he was letting her know what he wanted.

The gold of her eyes expanded, nearly swallowing the darker brown of her irises. "Yes," she murmured, letting him know she understood what he had silently asked and wanted the same.

Blood surging inside him, he swept her up in his arms and carried her down the hallway past Benjamin's bedroom and to the master bedroom on the right.

She'd left on a small lamp on the nightstand, its pale golden light spilling soft illumination around the room. Johnny gently placed her on the bed, the poppy flowers of the bedspread perfectly matching the crimson of her dress.

With his gaze holding hers, he grabbed the bottom of his T-shirt and pulled it over his head. He dropped the shirt onto the floor, then joined her on the bed.

The pleasure he'd gained by smoothing his hands over the back of her dress was nothing compared to the slick, cool material against his bare chest.

His lips sought hers and she tangled her hands in his hair, pulling him closer…closer still. Beneath the smooth bodice of her dress, he felt the hardness of her nipples, attesting to her state of arousal.

Their tongues danced, flicking and rolling around each other in a tango of temptation. His hands stroked down the sides of her, loving the curves of her body, the fragrance of her that filled his senses.

He broke the kiss and stood once again. "Turn over and let me unzip you," he said.

Her eyes flamed with the same fires that lit him and she turned over on her tummy, allowing him access to the zipper that ran from the top of the dress to her lower back.

Johnny unzipped it slowly, teasing not only her, but himself with each inch of revealed bareness. And with each inch he exposed, he paused and kissed the smooth skin, loving the taste of her.

When he reached the end of the zipper, she turned over and he pulled her to a sitting position. With infinite gentleness, he removed the dress from her arms. It fell to her waist, revealing a lacy red bra. She lay on her back, allowing him to pull the dress from beneath her and completely off her body.

"Turn off the light," she said, her voice husky and low. She splayed her hands across her stomach, as if self-conscious. He could guess what she was thinking, that her body wasn't the same as it had been ten years before. But, she was as lovely as he'd remembered.

"No, I want to see you," he replied. "I *need* to see you." He'd made love to her so many times in the darkness of night, in the fantasy of his dreams, he wanted— no, needed—the reality of the light so he would know this was not just another dream.

He stood once again, this time to quickly unbutton his jeans and kick them off. His briefs followed and when he once again returned to the bed, he gently removed her panty hose, pulled off her wispy red panties, then unsnapped the bra and removed it as well.

Naked, they hugged and their lips met in a kiss of ravenous hunger, of unbridled passion. Johnny felt himself getting lost in a haze, and he welcomed the unconsciousness, the lack of clear thought.

His hands sought and found her breasts, and he touched the turgid tips, reveling in Marissa's gasp of pleasure. He moved his mouth along her jaw, across her collarbones and touched one of her nipples with the tip of his tongue. She moaned, a throaty moan that sent sweet memories rushing through him....memories of other times they had made love, and she had moaned her pleasure against his throat.

As he kissed her breasts, teasing and nipping their peaks, her hands tangled in his hair, then swept down his back, leaving trails of fire each place that she touched.

Johnny knew he had little control, that his years of abstinence would make the final act over almost before it began.

He caressed the length of her body, wanting to take her over the edge before he sought his own ultimate pleasure. His fingers moved down her stomach, pausing as he encountered slight ripples that marred the smoothness of her lower abdomen.

Stretch marks. He knew instantly that it was these she had been trying to hide with her hands, why she'd wanted the light off.

He kissed each one lovingly, knowing that those marks had been part of the process of Benjamin's birth. She cried out, a soft whimper of delight as his fingers touched her intimately. She was ready for him, hot and wet, and her hips moved against him, her back arching as his touch grew faster.

He watched her face, loving the deep flush of her cheeks, the golden glow of her eyes as their gazes locked. Her lips were reddened and swollen from their kisses and he thought she'd never looked as beautiful as she did at this moment.

And then she was there…stiffening against him. She closed her eyes and her fingernails dug into him as she rode wave after wave of pleasure.

He didn't give her time to catch her breath. Instantly he entered her, closing his eyes and desperately trying to hang on to control as her muscles tightened around him.

For a long moment he didn't move, afraid that any sort of movement would take him over the brink. He was surrounded by her…her scent…her heat…the very essence of her filled him, and momentarily cast away the darkness that had been inside him for so long.

He heard the thunder of a heartbeat, but didn't know if it was hers or his own, and in any case, it didn't matter. Nothing mattered but their union. Her hips moved against his, and he matched her rhythm with deep strokes of uncontrollable desire.

Faster…deeper…they moved in perfect unison, taking and giving as they reached for release, sought a momentary eternity in each other's arms.

Afterward Johnny rolled over on his side and pulled her into his embrace. Marissa knew making love with him had probably been a mistake, but she had no excuse other than she'd wanted him.

She'd endured too many years alone, too little physical contact with members of the opposite sex, and too many fantasies about making love with Johnny one last time.

There would be no self-recriminations. She'd wanted

him, and she was old enough, smart enough to be able to make love to him and not involve her heart. She couldn't afford to give him her heart ever again.

Making love with Johnny was everything she'd remembered. She couldn't deny that his skill and his passion had made making love with him an unforgettable experience.

And now, she couldn't ignore how good it felt to rest her head upon his firm, muscled chest, how much she liked the feel of his strong arms holding her.

She touched him just beneath his hipbone, where a scar slightly puckered his skin. "It really is in the shape of a heart," she murmured.

"Yeah, old Tornado definitely got the best of me." His breath fanned the top of her head. "Still mad at me?" he asked softly.

"Yes...and no," she answered, unable to recall the anger that had assailed her when she'd first arrived home from her date. What difference did it make what he'd told Frank? She knew with certainty that although Frank had seemed to be a nice, attractive man, he wasn't the man for her.

Just as Johnny wasn't the man for her—though he was closer. Still, even knowing that there were questions she needed answered. For the past ten years there had been the ghost of a tragic girl in Marissa's heart. For all of those years she'd wondered about Sydney and Johnny's relationship and always...always she'd been afraid of the answers.

"Johnny?"

"Hmm?" He stroked her hair with a gentle touch.

"Tell me about Sydney."

His hand froze, and she felt his body tighten and fill with tension. She raised her head and looked at him. His gaze was dark and cold, cutting through her. Despite her desire to the contrary, she didn't look away. She held his gaze, knowing it was time she heard about the events, the emotions, the winds of fate that had brought them to this place, this here and now.

He disentangled from her, swung his feet over the side of the bed and sat up. He raked a hand through his hair and looked at her once again. "That question comes about ten years too late."

Marissa reached out and placed a hand on his arm. "Please, Johnny."

He frowned and dragged a hand across his jaw. "What do you want to know?" His voice was flat...emotionless.

"When? How did you meet her?"

He stretched out beside her once again, this time not touching her. He propped himself up on an elbow, staring not at her, but at some point over her head.

"I met her a couple of months before I met you. It was late one evening, near sunset, and I was out working the fields near the old shed. My tractor broke down. As I worked to get it running again, I heard the sound of somebody crying. I found Sydney in the shed."

Marissa scrunched the pillow beneath her to raise her head higher, then pulled the sheet up to cover her nakedness. "Why was she crying?"

He frowned. "She never told me. But she seemed so young, and so lonely. We talked that night for hours. It was like she was starved for conversation with somebody her own age. Her mother and Brad kept her so isolated, and her sister, Gillian, was nothing more than a little kid at the time."

He sighed, a deep, mournful sound that made Marissa want to draw him into her arms, but she didn't. She simply waited for him to continue.

"Sydney needed a friend, and I tried to fill that role for her. About three nights a week, I'd find a red scarf tied to my tractor. That was her secret signal letting me know that she'd managed to sneak out of the house and was waiting for me in the shed."

He fell silent for a moment, his features soft and reflective. "She was like the little sister I never had. She seemed so innocent, so out of touch with the rest of the world. And yet there was a deep unhappiness in her, shadows of secrets in her eyes that I couldn't get her to share with me."

"You loved her?" she asked the question even though she now knew the answer. He hadn't loved Sydney as she once feared he had. Marissa had been wrong all those years ago...wrong to believe that Sydney had somehow been her rival for Johnny's affections.

His eyes were dark, tortured as he gazed at her. "I loved her, but it wasn't a romantic love. There was no desire between us, nothing physical, nothing more than deep friendship."

He rolled over onto his back and crossed his arms behind his head, staring up at the ceiling as if lost in another world. "That night...the night of the prom...was the night Sydney was killed." He closed his eyes and was silent for a long moment.

In the passing of those seconds, Marissa looked at him, remembering that prom night when he'd looked so handsome he'd stolen her breath away. He was just as handsome now...although older, with life experience stamped onto his features. He now had a maturity in his eyes, and to his face, that was every bit as breathtaking.

"After I dropped you off at your house, I went back home. The scarf was tied to the tractor. Even though it was late, I figured Sydney would still be at the shed. It had become her retreat from her family, her little home away from home.''

''How was she able to get out of her house and spend so much time at the shed?'' Marissa asked curiously.

A whisper of a smile crossed his features. ''Sydney was nothing if not resourceful and apparently her mother was an early to bed kind of woman. Sydney would go to bed, then sneak out her window and down an old trellis. She figured as long as she was back in her room by dawn, nobody would know she'd been gone half the night.''

With one hand, he rubbed a circular pattern at his temple, as if trying to ward off the approach of a headache. ''Anyway, that night, like a hundred other nights, I went to the shed. She always brought a lantern with her, and I saw the light seeping out the cracks of the wood. I found her there…lying on the ground. At first I thought she must be asleep.''

Up until this point, his voice had remained a flat monotone. Marissa felt his building tension, saw the anguish that twisted his features and her heart ached with his misery. ''She wasn't asleep,'' his voice no longer lacked emotion, but rather drowned in it. ''I tried to rouse her. I called her name, then picked her up in my arms. She was dead. I had only a moment to realize it before the sheriff and his boys moved in on me.'' He released a sigh, then drew several deep breaths of air.

''How did the sheriff know to go to the shed?'' Marissa asked.

''An anonymous phone call. Somebody called the sheriff from the Roundup and told him he thought somebody was being hurt at the old shed.''

Johnny sat up. ''I've thought and thought about it, and what I think happened is that the killer left Sydney and went to the Roundup. Whoever he was, somehow he knew Sydney was expecting me to show up and when he saw my truck pass as I was going home, he called the sheriff and set me up as the killer.''

"But why? Why would anyone want to kill Sydney?"

Johnny smiled ruefully. "If I knew that, I'd be that much closer to finding out who killed her."

"Then who would want to set you up for such a heinous thing?"

Again Johnny smiled, but the gesture held no joy, only a sharp bitterness. "Why not me? I was young, poor, had a reputation for getting into trouble. I made a perfect patsy."

Marissa sat up and shoved her hair away from her face. She owed him an apology. For years she'd believed he'd been two-timing her with Sydney. That belief had caused her to back away from him, kept her from seeing him while he was in jail.

"Johnny, I'm sorry." For a moment she wondered if he'd know what she was apologizing for.

His features hardened and his eyes glittered with a cold-blue intensity that sliced through her. "Your apology, like your questions, comes ten years too late."

"But, Johnny, I thought you and Sydney...I believed you had deceived me, that you were romancing Sydney at the same time you were romancing me. That's why I didn't go to see you when you were arrested. That's why I never came to visit you in jail."

In one smooth motion, Johnny stood and grabbed his clothes. He pulled on his briefs, quickly followed by his jeans.

"Johnny?"

He didn't answer. He picked up his shirt and yanked it over his head.

"Johnny? Please..." She needed him to say something, anything to absolve her from the knot of guilt that suddenly thudded like a fifty-pound weight in the pit of her stomach.

"Please what?" He glared at her, his eyes once again blazing hot flames of blue heat. "Please tell you all is forgiven? I can't do that, because I can't forget those hours…days…weeks…I spent waiting for you to come and see me, praying that you'd show up and tell me you believed in me."

"Johnny, I was young…scared. My heart had broken and I couldn't see anything but my own pain."

He laughed, an ugly, bitter sound that pieced through Marissa's heart. "You think I wasn't? I kept thinking everything would be fine as long as you came. I could have endured whatever was ahead if I knew you stood beside me." He turned and left the bedroom.

Marissa flew from the bed, cursing as her feet tangled in the sheet and she nearly fell. Grabbing her robe, she raced after him, not wanting to leave it like this…needing him to understand. She pulled her robe around her as she ran.

She caught up with him at the front door and grabbed his arm. "Johnny, can't you understand how devastated I was to think that you were making love to me, then leaving me and making love to Sydney?"

He paused and turned back to her, his eyes cold as the snows in the mountains of Montana. "You can try to fool me by pretending that's the reason you didn't stand beside me, but I know the truth." His voice was laced with a combination of hurt and anger.

"What truth?" she asked softly and dropped her hand from his arm.

"The truth is you were ashamed. You didn't want your friends to know, your family to know that you'd been seeing that poor trash Johnny Crockett. It's bad enough you thought I could be so duplicitous as to two-time you with Sydney. But, what's worse than that, what I'll never be able to forgive, is that deep down in your heart, you weren't one hundred percent certain that I didn't murder Sydney Emery.''

He didn't give her a chance to respond. Instead he stormed out the door and into the dark of night.

Chapter 10

Marissa groaned beneath her breath as the bell sounded over the door announcing her first customer of the day. The last person she wanted to see first thing on a Monday morning was Millie Creighton.

The older woman wore one of her many infamous hats, this one a wide-brimmed straw covered with sunflowers and realistic bumblebees. Nobody in the town of Mustang knew why she wore the crazy hats, but she had been for so long they had become as much a part of her as her double chin.

Millie approached her with a vacuous expression and a friendly smile, but Marissa knew beneath the superficiality and ridiculous hat was a mind as sharp as a cattle prod.

"Good morning, Millie," Marissa forced a welcoming smile to her face.

"Morning, dear." Millie set down her purse on the

counter. "I need to order a fresh-cut flower arrangement. My dear friend Gloria Townsend is in the hospital."

"I hope it's nothing serious," Marissa replied, contrite that she'd assumed Millie's visit was for gossip purposes.

"Gallbladder," Millie replied. "I was on my way over to the hospital and thought I'd stop and get a nice bouquet…something festive, to bring her."

"Do you have any particular kind of flowers in mind?"

"No. I trust your judgment." She beamed at Marissa. "You do such wonderful work."

"Do you know about how much you want to spend?" Marissa asked, her mind already whirling with possibilities for a nice arrangement.

Within minutes, Marissa was busy working and Millie was seated on an upholstered chair chosen with the comfort of customers in mind.

"Lovely program that the children put on the other night, wasn't it?"

Although Millie smiled at her innocently, Marissa heard the rattle of a coiled snake in the seemingly innocuous question.

"I always enjoy the school plays," Marissa replied.

"That boy of yours sure can sing," Millie said, the words filling Marissa with a burst of warm pride. "I couldn't help but notice you attended the performance with Johnny Crockett. It's not everyday you see the daughter of the mayor with a convict."

The warmth that had momentarily filled Marissa seeped away as she realized she'd been right initially. Gloria Townsend might truly be in the hospital, but Millie was here for more than flowers. She was nibbling for gossip for her society column in the *Mustang Monitor* newspaper.

"Ex-convict," Marissa replied stiffly. "An innocent man who was wrongly convicted and served ten years in prison."

"How is he adjusting to civilian life?" Millie asked, obviously not put off by Marissa's cool tone.

"You'd have to ask him." Marissa cursed inwardly as she clipped the stem of a daisy too short for use. She tossed the ruined flower in the trash and grabbed another one.

"I couldn't help but notice that your son and Johnny appear to share common features."

"That's not unusual in a father and son." Marissa stopped working and glared at Millie. "And if you put that fact in your column, I will see to it that your column is pulled and you'll be out of a job."

Millie reared back in the chair and huffed indignantly. "Well, there's no reason to get all hostile."

"I promise you, if you write a column about Johnny and Benjamin, I will not only get hostile, I'll get even," Marissa retorted.

Again Millie huffed indignantly, the motion causing the bees on the top of her hat to vibrate and emit a tiny buzzing noise. "I would never do anything to harm that sweet little boy of yours."

"It's not just Benjamin I'm worried about. I don't think it's in Johnny's best interest for his name to be mentioned in the paper. He's having a difficult enough time trying to clear his name. He doesn't need any publicity."

"He's trying to clear his name?" Interest colored Millie's tone. "What exactly is he doing?"

Marissa cursed herself for saying anything at all. She poked the last flower into the arrangement, then shook her head. "No more, Millie. If you want information about Johnny, then you need to go talk to him."

With a sniff of dissatisfaction, Millie paid for the arrangement, then left, bumblebees bouncing and buzzing with each step.

When she was gone, Marissa sank down into the chair behind the counter. She rubbed her eyes. They felt gritty with exhaustion. It had been near dawn when she'd finally fallen into an exhausted sleep. Johnny's words, his accusations, had whirled around and around in her head. She tried to tell herself he was wrong, that she hadn't been ashamed of him or their relationship. He was wrong to think that any part of her believed for a minute that he'd harmed Sydney. But, the inner voice that denied it all was weak and reedy, not strong with conviction.

She'd told herself for all these years that Johnny had betrayed her, that he'd been two-timing her with Sydney. It had been the excuse that had kept her away from him and it had been the reason for the anger that had sustained her the last ten years.

Last night, he'd taken away her anger, banished it with the truth…a truth she could have discovered ten years ago if she'd had the nerve to ask for it.

Had she stayed away from Johnny because she'd been afraid of what people might say? What they might think of her? Had there been a tiny place in her heart that wasn't sure of his absolute innocence?

It frightened her that the answer might be yes. And if that were true, it spoke poorly of her, spoke dismally of the love she'd thought she'd felt for Johnny. It made her the kind of person she didn't want to be.

She also now knew at least part of the root of Johnny's rage. He might have kissed her with desire the night before, might have made love to her with exquisite skillfulness and tempestuous passion, but his heart beat with loathing where she was concerned.

And despite the fact that her body ached for his again...and again, he'd made it crystal clear that he would never, could never forgive her, that his heart would always be closed off and unattainable to her.

She stood and rubbed her temples, the turmoil of her thoughts creating an ache of confusion to pound a maddening rhythm. She didn't want to care about Johnny, but she did. She didn't want to want him, but God help her, she did.

Their lovemaking the night before had only confirmed the reality of her memories, and the reality was that their bodies were born to love each other, created as perfect male/female counterparts.

"Enough," she said. She'd spent enough time thinking, obsessing, remembering and pondering Johnny. Last night had been an aberration, an anomaly that would not be repeated. Knowing now that Johnny hated her, that he would never be able to forgive her, let her know that making love with him again would only complicate their relationship further.

She jumped as the phone rang. "Flowers By Marissa," she said into the receiver when she answered.

"Good morning, Marissa."

She instantly recognized the pleasant, clipped tones of Rachel Emery. "Good morning, Mrs. Emery."

"I was wondering if perhaps you would have an opportunity to meet with me here at the ranch sometime today," Rachel said.

Marissa frowned thoughtfully. She assumed Rachel wanted to discuss the floral decorations for the upcoming prom. "I could close up the shop around noon and drive out there, if that would work for you."

''That would be fine. I'll see you then.'' Rachel, rarely one for small talk, hung up.

Marissa had been expecting a call from Rachel concerning the prom decorations, although she was rather surprised by Rachel's desire to meet at the Emery home. The past four years Marissa and Rachel had made the arrangements with a flurry of phone calls to one another.

At quarter after twelve, Marissa hung the Closed sign in the shop window and headed toward the Emery place. It was a pleasant drive, a warm breeze signifying the promise of summer just around the corner.

However, Marissa wasn't enjoying the beauty of the day, instead she found herself playing and replaying the night before…the night of loving Johnny.

It would be easy to blame him for seducing her into doing something she hadn't wanted to do. But, she knew that wasn't the truth. The truth of the matter was that she'd wanted to make love with him again, she'd hoped that by doing so, she could finally put him behind her, forget her first love in anticipation of finding a new, more mature love that would last a lifetime.

But somehow, the night with Johnny had not moved him out of her heart, rather it had simply added to her confusion where he was concerned.

She shoved thoughts of Johnny out of her head as she turned down the short, tree-lined lane that led to the Emery mansion. Although she'd admired the huge, two-story house a hundred times in passing, this was the first time she would be admitted inside.

Pulling up front, she took a moment to admire the structure. Elegant, with a sweeping veranda and huge columns, the house whispered of longevity and wealth. Burton Emery, Rachel's dead husband, had amassed a fortune both in ranching and by dabbling in real estate.

A widower with a son, it had been big news when he'd wed Rachel, a woman who'd become an instant step-mother to Bradley. Sydney was eleven, Gillian only a year old when Burton had died of a heart attack. Nineteen-year-old Bradley had taken up the reins of responsibility and stepped into his father's shoes.

It was obvious the ranch continued to prosper, Marissa thought as she got out of her car. The outbuildings were in pristine condition and several handsome horses pranced proudly in the large corral.

Marissa knocked on the front door and was ushered into a formal living room by the housekeeper. "Mrs. Emery will be with you momentarily," she said as she directed Marissa to one of the wing-backed chairs in front of a marble fireplace.

Marissa nodded and sank down on the chair, a little intimidated by the grandioseness of her surroundings. She wasn't certain if it was the magnificence of her surroundings that caused a flutter of anxiety in the pit of her stomach, or the knowledge that Rachel Emery had probably heard by now the gossip of Marissa's relationship to Johnny. In any case, as she sat waiting for the lady of the house to appear, her stomach rolled and kicked as if protesting the lunch she hadn't yet eaten.

The room was overly warm, with the midday sunshine streaming in through the open curtains. She shrugged out of her jacket and folded it across one arm, grateful that her blouse beneath was sleeveless.

"Marissa." Marissa jumped up from her chair as Rachel swept into the room. "Thank you for finding time for me today," she said as she gestured Marissa back into the chair. She sat opposite Marissa, her white hair a perfect foil against the navy fabric of the high-backed chair behind her.

"No problem," Marissa replied. "I often close shop for an hour or so at this time of the day."

"Would you care for something to drink?"

"No, thank you. I'm fine," Marissa replied.

Rachel nodded, then looked at the housekeeper who waited in the doorway. "That will be all, Alma," she said, then waited for the woman to close the large wooden doors, giving Marissa and Rachel complete privacy.

Despite the warmth of the day, Rachel was impeccably dressed in a high-necked, long-sleeved blue dress that perfectly matched her eyes. Her makeup was understated and her jewelry tasteful. Marissa had never seen the older woman when she wasn't turned out flawlessly.

Rachel stood and walked to one of the windows, her back to Marissa. "Summer is just around the corner," she observed. "Sydney always loved the summer."

The fluttering in Marissa's stomach intensified. She wasn't sure how to answer, so said nothing at all. Rachel remained with her back to Marissa. "I miss her, you know. She was my firstborn, so bright and so beautiful."

Marissa heard the deep grief in Rachel's voice and compassion replaced anxiety. How horrid to lose a child to murder. Marissa couldn't imagine the depth of pain Rachel carried with her every waking hour, every dreaming moment.

Rachel turned away from the window and faced Marissa. "Forgive me," she said with the dignity that was as much a part of her as her hollow blue eyes. She once again sat in the chair opposite Marissa. For a long moment she said nothing, but her expression was one of a woman contemplating her next words. She leaned forward, a sudden fervor in her eyes. "Marissa…"

The double doors swung open and Brad strode in.

"Well, well. Alma told me we had a guest." He smiled at Marissa…seemingly a different man from when she'd last seen him with rage contorting his features as he'd threatened Johnny.

He walked around to stand behind his stepmother and placed a hand on each of her shoulders. "Mother, did you offer our guest refreshments?"

"She did," Marissa replied. "And I told her I'm fine." Marissa shifted in her seat, aware that Brad seemed to have brought with him an electrical charge that filled the air with tension.

"Please, don't let me interrupt," Brad said as he walked over to the wet bar in the corner of the room. As he splashed scotch into the bottom of a glass, Marissa turned her attention back to Rachel.

Rachel's face seemed paler, more strained as she once again focused on Marissa. "We understand that you have some sort of a personal relationship with Johnny Crockett." Her voice, normally soft and polished, was halting and filled with stress.

Warning bells went off in Marissa's head as she realized it wasn't just prom and flower business that had brought her here. "Johnny is my son's father," Marissa said.

"Then you have some degree of influence on him," Brad exclaimed.

Marissa smiled at his obvious misconception. "Nobody has influence on Johnny. He's definitely his own man."

"He's definitely a man we want out of Mustang," Brad replied.

"I think Johnny is well aware of your sentiments where he is concerned." Marissa looked searchingly at

Rachel. "Is that why you asked me here? To see if somehow I can make Johnny leave town?"

"He's asking questions, bothering our ranch hands," Brad replied. He took a swallow of his drink then continued, "He's upsetting my mother with all his digging into the past."

Marissa didn't look at Brad, but rather kept her attention focused on Rachel. "He's digging into the past because he didn't kill your daughter." Marissa knew now what she'd always known, that Johnny wasn't capable of the act of murder. He'd been wrong when he'd accused her of having doubts about that particular issue.

"Spoken like a woman who's bedding the man in question," Brad said with a hint of a sneer.

"Bradley," Rachel admonished. She sighed wearily, looking smaller and more fragile than Marissa had ever seen her before. When she looked back at Marissa, her face reflected weary resignation. "We were hoping that you could convince Johnny to leave things alone, stop asking questions that dredge up the pain, the horror all over again."

"I can't do that," Marissa replied, then raised her chin a notch higher. "I won't do that. I believe in Johnny's innocence, and unless he asks questions, digs deeper, the real killer will never be found."

It was at that moment that Marissa realized her feelings for Johnny ran deeper than she'd acknowledged to herself. She cared about him more than she'd ever cared about any man, and she would do whatever she could to help him prove his innocence.

"You tell him to keep the hell away from my men," Brad exclaimed.

Marissa gazed at Rachel, ignoring Brad's outburst. "I'm sorry if this is painful for you, Rachel, but on that night ten years ago, when Johnny found Sydney in the shed, she was already dead." Marissa stood. "He didn't kill her, and I intend to encourage him to keep digging, keep asking questions. He spent ten years in prison for a crime he didn't commit, meanwhile, the real killer has continued life, comfortable in the knowledge that he got away with murder. I intend to help Johnny change that."

She turned and started for the door, but hesitated when Rachel called after her. Marissa turned back to look at the older woman. "We've decided this year not to use flowers for the prom decorations, so I'm afraid we won't be needing your services."

Marissa stared at Rachel in shocked surprise. "I...I don't understand," she said even though she understood perfectly well. If she wasn't willing to use her influence with Johnny, then she would be punished by losing the large prom account.

Rachel's cheeks pinkened slightly and she didn't meet Marissa gaze. "We've decided to do things differently this year. I'm sorry."

Brad again moved to stand behind his stepmother, his hands once more settling on her shoulders. "Alma will see you out," Brad said.

As if by magic, the housekeeper appeared at the door. "This way," she said and Marissa followed.

Within minutes Marissa was again in her car and headed back into town. The loss of the prom account was difficult to swallow. Providing flowers for the school dance had been one of the few big money occasions throughout the year.

Losing the account would mean she would have to tighten her belt, watch how she spent each and every penny. While the flower shop had been a moneymaker for the last four years, the profits weren't huge and there had been times in the past she'd had to borrow money from her parents to get through a month or two when Benjamin needed something not in the budget.

"It's nothing short of blackmail," she breathed aloud. She would have had the school account if she'd agreed to pressure Johnny. But, her integrity couldn't be bought.

It was bought ten years ago, a little voice murmured insidiously, when she'd turned her back on Johnny, and her payoff had been no awkward questions, no sly looks or grins. She'd held her silence, and withheld her support because she'd been afraid of what people would think.

Shame coursed through her as she recognized the truth. She'd tried to tell herself for years that she'd turned her back on Johnny because she believed he'd slept with Sydney.

But, the truth was, she hadn't wanted her name to be tangled with the dirt-poor, bad boy who would probably go to prison. She'd stayed away not because he was dirt-poor, or because he had a reputation as a teen with a chip on his shoulder, but because she'd known the kind of reprisals she'd face for being involved with him... reprisals she'd been too weak to face.

"I'm sorry, Johnny," she whispered. She'd said those same words to him the night before, and he'd thrown them back in her face. She'd given him too little, too late.

He might have loved her once, but she'd thrown his love away. Even if she wanted the two of them to try again, which of course she didn't, she had a feeling Johnny didn't believe in second chances, especially where she was concerned.

What she didn't understand was why this thought brought with it a yawning black hole that ached with regret, throbbed with loss, a black hole that took up residency in her heart.

Chapter 11

Johnny sat on the ground beneath a leafy tree to eat the lunch he'd packed for himself that day. Cameron Gallagher only had half a dozen hands working for him, and the others had driven into town for lunch at the café. They'd asked Johnny to go with them, but he'd declined, explaining that he'd brought his lunch.

It had taken Johnny less than an hour to come to the conclusion that he liked and respected Cameron Gallagher. Although apparently not one to small talk, he'd worked side by side his hands, treating then all like valued partners instead of inferior underlings.

The Gallagher ranch seemed to be still in its infancy. A new barn was half-built and looked to be twice the size of its older, sagging counterpart. Although there were no cattle, there was a small herd of purebred horses cavorting in the tall grass of one of the pastures.

Johnny ate his ham and cheese sandwich slowly, enjoying the warm breeze that fanned his face, bringing with it the scent of sweet green grass and dark, rich earth. How he had missed the smell of Montana while in prison. He'd ached for the sight of the wide, blue sky and the feel of the sun warming his face.

He finished his sandwich and pulled an apple from the paper bag that had held his lunch. He bit into the sweet, juicy fruit and tried to keep thoughts of Marissa at bay.

He didn't want to think about her, about last night and their lovemaking. Every time he thought about it, he was assailed by conflicting emotions. It was much easier to focus on the anger that had propelled him out the door and into the night...an ever-present anger that had begun ten years before and grown harder, colder each and every day since.

"Hi."

Johnny jumped in surprise at the childish voice coming from behind him. He leaned out to look around the tree trunk and saw a little girl peering back at him.

"Hi, yourself," he replied.

She came around the tree and plopped down in the grass next to him. "My name is Rebecca, what's yours?" She had gamine features and chin-length, pale blond hair. She offered him a smile that displayed a missing front tooth.

"I'm Johnny," he replied.

"You're new, aren't you?" She eyed him steadily. "Are you a good cowboy or a bad cowboy?"

"Definitely a good one." He bit back a smile. She was a cutie, six or seven years old and dressed in denim jeans and a cowboy shirt with white fringe and pink pearlized buttons. Her feet were clad in a pair of shiny red miniature cowboy boots.

"You got anything in that bag that a cowgirl might like to eat?" she asked.

Johnny dug into the bag. "I've got some corn chips," he offered.

She nodded and took the snack-size bag he held out. "Thank you, Mr. Johnny."

For several moments they were silent, Johnny finishing his apple and his tiny lunch mate eating the corn chips with crunchy relish.

When she finished the chips, she wadded up the bag and gave it back to Johnny. "You have any kids, Mr. Johnny?" she asked.

"I've got a son. His name is Benjamin," Johnny replied. "Is your daddy Cameron Gallagher?"

"Yup." She frowned. "Except he's not my real daddy. My real daddy died and then me and Mom met Mr. Lallager, then Mr. Lallager 'dopted me." She smiled, a beatific smile of happiness. "And now Mr. Lallagher is my daddy. And I love him more than anything in the whole wide world…'cept my mom."

In the distance a woman stepped out on the back porch. "Rebecca?" she called.

"I'm here, Mommy." Rebecca stood and waved to her mother.

"Come inside. It's time for lunch," the woman called out.

"I gotta go," Rebecca said to Johnny. "Me and Mommy and Daddy always eat lunch together when I'm not in school." With a cheerful wave, she turned and ran for the house.

Johnny watched her go and smiled. Cameron Gallagher was one lucky man. From what Rebecca had said, at noon every day he went home to enjoy the midday meal with a woman who loved him and a little girl who thought he hung the moon.

And at night, Cameron probably tucked his little girl

into bed with hugs and kisses, then went to his own room where his wife awaited him. They would make passionate love, then fall asleep in each other's arms.

It was exactly the kind of life Johnny had always dreamed of for himself. A ranch, a wife and half a dozen children to fill the house with laughter and love. From the time he was small, a lonely fatherless boy being raised by a beaten-down mother who worked too hard on a failing ranch, he'd dreamed of building a life much different than what he'd had. He'd wanted to be a successful rancher, a faithful husband, and a loving, supportive father.

The moment he'd met Marissa, he'd known she was the woman he wanted to build those dreams for, the one he wanted to live with for the rest of his life. Unfortunately, fate had other plans for him.

He stood, irritated with his thoughts of Marissa and what might have been. Even though he'd smelled her on his skin when he'd first awakened this morning, despite the fact that his body had still tingled with the memory of their impassioned joining, he knew there was no way for him to get past his anger, past his heartache and forgive her.

Making love to her had been a mistake, one he didn't intend to repeat. He needed to be in her life, like an ex-husband who needs to maintain contact for the relationship with the child. At least until Benjamin was eighteen, he and Marissa would have to deal with each other. But, there would be no more physical contact between them.

He threw his lunch bag into the cab of his pickup, then sat down to wait for the rest of the crew to return from lunch.

As he waited, he thought of what little Rebecca had

said to him, that she wasn't Cameron's birth child, but rather had been adopted.

Some day would Marissa marry some man who would want to adopt Benjamin? Would the day come when Marissa would try to convince Johnny that the best thing for Benjy would be for him to relinquish his parental rights? And if that day came and Johnny realized that would be best for Benjamin, would he be able to do it despite the breaking of his own heart?

With enormous relief he saw in the distance the truck carrying the other workers back from lunch. Nothing like hard work to keep thoughts at bay. And at least for today, Johnny wanted no more thoughts of Marissa and the dreams she'd shattered.

They worked until dusk, then called it a day. As Johnny drove back to his place, his muscles ached from exertion, but it was the good ache of hard work and chores accomplished. If only he'd gained the sore muscles from working on his own land, building his own place.

A couple more weeks, he promised himself. The prom kicked off the weekend in two weeks and hopefully he'd win the purse for bull riding and that would be the beginning of a new future for him.

As he pulled up in front of his place, for a long moment he sat and stared at the house. It didn't look warm and welcoming, but rather abandoned...deserted. No lights shone from the windows to ward off the coming night. No scents of cooking, no sound of laughter would greet him as he walked through the door.

He tried to tell himself it didn't matter, he was accustomed to being alone. There were times he felt as if he'd lived all of his life alone.

As a child, he'd suffered the emptiness of knowing his

father had turned his back on him. As a young teenager he'd endured peer taunts because of his worn clothes, his lack of spending money.

In the pain of that isolation, he'd developed a tough-guy attitude and a chip on his shoulder that had further separated him from everyone else. Then, with his arrest, he'd spent ten agonizing years alone in a jail cell, learning to live with his aloneness.

So why did he ache with emptiness as he sat staring at his lonely house? Why did he yearn for the laughter of children to fill the air? If he was so damned comfortable in his aloneness, why did he fantasize the sweet scent of perfume in the air, small, dainty hands to stroke his face as a woman kissed him hello after a hard day's work? And why in the hell did the woman in his fantasy have Marissa's face?

He got out of his truck, slamming the door with more force than necessary. Damn Marissa with her winsome smile and sexy ways. Damn her with her musical laughter and soft sighs. Despite his intentions to the contrary, she twisted him up inside, made him want her over and over again even while his anger with her simmered deep inside him.

Too restless to sit around the house, and with the refrigerator disappointingly empty, he decided to drive into town for dinner.

It was late enough that Johnny had missed the dinner rush so he had no problem finding a booth near the back where his presence would be as unobtrusive as was possible. He ordered the dinner special, knowing the diner was known for large portions of their nightly special at reasonable prices. Tonight the special was meat loaf with mashed potatoes and green beans.

Johnny ate slowly, eating not only his dinner but the

hours of the evening between dusk and sleep...the heart-ache hours of the day.

Conversation swirled around him as other late diners wandered in for a meal. He couldn't help but overhear snatches of conversations, pieces of other peoples' lives. Somehow it all just made him more lonely.

He'd just finished his meal and was about to get up when Marissa and Benjamin walked in. "Dad!" Benjamin exclaimed in delight and raced over to Johnny's booth. Marissa followed more slowly, her footsteps dragging as if with dread.

"What are you doing here?" Johnny asked his son.

"Mom promised me a hot fudge sundae if I cleaned my room really, really good." Benjamin grinned widely as his mom reached them. "Hey, Mom, why don't we just sit here with Dad?"

Initially, as Marissa had dragged her feet approaching him, he'd assumed she was probably angry because of what he'd said to her before storming out of the house the night before. He figured she blamed him for their lovemaking, somehow made it his fault, believed that he'd seduced her into something she hadn't wanted to do.

But, instead of anger, he saw contrition in her eyes, and instead of blame, he saw penitence. "Mind if we join you?" she asked, although it seemed a mute point since Benjamin had already done just that.

He indicated the seat across from him. She slid in next to Benjamin, looking as ill at ease as he felt. Dammit, he'd come here to escape her presence in his thoughts, and here she was, a full-blown reality looking far too luscious in a pair of tight jeans and a coral-colored T-shirt advertising her flower shop.

She smiled, a tentative, hesitant smile that somehow

pierced the armor he'd spent the entire day erecting around his heart. "Did you work at Cameron Gallagher's place today?" she asked.

He nodded.

"How did it go?"

He shrugged. "It went. Cameron seems to be a fine man."

"He used to be a bounty hunter, you know," Marissa said.

Surprise shot through Johnny. "A bounty hunter?" His respect for the man rose by leaps and bounds. Apparently Cameron Gallagher had at one time worked for the principles of the law, and as far as he knew, Johnny had worked against those principles, but it hadn't stopped Cameron from hiring him.

The waitress appeared at their table and Benjamin and Marissa each ordered a hot fudge sundae. Johnny ordered nothing, explaining to his son that he'd just finished a big meal.

"I have a ball game Wednesday night," Benjamin said when the waitress had departed. "You'll come to it, won't you, Dad?"

"Of course I'll be there," Johnny said without hesitation, warmed by the light of devotion that shone in his son's eyes. "What time?"

"Seven o'clock," Marissa answered. "At the ball field by the grade school." She dug into her purse and pulled out a dollar. "Why don't you go put this in the jukebox and pick out some good music?" She handed the dollar to her son.

He gave her a knowing look. "You want to talk to Dad by yourself, right?"

She smiled self-consciously. "Right."

"Okay. I'll go play the jukebox, and I'll take a few minutes picking out the songs."

Marissa got up to let Benjamin out and when she slid back in across from Johnny, her gaze didn't meet his. "I've been doing a lot of thinking since you left last night," she began.

Here it comes, Johnny thought, the recriminations and the denials.

"You were right...and you were wrong."

He looked at her in surprise. "Wrong about what?"

Marissa's gaze locked with his, her eyes a beautiful deep brown and filled with emotion. "Johnny, I never believed you had anything to do with Sydney's death. Never, for a single instant did I entertain a doubt in my mind about that."

He believed her. The truth was on her face, shining from her eyes, and he felt one of the cold fingers around his heart let go, allowing warmth to seep through him. He hadn't realized until this moment how important it was to him that she, of all people on the earth, believed him incapable of Sydney's murder.

"And," she continued, her gaze once again skittering away from his. "You were right when you said I was using the belief that you'd made love to Sydney as an excuse." She stared down at the tabletop. "I was scared, Johnny. I was young, and stupid and scared."

He sat back, surprised by her confession. Before he could say anything she held up a hand to still him. "I was never ashamed of my feelings for you, Johnny. I didn't tell my parents we were seeing each other because I knew they would disapprove and try to make me stop seeing you. I didn't tell my friends because I didn't want to share what was so special to me with anyone."

She sighed and raked a hand through her tumble of

curls. "When Sydney was found murdered and you were arrested, I was afraid…afraid of what people might think if they knew I was seeing you, afraid that I would get tangled up in Sydney's murder investigation. Shame wasn't part of our relationship, Johnny. Until now." Again her gaze met his. "And now I'm ashamed of the girl I was and how I let you down."

Johnny refused to allow himself to be moved by her words, by her repentance. Too many years had passed, too much anger and sorrow had wrapped together in his heart and created an impenetrable, protective barrier.

"What do you want me to say?" he asked softly. "What in the hell kind of difference does it make now?"

"I don't know. I thought it might help for you to understand."

"Help with what?" he demanded. He drew a deep breath and leaned forward. "Now let me make you understand something, Marissa. Ten years ago I loved you more than anyone or anything on this earth. And when I needed you most, you weren't there." The cold fingers that remained clutching his heart constricted more tightly, squeezing the warmth out of him.

He sat back once again, eyeing her with the dispassion of a man accustomed to circumventing emotions. "I won't lie to you. I wanted you last night, and I still want you today. I like making love to you. But don't make any mistake…it means nothing emotionally to me. I can't just let go of the past, pretend that it didn't happen. That your running away from me wasn't the biggest blow I suffered. I don't know that I can forgive you, Marissa." He saw her immediate reaction to his words, each like a slap across her face.

She swallowed visibly, but had no chance to reply as

the waitress arrived with their ice cream order and Benjamin trailed at her heels.

Benjamin scooted into the seat next to Marissa and smiled at Johnny. "You want to share my sundae, Dad? I'll share with you."

Benjamin's words, so sweet, so loving, suddenly made Johnny feel far too vulnerable. Somewhere, in the mess that was his life, he must have done something very good to deserve Benjy. "No, thanks, son," he said and slid out of the booth. "I'm really tired, so I think I'm going to head on home."

"You won't forget my game on Wednesday night, will you?" Benjamin asked.

Johnny flashed him a smile. "Not a chance." With a curt nod to Marissa, he walked to the cashier, paid for his dinner, then left the restaurant.

He drove home slowly, carefully distracting his thoughts away from the conversation he'd just had with Marissa. He didn't want to think about her. He was tired of thinking about her.

At least she now understood where he was coming from where she was concerned. She knew not to expect anything more from him than physical pleasure and shared parental duties. No emotional ties, no painful recriminations. The past was gone and there was no going back for the two of them. She'd forfeited his love through abandonment and there was no absolution for her sin.

By the time he arrived back at his place, dusk had fallen and the ebony shadows of night clouds stretched to steal the last pale glow of twilight.

Johnny left his truck and sank down on the front porch, staring out over the ranch that held such a large portion of his heart.

If he didn't win the bull-riding contest, he didn't know

what the future might hold. He needed to give Benjamin something, and he wanted this land to be his legacy to his son. But a ranch without livestock, land without fields of grain, was nothing more than an empty promise.

Johnny stood. Despite his aching weariness, in spite of the deepening shadows of night, he was too restless to go into the emptiness of the house. Maybe a walk would work off his unsettled energy and make sleep come easy.

He walked with no specific destination in mind. As he walked, he breathed deeply of the night-scented air, watched the stars overhead winking on like a million miniature crystal lamps.

Marissa's words in the diner had surprised him. He hadn't expected a soul-shattering admission of guilt from her. But in effect that's what she'd done, confessed to letting him down, acknowledged her desertion of him.

First his father, then Marissa, followed by his mother's death. Seemed most people in his life had walked out on him in one way or another. Doesn't matter, he thought. He didn't need anyone other than Benjamin. His son wouldn't leave him.

He stopped walking, recognizing where he was by the dark outline of the structure in front of him. The old shed. This was the place where his life had finally come unraveled, where all had been lost.

Sydney. Her name rang in his head, a distant echo of friendship lost, of youth stolen. It was hard to feel sorry for himself. He'd lost ten years, but she'd lost her very life.

He froze, his breath catching in his chest as a pale light flashed from within the structure. Somebody was in the shed. But who would be out here in the dark…and why?

Johnny eased closer, heart pounding furiously. Drawing a deep breath, he shoved open the door and froze once again. "Sydney..." The name whispered from him in shock as he stared at the blond-haired girl who stared back at him in equal surprise. Sydney...she held a flashlight in one hand and something he couldn't quite see in the other. Sydney.

But, of course it wasn't Sydney. Sydney was dead. His mind worked frantically to make sense of the young woman's presence. "Gillian," he said in realization.

His voice broke the inertia that had held her. With a small cry, she turned and slipped through the back of the shed where a board had rotted and fallen to the ground.

"Gillian, wait!" he cried, hurrying after her. "Please...I just want to talk to you."

As he tried to slide through the same opening in the structure as she had, she looked back at him. In her eyes he saw more than fear, he saw abject terror.

He stopped struggling and instead watched as the beam from her flashlight was swallowed up by the darkness of the night.

Gillian. Johnny stepped back into the interior of the shed, his mind reeling. Dear God, she had looked so much like Sydney. The same pale hair, the same petite features....

What had she been doing out here? Johnny stared around him in confusion. Moonlight spilled through the gaps in the wooden slats and he saw that the dirt floor had been torn up, as if Gillian had been digging for treasure.

What could she have been looking for?

Bending down, with the aid of the bright moonlight that illuminated the night, Johnny ran his hands across the ground. It appeared as if she'd dug around in every inch of the floor. If there had been something buried here, she'd found it, for Johnny could see nothing in the dirt.

What had she held in her left hand? The flashlight had been in her right, but she'd had something in her left. Something she'd found out here? Something that had been buried?

Johnny left the shed and walked slowly back toward his house, his heart as heavy as the full moon hanging low in the sky. Gillian had looked at him with such fear. He knew it was because she believed he'd cold-bloodedly killed her sister.

He had to clear his name. Somehow, someway, he had to find out who had really killed Sydney. Otherwise he would never rid himself of the black shadows of night that filled his heart.

Chapter 12

"I can't believe they aren't letting you decorate the prom," Lucy said as she poured herself another cup of coffee. "You've provided flowers for the prom ever since you've owned this shop."

Lucy and Marissa sat in the backroom of the flower shop and Marissa had just related to her friend her conversation with the Emerys the day before.

It had become habit for Lucy to stop in every Tuesday, on her day off at the diner, and share a little friendly morning gossip and coffee with Marissa.

Marissa frowned into her mug thoughtfully, her mind going over the conversation that had taken place at the Emery home. "I got the feeling that it was Brad's dictate rather than Rachel's. He seemed to be the one in control."

"Big surprise. He's always been a bully," Lucy replied as she once again sat down next to Marissa at the small work area.

"Rachel has really aged since last time I saw her. She looked so weary, so beaten-down yesterday."

"Maybe it's because the ten-year anniversary of her daughter's murder is in two weeks. Prom must be really hard on Rachel, since that's the night Sydney was found dead." Lucy stirred a large spoonful of sugar into her coffee. "I mean, this time of year has got to be particularly hard on her." She took a sip of the brew. "What did Johnny say about all this?"

"I didn't tell him, and I don't intend to tell him." Marissa tried to shove away the memory of his expression when he'd told her he couldn't forgive her, he'd never forgive her.

She sighed and threaded her fingers through her hair. "What's the point? He already knows the Emerys don't want him in Mustang. He knows they're angry that he's stirring up the murder again."

"Yeah, but he should also know the price you're paying for standing up for him to the Emerys," Lucy observed.

Marissa smiled ruefully. "Maybe it's a weird form of delayed justice or something." Lucy looked at her blankly, obviously not understanding. "Ten years ago I didn't stand up for Johnny because I was afraid of the reprisals I might have to face. I'm just doing now what I should have done back then."

Lucy fluffed her blond curls, settled back in her chair and eyed her friend thoughtfully. "Are you sorry he came back here?"

"I went to the prison three weeks before he was released and tried to talk him into settling someplace else," Marissa confessed.

Lucy's round blue eyes widened in surprise. "You're kidding me," she gasped.

Marissa shook her head. "I didn't want him to know about Benjamin. I was afraid of the changes that would happen to my life if he came back here."

"And now?"

"And now I know Johnny belongs here in Mustang as much as I do, and I had no right to try to discourage his choosing to come home." She stared into her coffee mug, conflicting emotions warring inside her. "There's no doubt about it, things would have been easier if he'd never come back here. But when I see him with Benjy, see the love they have for each other, I'm glad he's here, no matter what price has to be paid."

"Word through the grapevine is that he's going to compete in the rodeo," Lucy said.

Marissa frowned. "Don't remind me. I get upset every time I think about him taking such a risk."

"But it isn't that big of a risk," Lucy said, then continued in explanation. "I mean, Johnny was a terrific bull rider years ago."

"Yeah, but it still worries me."

Lucy narrowed her eyes. "He's getting to you, isn't he?"

This time it was Marissa's turn to look at her in surprise. "What do you mean?"

"Johnny. He's getting under your skin. You're falling in love with him again."

"Don't be ridiculous," Marissa scoffed. She got up to get herself more coffee, too unsettled by Lucy's words to remain seated.

She poured herself a second cup, but instead of returning to the table, she began to pace back and forth in the small work area. "I can't deny that I care about Johnny. After all, he is the father of my son. We share a certain history. But I'd be a fool to let him get into my heart."

Lucy grinned. "Then you're a fool."

"No, I'm not," Marissa objected, a heated flush sweeping over her face. "And trust me, I know what a fool I'd be to fall in love with Johnny again. There's a part of him that hates me, a part of him that can't forgive me for not being there for him years ago."

She set her mug down on the counter, but didn't stop her pacing back and forth. "He's let me know in no uncertain terms that he would never be able to get past his bitterness where I'm concerned. Trust me, Lucy. I have a firm grip on my heart where Johnny is concerned."

Lucy nodded, as if Marissa had finally managed to convince her. "Speaking of your heart...what did you think of Frank?"

"He was nice, very mellow and pleasant."

Lucy shot her a look of disgust. "You sound like you're describing a glass of buttermilk."

Marissa shrugged. "What do you want me to say? He's a nice, handsome guy, but there were no sparks, no chemistry."

"Too bad. He really liked you. He's planning on coming back to town next weekend and wants to ask you out again. This time just the two of you, without Derrick and me."

"Oh, Lucy, tell him not to. I'll just have to turn him down and that's always so awkward." Once again Marissa sank down on the chair next to her friend. "I don't want to lead him on or waste his time."

She tried not to think about the chemistry, the sparks that had exploded after her date with Frank...sparks that had ignited into full-blown flames of desire with Johnny. "It's not fair to Frank for me to see him again."

"Okay, so I'll fix you up with somebody else. At least

you broke the dating ice by going out with Frank. I've got a dozen single men who would love to ask you out," Lucy said cheerfully.

"I don't think I'm ready," Marissa replied, the very idea of another date turning her stomach. "I need more time to get used to the idea of dating."

"More time?" Lucy eyebrows flew upward in disbelief. "My goodness, Marissa. You've had ten years. How much longer do you need?"

"I don't know," Marissa said, her voice sharp with the beginnings of irritation.

"Okay, okay. Don't get excited." Lucy held up her hands in surrender. "I was just trying to help."

Marissa smiled an apology. "I know, and I'm sorry for getting snappish. I've just got a lot on my mind."

Lucy's expression instantly turned sympathetic. "Is losing the prom account going to make things financially difficult?"

"It's going to make things tight, but I'll get by. Benjamin will just have to wait a little longer for that computer he wants."

Lucy finished the last of her coffee and stood. "Guess I'd better get out of here and let you get to work."

"You don't have to hurry off. It's been a slow day." Marissa said the words out of politeness, instead of any real desire to get Lucy to remain. The entire conversation had unsettled Marissa, bringing with it too many thoughts of Johnny, his alleged crime, and her own feelings toward him.

She walked with Lucy to the front door of the shop. "Maybe we can catch a movie this weekend," she suggested, realizing it had been a while since she and Lucy had shared a ladies' night out.

"Sorry, not this weekend." Lucy smiled, a rapturous

smile that transformed her features from pretty to beautiful. "Derrick and I are driving to Butte to meet his parents. We're leaving Friday and won't be back until Sunday."

"Sounds serious."

"I think it is." Lucy smiled again. "I'm crazy about him, Marissa. I've never felt this way about anyone before."

Marissa gave Lucy an impulsive hug. "I'm so happy for you, Lucy," she said, fighting against a new wave of loneliness that threatened to overwhelm her.

Later, after Lucy had left, the loneliness crept into Marissa's heart once again. She was glad Lucy had found somebody she loved and who seemed to love her back. That was the way it was supposed to work.

However, Marissa couldn't help the rather selfish jealousy that assailed her. Lucy had been a good friend for years, and even though Lucy had dated a lot during those years, she'd always made herself available to help Marissa fill lonely nights. At least once or twice a week the two would go shopping, or to dinner, or to a movie together, but Marissa had a feeling those times now would be few and far between.

Marissa would miss those nights shared with her friend, but she couldn't begrudge Lucy her happiness in finally finding the man she believed would fill all her needs, the man who would share in her future.

Deciding to dust the glass shelves that held an array of artificial flower arrangements and a variety of empty vases, Marissa got to work, hoping that keeping busy would clear her mind of all other thoughts.

By the next evening when Benjamin's ball game rolled around, Marissa was exhausted. Since her talk with Lucy, she'd deep cleaned each and every inch of the shop, taken a much-needed inventory and had stayed up late the night before cleaning her bedroom and storing away winter clothing.

"Do you think Dad will show up?"

Marissa turned into the elementary school parking lot, then shot a quick glance at her son's hopeful face. "He said he'd be here, so I'm sure he will."

"You think he'll like watching me play ball?"

Marissa smiled. "I'm sure he'll love it."

Benjamin nodded, his face lit with eagerness. "It will be the first time he's seen me play. I hope I do really good tonight."

Marissa parked her car, then smiled at Benjy. "Honey, you just do your best, and that will be more than good enough for your dad."

Benjy nodded and scrambled out of the car. "I'll see you after the game, Mom."

As he hurried to join his team in their dugout, Marissa walked toward the spectator stand, a small set of bleachers where several parents were already seated.

Marissa nodded and waved to those she knew as she sank down in the middle of the first row of bleacher seats. As Benjy's team ran out onto the field and began to practice, Marissa watched her son with pride.

He looked so cute in his little red-and-white uniform, his enthusiasm apparent in the smile that curved his lips, the way he practically vibrated with energy. He was always excited before a game, but his excitement level this evening seemed particularly high, and Marissa knew the reason why.

Johnny.

In the short time he'd been back in town, he'd captured his son's heart completely. And she knew Johnny loved his son with all the devotion a father could give. They needed each other and Marissa knew Johnny gave Benjamin the emotional support a boy needed from a father.

As the practice session continued on the field, she was aware of Benjamin looking toward the bleachers every few minutes, and she knew he was looking for his dad.

A caravan of minivans pulled into the parking lot, delivering the opposing team from their nearby hometown. Within minutes the bleachers were three-quarters filled and the teams were once again in their respective dugouts for last minute inspiration from their coaches.

Where was Johnny? She, too, watched the parking lot anxiously, hoping—praying—that his truck would appear. There was no way she'd believe that he would let his son down unless something dire kept him away.

As the teams all left the dugouts to take their positions on the field, Marissa breathed a sigh of relief as she saw Johnny's truck pull into the parking area.

Marissa's heart thudded wildly in her chest as she watched Johnny approach. Clad in a tightly fitted pair of jeans, a white T-shirt, and with his familiar black cowboy hat planted firmly on his head, he looked like the young man she'd fallen in love with…the hero who'd saved her from Brian Theron's drunken advances…the man who'd danced with her in the woods on a prom night years ago, then had made beautiful love to her.

It was at that moment, Marissa realized she'd lied to Lucy—just as she'd been lying to herself all along. She didn't have a firm grip on her heart, she didn't have her heart in her possession at all. She'd given it to Johnny ten years ago and he still owned it. She was still in love with Johnny.

Johnny swept his hat off his head as he approached the bleachers where Marissa sat. He tried not to notice how pretty she looked in her jeans and a bright red T-shirt that acknowledged her as a Mustang Mavericks supporter.

Instead he averted his attention from her to the field, where Benjamin waved from his spot on the pitcher's mound. Johnny was here for Benjamin, not for Marissa, he reminded himself.

He had two things on his mind...Benjamin's game, and the conversation he'd had earlier in the day with Brett Enderly, one of the men who'd been a suspect in Sydney's murder. Johnny had finally caught up with Enderly, who no longer worked for the Emerys, but now worked as a trash collector for the town of Mustang. He shoved the conversation to the back of his mind, wanting his full attention on his son and the ball game getting ready to begin.

Johnny sat down next to Marissa, knowing that's where Benjamin would expect him to sit. As her perfume filled his senses, and she smiled her damnable sweet smile at him, tension swelled inside him.

"Benjamin will be so glad you came," she said.

"I wouldn't have missed it for anything," he replied curtly.

"That's what I told him." She smiled at him again and Johnny felt his desire for her surge up from within. But, it was a desire he had no intention of acting on. Instead, he turned his complete attention to the game getting ready to begin.

Once the game began, it didn't take Johnny long to get caught up in the excitement. The kids played their hearts out, and the spectators verbalized both their support and their disappointment with each play.

Although Johnny had intended to keep emotional distance from Marissa, it was impossible not to share pride in their son, and the excitement of cheering his team toward victory. When Benjamin hit a home run, driving in two runs to put the Mavericks in the lead, Marissa squealed her happiness and threw her arms around Johnny.

In those brief moments of celebration and intimate closeness, Johnny's desire for her once again rocketed through him.

When would he stop wanting her? When would he finally be able to talk to her, spend time with her and not feel the responding heat and passion she always seemed to provoke in him? He hoped that day would come soon, because in his present state, each moment he spent with her was a curious kind of torture.

The game ended with the Mavericks winning by one run. Benjamin came running over to where Johnny and Marissa sat, whooping and hollering with joy. ''Did you see me? Coach said I did a great job tonight,'' Benjy said excitedly.

''Better than great,'' Johnny replied as he tousled his son's hair. ''You were fantastic. Your fastball whizzed by those batters so accurately they couldn't get a handle on it.''

Benjamin turned to Marissa. ''Mom, Coach is taking us all out for pizza. He says he'll bring us all home later. I can go, can't I?''

Marissa laughed. ''Of course you can go. I'll just meet you at home later.''

''Great!'' Benjamin gave both Johnny and Marissa a wide grin. ''I gotta go,'' he said as the coach called for all the players to join him at the dugout. ''See you later, Dad. Thanks for coming. Bye, Mom.'' He turned and, with a stir of dust, raced off.

''Want to go to the diner and get a cup of coffee?''

The words of invitation fell from Johnny's lips almost as if of their own volition.

"A cup of coffee sounds good," she agreed. "I'll meet you at the diner in about fifteen minutes."

Just drive on home, Johnny told himself once he was back in his truck. Why the hell are you meeting Marissa for coffee? Despite his chiding, the truck headed for the diner instead of for his house.

Marissa was already seated at a booth when he arrived. He joined her and they both ordered coffee from the waitress. As Johnny sipped his, he tried not to notice the flush of color in Marissa's cheeks, the way her T-shirt clung provocatively to her breasts, how her hair was in charming disarray as if tousled by a lover's hands.

Of all the single, available women in Mustang, why did it have to be this one that heated his blood? Why did it have to be Marissa who stirred him on such a primal level?

"The game was fun," he said in an attempt to start a conversation that would keep all other thoughts in check.

Marissa nodded. "I enjoy going to the games."

An uncomfortable silence grew between them, a silence thick with tension.

"I thought…"

"It seems…"

They started to speak at the same time, stopped, then laughed. "Go ahead," Johnny said.

"I was just going to say that it seems like everyone is getting used to having you around. I didn't notice anybody paying much attention to you when you showed up at the game."

Johnny smiled. "I guess I'm old news by now."

"What were you going to say?" Marissa asked curiously.

"I was just going to say that I thought your friend worked here…Lucy?"

"She does, but she works the day shift."

Johnny signaled for a refill from the waitress. She poured them fresh coffee, then left and another long silence built between Johnny and Marissa.

"I talked to Brett Enderly today," Johnny said, and as soon as the words left his mouth, he knew it was why he'd invited Marissa for a cup of coffee. He wanted to bounce the conversation he'd had with Brett off her.

"Brett Enderly?" She frowned thoughtfully. "Who is he?"

"One of the five original suspects in Sydney's murder. He used to work for the Emerys but now collects garbage."

Marissa leaned forward, her eyes lit with excitement. "Did he tell you anything you can use to help clear your name?"

"At first he didn't want to talk to me at all." Johnny paused a moment to sip his coffee, remembering the man's reluctance to speak with him. "He told me he couldn't afford to lose his job, that the power of the Emerys was long reaching."

"So, he didn't tell you anything?" The brown of Marissa's eyes deepened with disappointment.

"He finally told me a little, enough to get my brain working. Apparently he started working for the Emerys when Sydney was twelve years old, and he quit working for them when Sydney was sixteen."

"Why did he quit?" Marissa still leaned forward, her features radiating interest. Johnny wished she'd sit back, widen the distance between them so he couldn't smell her, couldn't so easily reach out and touch her.

Johnny took another sip of his coffee, as if the brew

would protect him from his own desire where Marissa was concerned. "He said he quit because he couldn't stand to see the way Brad treated Rachel, Sydney and Gillian."

"And how did he say Brad treated them?" Marissa asked softly.

"He said they were treated like prisoners in a prison with a sadistic warden. He said he saw Brad slap Sydney, twist her arm, kick her. Brett told me that not a day went by that Brad wasn't tormenting one of the girls in one way or another. The day he quit it was because he saw Brad whip Sydney. She was back-talking him and as she turned to walk away, he snapped that whip and laid open not only her dress, but the flesh of her back."

Marissa gasped, the horror in her eyes the same emotion Johnny had felt when Brett had told him what he knew. "Oh my God!" she gasped.

Johnny expelled a deep breath and raked a hand through his hair. "You know, I've had all afternoon to think about what Brett told me. Brett's words made me remember that Sydney never wore short sleeves or shorts. No matter how hot it was, all of the time I was meeting with her, she always wore long sleeves and slacks."

He shook his head, anger welling up inside him. "I should have known. I was supposed to be her friend. I should have realized things were bad for her, that she was scared and physically abused."

"Johnny." Marissa reached across the table and captured his hand with hers. "How could you know? If Sydney didn't tell you, how were you supposed to know?"

The guilt that had been eating at Johnny since his conversation with Brett reared up in full force. "The signs were there, I just didn't see them, but I should have. The clothes she wore, the fear I always saw in her eyes. One night she had a bruise on her chin. She told me she fell on the stairs and had bumped it, but her story didn't sound right. Still, I didn't pursue it. She seemed so damned fragile.''

"You can't blame yourself, Johnny.'' Marissa squeezed his hand, her eyes filled with compassion for him...for Sydney. "She wouldn't want you to beat yourself up, Johnny. I'm sure your friendship with her brought tremendous joy to her life. That's what you need to remember.''

His guilt ebbed somewhat with her words and he looked at her gratefully. "I think Brad killed her,'' he finally said.

"You need to go to Jesse. Tell him what you've found out and let him reopen an investigation.''

Johnny pulled his hand from hers and frowned. "The sheriff isn't going to reopen an investigation based on speculation. And right now, that's all I've got. In my gut, I believe Brad killed her, but that's not enough to go on. The sheriff will want to know why Brad might have killed her, and I don't have an answer for that.''

"But Brett could tell Jesse what he told you,'' Marissa protested.

"Brett won't repeat what he told me to anyone. He already told me that. Brad Emery has this whole town running scared because of his temper and his power.'' Johnny sighed again, deep and long, knowing the sigh reflected the hopelessness that echoed hollowly inside him. "Maybe I'm a fool,'' he said.

"What are you talking about?''

He shrugged. "Maybe I'm a damned fool to be spinning my wheels trying to clear my name. Maybe you were right all along, maybe I should just forget it and get on with my life.''

"Okay, then I'll go home and try to explain to Benjy why his father is a quitter," Marissa said, trying to inspire him.

Johnny looked at her sharply. "Hell, Marissa, you're the one who kept telling me to leave things alone, get on with my life, stop trying to change the past."

Her cheeks flushed with color. "And I was wrong." Again her hand reached for his, clasping his warmly. "Oh, Johnny, I didn't want you stirring things up because *I* was afraid, but I'm not afraid anymore."

She drew a deep breath. "This is bigger than me and my fears, or Benjamin or even you. This is about a girl who was murdered. If you're right and Brad killed her, then he should be in jail. And if you're right, and he's an abusive monster, then you need to dig deeper, find out the truth not just for yourself, but for Rachel and Gillian as well. They've continued to live with his torture for ten years."

Johnny closed his eyes and curled his fingers so that instead of her clasping his hand, he was holding hers. This was why he'd wanted her to come for coffee, he'd known instinctively that she would give him the strength to continue.

"That's why Brad has been so crazed to get you out of town," she continued. "Because you're getting too close. More than anyone else in town, you pose a threat to him because you know you're innocent."

Johnny nodded. He knew he should pull his hand back from hers, but he didn't. He kept her hand captive in his, as always marveling at the smallness of hers. Small hands for a strong woman. He was glad his son had been raised by her, knew that Marissa had the character traits he'd want instilled in his son.

"What are you going to do now?" she asked.

"I'm going to turn up the heat," Johnny replied, finally releasing his hold on her hand. "I'm going to let Brad know that I'm coming after him, hope that somehow he makes a mistake of some kind that will trip him up." He eyed Marissa steadily. "I can't promise that things won't get rough," he warned. "The harder I push, the more angry Brad will get. I don't want you and Benjamin to get caught in the cross fire."

"Don't you worry about us," she replied. "We'll handle whatever happens. You do what you have to do. You have my complete support."

Again a whisper of desire shot through Johnny as he gazed at Marissa, but it was desire tempered with the knowledge that she hadn't handled things well in the past. And just like the past, he had a feeling when the going got rough, Marissa would once again abandon him. And that knowledge effectively tempered any desire he might have for her.

Chapter 13

"I'm worried about you." Jeffrey Sawyer eyed his daughter from across the table. They had just finished clearing the dishes after the evening meal. Benjamin and Marissa's mother had gone for an after-dinner walk, leaving Marissa and her father alone to share coffee at the table.

"Why?" Marissa asked in surprise.

"You look tired. You have dark circles under your eyes."

Marissa smiled ruefully. "Thanks, Dad, you always did know how to sweet-talk a lady."

"I'm serious, Marissa. I know things have been rough for you lately. I've heard the talk around town. I know how angry Johnny has made the Emerys, and I know your shop has been blackballed by them and everyone who is afraid of them." He smiled at her, a smile she'd grown up seeing from her father, one of support and boundless love. ''You don't have to pretend that all is well with me, Marissa.''

Marissa started to protest, then sighed wearily. ''Okay, things have been a little rough the last couple of weeks. But with the rodeo starting tomorrow and all the tourists in town, the shop is still doing a little business.''

''A 'little business' won't pay your bills. Your mom and I could loan you some money to tide you over.''

Marissa smiled and shook her head. ''No, Dad, that's not necessary. I'm doing okay. I'm just tired.''

She couldn't very well tell her father that most of her weariness wasn't due to money worry, but rather to thoughts of Johnny. Thoughts of him kept her tossing and turning all night.

For the last two weeks she'd seen him only when he'd come to pick up Benjamin or bring Benjamin back home. The night they'd shared coffee after the ball game had been the last time she'd felt she shared any kind of emotional connection to Johnny. Since that night, it was as if he'd turned off where she was concerned. He kept his distance, both physically and emotionally, and in that distance Marissa ached.

''Folks are saying that Johnny is accusing Brad Emery of Sydney's death,'' Jeffrey said, interrupting Marissa's troubling thoughts.

''That's true.''

Jeffrey's frown deepened. ''Brad is threatening to take Johnny to court, sue him for slander.''

''You can only win a slander suit if what the other person is saying about you isn't true. In this case, Johnny truly believes Brad killed Sydney, and so do I.''

Jeffrey raked a hand through his thick, sandy hair and leaned back in his chair with a thoughtful frown. ''It certainly wouldn't surprise me to find out that Brad had something to do with that poor girl's death. He's always been a mean cuss.''

Marissa absently tapped two fingers on the tabletop. ''I don't understand the people in this town. Everyone I've talked to seems to know that Brad is mean and hateful, but nobody seems willing to believe he killed Sydney.''

''Oh, there are plenty of people in Mustang who would believe Brad capable of such a crime, but none of them would be willing to point a finger of accusation at Brad.''

''Johnny is willing, and that's exactly what he's doing,'' Marissa exclaimed.

Jeffrey smiled at his daughter, the patient, tolerant smile of a knowledgeable adult for a foolish child. ''Johnny can afford to. He has absolutely nothing to lose. The only thing worse than a bully, is a bully with money and control.'' Her father's smile fell away. ''What bothers me is that while Johnny is trying to clear his name, he's taking you and Benjy down with him.''

Marissa laughed. ''You don't have to worry about Benjy. Apparently the younger generation isn't feeling any of the tension or fear that's in the air. Besides, Benjy thinks Johnny hung the moon.''

''And what do you think?''

To Marissa's horror, tears blurred her vision, then spilled onto her cheeks. ''I love him, Dad,'' she confessed through her tears. ''I love him but he doesn't love me, and I don't know what to do about it.''

Jeffrey left his seat at the table and walked around to his daughter. In a gesture reminiscent of Marissa's youth and of childhood hurts, he pulled her up from her chair and into his embrace.

In his loving, familiar arms, Marissa could no longer hold back her heartache. Sobs of pain ripped through her as her dad stroked her hair in the same way he had always tried to soothe her pain.

Her tears came fast and furious, eventually subsiding. "I'll tell you one thing," he said softly as he continued to hold her close. "If Johnny Crockett doesn't love you back, then he's stupid…too stupid for you to love."

Marissa laughed despite her tears at the utter indignation in her father's voice. She stepped back from him and swiped the remaining tears from her eyes, her laughter only momentarily easing the heartbreak that ached in her chest.

"Oh, my little girl." Jeffrey reached out and placed the palms of his hands on her cheeks. "I knew this day would eventually come…the day when you'd have a boo-boo that Daddy's hugs and kisses couldn't fix."

Marissa saw her own pain reflected in her father's eyes as he continued. "A father can give his daughter advice, he can guide her through the rough patches of life, but no matter how much he'd like to, he can't heal a heartache…only time can do that."

Time. Marissa didn't have the heart to remind her father that it had already been ten years. How much more time would it take for her heart to heal from its run-in with Johnny?

An hour later Marissa drove home by herself. Benjamin had been invited to spend the night with her parents. "Let him stay here tonight. You can pick him up on your way to the rodeo in the morning," her mother had said. "Maybe this way you can get a good-night sleep."

A good-night sleep. Marissa couldn't remember the last time she'd had one of those. Maybe she'd take a long hot bath when she got home. Hopefully a hot soak would encourage her body to relax and promote the possibility of a good-night sleep.

As she drove through town toward her house, signs of both the imminent rodeo and the high-school dance were everywhere. Cowboys were everywhere, walking the sidewalks with jangling spurs and leather boots. Interspersed among the macho men were youthful couples decked out in fancy dress and heading toward the high school where the dance would begin within an hour.

It was unusual for the two events to be taking place the same weekend, but as mayor of Mustang, Marissa's father had pursued the rodeo with a vengeance despite the fact that it was scheduled to occur the day after prom. Jeffrey knew the rodeo would attract tourists and bring much-needed revenue to the businesses of the small town.

As she drove by the high school, a sharp burst of anger swept through her. She should be inside there right now, putting last minute touches on floral decorations. She should have spent the week making table arrangements with bright blue and gold ribbons, the school colors.

It wasn't fair. However, Marissa knew as well as anyone that life was rarely fair. If it were, then Johnny wouldn't have gone to prison for a crime he didn't commit. Instead he and Marissa would have married, and Benjamin would have been raised in a happy, loving two-parent home.

An hour later she got out of the bathtub, no more relaxed and unstressed as she'd been when she'd gotten into the tub.

Prom night. Ten years ago tonight had been the last night she and Johnny had made love when she'd felt that both their hearts beat in unison. On that night, neither of them had known the fateful winds that would render them apart. On that night, they'd just loved each other with the exuberance and the innocence of youth.

Instead of pulling on her pajamas, Marissa dressed in a long cotton dress with a springtime floral pattern. It was just a few minutes after eight, far too early for bed. Dressed, and with her hair dried and pulled back and gathered at the nape of her neck with a piece of ribbon, she sat down on the sofa and picked up the phone. She quickly punched in Lucy's number, hoping she could talk her friend into getting a cup of coffee at the diner or maybe seeing a movie.

Lucy's phone rang three times, then her answering machine clicked on. Marissa left a message for Lucy to call her back, but figured since it was Friday night Lucy was probably spending the evening with Derrick. She waited until nine, then tried one more time to reach Lucy, but again got the machine.

Making a decision, Marissa grabbed her purse, a sweater and her keys and left the house. No reason why she couldn't go see a movie by herself, she reasoned.

However, by the time she reached Mustang's small movie theater, she'd changed her mind and drove right on by. It was too pretty of an evening to spend cooped up in a theater.

Instead she decided to enjoy a short drive, then go back home and head to bed. She drove aimlessly, with her windows down and the warm, fragrant evening air caressing her face and shoulders.

Night fell, bringing with it a sky full of stars and still Marissa was reluctant to call an end to the day. She didn't realize her final destination until she arrived there.

She found an empty parking space in the very back of the high-school parking lot. She parked, shut off her engine, and wondered if she'd lost her mind. What was she doing here? Why had she come?

Even as the questions fluttered through her mind, she

knew the answers. She wanted to sit in the woods behind the school and listen to the band play their music. She wanted to remember how happy she'd been on that night so long ago when she and Johnny had met in the woods and shared their own private prom night.

She grabbed her sweater from the passenger seat, draped it around her shoulders and got out of the car. The night wrapped around her with the warmth of a lover's embrace. She stood for a moment, breathing in the air, listening to the noise emanating from the high school.

She could hear the soft murmur of young people talking and laughing, their muted voices mingling with the vociferous sound of insects from the dense woods nearby.

The night sounded like, smelled like, felt like it had ten years before, and a wistful longing for what once had been, for what might have been filled Marissa's heart.

As she walked toward the woods, the band began to play, the sound traveling out of the open gym windows to spill into the night. The song was a slow, romantic love song and she could easily imagine the young couples moving to the rhythm, their arms entwined as they gazed into one another's eyes.

It took Marissa only moments to find the small clearing where she and Johnny had once danced together. Trees' branches provided a leafy balcony overhead and among the leaves, the stars winked and shone their brilliance.

She sank down into the sweet, lush grass, unmindful of any grass stains that might mark her dress. She just wanted to dwell in the memories that unfolded rich and vivid in her mind...memories of love found, then lost forever.

Johnny drove aimlessly, trying to ease the attack of anxiety that struck him as he thought of the rodeo the next day. All or nothing. He had to win that bull-riding event or he'd have nothing...be nothing. Unless he could make a success of the ranch, he would always be that poor, fatherless Crockett kid, if not to the people in Mustang, then to himself.

Although he tried to still the zinging of his nerves, he was grateful for the nervousness. A man who didn't respect the bulls, a man who didn't have a healthy fear of the bulls, wasn't a bull rider for long.

The last two weeks had been hell. Besides working at the Gallagher ranch every other day, Johnny had spent hours trying to talk to anyone who might know anything about Brad Emery and any whisper of abuse Sydney might have suffered at her stepbrother's hands.

He'd spoken to Dr. Williams, Mustang's only doctor. Henry Williams was old as dirt, but as ethical as they came. Despite the fact that Sydney was dead and gone, the doctor insisted he could tell Johnny nothing of her general health or any injuries he might have treated because of doctor/patient confidentiality.

He'd talked to neighbors, ranch hands, store clerks... anyone who might have seen or heard something that would corroborate Johnny's theory. All were reluctant to talk. Johnny wasn't. He told each and every person he spoke to that he believed Brad had killed his stepsister in one of his temper rages.

Johnny had gained few answers, but he knew he was getting to Brad. He could tell by the recent attacks of vandalism that had taken place on his property. His fencing had been cut in two different pastures and the carcass of a dead coyote had been left on his porch.

Johnny saw each attack as a measure of his success, the result of a frightened, guilty Brad threatening Johnny, who threatened Brad's facade of innocence. Johnny knew an explosion was coming, that the tension between the two men was building to a dangerous level. He had no idea when the explosion would come or in what form, but he was ready…ready to point a finger of guilt to Brad Emery for the death of Sydney.

Johnny felt as if another explosion was just as imminent…an explosion between Marissa and himself. Despite the fact that he refused to let her back into his heart, she still burned in his soul, filling him with needy hunger each time he saw her.

She haunted his soul as much as Sydney did. Sydney haunted him with cries for justice. Marissa haunted him with cries of passion, with whispered words of love that tormented him with what might have been.

He turned his truck into the high-school parking lot, unsure exactly why he was here, but following a force that tugged at him.

Prom night. How many young couples, caught up in the romantic aura of the dance, would consummate their love for the first time tonight? Funny, prom night, instead of being his and Marissa's first night together, had been their last. The memory of that night still burned in his heart, as if branded in leather.

Unsure what force drove him, he parked his truck and got out. The night sang with the music of nature and the noise from the gym. Music and laughter, the sounds of youth…and hope…and sweet dreams of the future.

He kicked at the gravel beneath his feet and leaned against his truck. Had he ever been that young? That filled with hope and dreams?

Perhaps on that prom night so long ago when he'd danced with Marissa, held her in his arms and believed they had a future together. They'd spun fantasies that night, dancing and whispering of what their future held, the goals they'd reach together.

Pain tore through him, an ache of loss, of grief. He ached for the young man he'd once been, wished he could be that young man again, with all his hopes and dreams still intact.

Pushing away from the truck, the memories of that prom night with Marissa flooded through him, momentarily easing the ache of regret, the mourning of innocence. He walked away from the school building and toward the woods, wondering if by saying goodbye to this place, he could also get Marissa out of his soul.

It took him only a minute to come to the clearing and discover that the woman he'd come here to forget, sat like a beautiful statue in the center of the glade.

The starlight seeping through the tree branches overhead was bright enough for him to see that her eyes were closed. He could hear her humming, slightly off-key, to the same tune the band played, the strains drifting on a slight breeze.

For a long moment he remained just outside the clearing, hidden by the deep shadows of the trees that surrounded him. He took the opportunity to visually drink of her, to savor the length of her legs stretched out before her, to relish the slender lines of her body, the sweet swell of her breasts against the light cotton material of her dress.

What was she doing here? he wondered, then wondered the same about himself. Had he instinctively known she might be here? Had he hoped she would be? Was this the reason, the force that had pulled him here? The need to dance with her, to hold her in his arms, to love her just onc more time?

Without further hesitation, he decided to follow his

desire, and his desire was for her. He stepped into the clearing, a small branch crackling beneath his boot.

Her eyes flew open in fear. As she recognized him, he saw a glow in the depth of her eyes, a glow as hypnotic as a winter's fire. He felt that glow deep in the pit of his stomach, spreading warmth as it traveled throughout him.

He walked over to where she sat and offered his hand to her. "Dance with me, Marissa," he said softly. In one graceful motion, she came to her feet and into his arms.

She was a perfect fit, the top of her head reaching just beneath his chin. Her arms went around his neck, as his wrapped around her waist. With the sweet melody of a love song drifting through the trees, they moved as one, neither of them speaking.

Johnny closed his eyes, allowing only his sense of touch, his sense of smell to work. She smelled of spring flowers and summer nights, and her body molded to his as their feet moved them around the grassy dance floor.

His heart beat the same rhythm as hers, steady but faster than normal, a cadence of anticipation, a pulse of desire building.

"What are you doing here?" she asked, breaking the silence. Her breath was warm against his throat.

"I could ask you that same question," he replied.

She tilted her head back to look at him. "I'm not sure why I came here. It just felt right at the time."

He hesitated, then nodded. "Same here."

She bowed her head, tucking it beneath his chin once again. "What are we doing, Johnny?" she asked, her words a mere whisper.

He held her closer, more tightly. "Damned if I know," he admitted. It was as if all the elements in life had conspired to give them this single night and he wasn't sure whether to go with it, or to run from it.

She raised her head and looked at him once again. His lips claimed hers and he knew he wasn't about to run from it. Tonight he wanted nothing but to be that young man again, to hold Marissa in his arms, dance with her and make love to her. Tonight he wanted no tomorrows, no yesterdays, just this moment, with this woman.

Her mouth opened to welcome his kiss, and their feet stopped moving as the kiss deepened. Sweet…so sweet. Her lips were soft and yielding, giving way to heat as their tongues touched and retreated, then touched again.

Her fingers waltzed through his hair, knocking his hat from his head and to the ground behind them. He was vaguely aware that the band played a fast song perfect for dancing. But he no longer wanted to dance. He wanted to kiss her forever.

His hands moved from her waist up her back, pulling her breasts more firmly against his chest. He loved the way she felt against him, the swell of her breasts and the press of her thighs. His mouth left hers and he bent his head to touch his lips behind her ear, then down her throat.

Her breaths came more rapidly now, as did his. The sound of their growing desire filled the clearing, mingling with the night noises and the muted music that rode in the air.

When the music once again played soft and romantic, Johnny once again moved his feet, forcing her to dance with him. He didn't want them to move too fast, didn't want the night to end almost before it began.

He knew with a certainty that they would make love, knew it by the glow in her eyes, knew it by the way her body swayed with his. But, he wanted the night to move slowly, wanted to savor each and every moment with her.

Marissa seemed to sense his need to slow down, and

she moved an inch or two away from him, so their bodies no longer touched and it was easier for her to look at him.

"Are you nervous about tomorrow?" she asked.

"Yeah, but it's a good kind of nervous."

"What happens if you don't win, Johnny?" Her voice held worry.

He smiled, although her words caused a sick apprehension in the pit of his stomach. "I refuse to consider that possibility."

"Winning isn't everything."

He trailed a finger down her cheek. "In this particular case, winning is everything," he countered. "If I don't win, I have nothing to give Benjy. I might as well walk away from him just like my father did me."

"Oh, Johnny, when are you going to learn that you don't have to win? You don't have to be anything but who you are to earn Benjy's love."

There was no way she could understand the forces that drove him, no way she could ever relate to how important it was for Johnny to be more than who he was, more than what he was. "Enough talking," he said and once again tightened his grip on her. "I don't want to think about tomorrow or yesterday or anything else right now. I just want you to be with me like you were on prom night so long ago."

"You're the one who told me we can't go back," she reminded him.

"But we can...for this one night, we can." Once again his mouth covered hers, this time in a kiss that contained all the hunger of a lifetime.

She responded as if with the same hunger and once again Johnny lost the beat of the music as he responded to the rhythm of his own need. As the kiss continued,

Marissa's fingers worked at the buttons of his shirt. When they were all unfastened, she shoved the shirt off his shoulders and replaced the material with the warmth of her hands.

Her hands were everywhere, stroking across the broadness of his back, sliding across his flat abdomen, trailing upward to tangle in a patch of chest hair.

Johnny broke their kiss long enough to reach behind her and find the zipper on her dress. He unzipped it, and with a shrug of her shoulders, it fell to the ground around her feet, leaving her clad in a bra and panties.

He reached behind her once again, this time to grasp the ribbon that kept her hair confined. He tugged at it, releasing the spill of her curls into his hands. The starlight found the palest of strands and kissed them with a silvery light.

"You are so beautiful," Johnny said, his hands caressing over her shoulders, then down her arms.

She looked like a wood nymph, with her hair tousled by his touch and the kiss of the night wind. Her eyes glowed as if she'd managed to capture the twinkling of the stars.

Johnny unbuttoned his jeans, then took them off. He also removed his briefs, leaving him naked and exposed. He took her hand, then stretched out in the cool, soft grass, pulling her on top of him.

Their bodies, cool from the night air, quickly warmed as they touched and kissed, caressed and stroked. When her hand closed around him, intimately touching him, he couldn't stop the low moan that erupted from him. He felt as if her touch set him on fire, and every nerve in his body sizzled with desire.

"Do you have any idea what you do to me?" he murmured.

"Yes...the same that you do for me," she replied, her voice husky and breathless. "You fill me up, you make me whole."

Her words increased Johnny's desire. Pulling away from her touch, he rolled over so she was on the bottom. He reached beneath her and unclasped her bra, baring her breasts to his hands and his mouth. He flicked his tongue over first one, then the other nipple. She arched and tangled her hands in his hair, gasping aloud her pleasure.

Johnny reached down and touched her through her panties, wanting to bring her enough pleasure to last a lifetime. He loved the way she looked in the grip of passion...her cheeks flushed with color and her eyes didn't quite focus. Her head moved from side to side, and her breathing accelerated to fever pitch as his touch grew more intimate and his fingers slid beneath the silk material.

She was all heat and flames, and Johnny felt as if he were being consumed by her fire. With one smooth movement he removed her panties. "Yes," she whispered, opening her arms to welcome him. "Please, let me feel you inside me."

Johnny's head swam in a sea of desire, and any plan he had to continue their foreplay, died beneath her words. He entered her slowly, easing into her moist warmth. He closed his eyes, fighting back a wave of emotion so intense it brought tears to his eyes.

She'd said he filled her, but when they were joined as they were now, he felt full, whole...complete. He opened his eyes and gazed at her. "Johnny," she whispered, her hands reaching up to cup his face. "Love me, Johnny. Please love me."

He moved slowly at first, easing back from her then thrusting deep and lingering. She arched to meet him, her muscles constricting around him. Johnny closed his eyes once again, allowing the tantalizing sensations to overtake him. Her hands clutched at his shoulders, then rubbed down his back, her fingernails biting slightly with each of his thrusts.

With a suddenness that startled him, she pushed him off her, rolled him onto his back, then straddled him so she could set the pace of their lovemaking.

And the pace she wanted was fast and furious. Johnny met her demand as he felt himself lost to the sweet friction of their bodies. He felt her building, moving faster…closer to release, felt his own zenith approaching but held back, wanting to peak with her.

She stiffened, a choked cry bursting from her, and Johnny plunged over the edge at the same time, spilling himself into her as they clung to one another.

Once again Johnny was aware of the muffled sounds of the band, the clicks and whirrs of the night insects that surrounded them. They lay in each other's arms, the slight breeze cooling the heat of their bodies.

Johnny searched for something to say, words to fill the silence between them. He couldn't say "I love you," for although there would always be a place in his heart where he did love Marissa, there were too many other less positive emotions surrounding that place.

She stirred in his arms and lifted her head to look at him. "I'm scared, Johnny."

Her words surprised him. "Why?" he asked.

"I'm scared of you making Brad Emery so angry."

He tightened his arm around her. "I would never let him hurt you or Benjy," he replied.

"I'm not frightened for us, Johnny. I'm frightened for you. If he killed before, what makes you think he won't try to kill you to keep you quiet?"

Johnny frowned. "I won't go down easily. Besides, Brad is arrogant enough to think he's safe from anything I say. Right now, I'm irritating him, and he's irritating me, but he's too smart to show his hand by overtly threatening my life."

"But you know Brad isn't always in control. Sometimes his temper gets the best of him," Marissa replied.

"And that's what I hope will eventually happen," Johnny replied. "I hope I can make him mad enough that he'll slip, say something to incriminate himself." He stroked down the silky length of her back. "It's all I've got. Nobody is willing to come forward with any information about Brad's physical abuse of Sydney."

"You know even if you never get Brad, if your name is never cleared, it doesn't matter to Benjamin." She hesitated a moment, then added, "And it doesn't matter to me."

He saw in her eyes an emotion he didn't want to see. He averted his gaze from hers. She sat up and grabbed her underclothes. "We've got to stop doing this, Johnny," she said, her voice strained. She put on her bra, then stood and stepped into her panties.

"But we're so great together," he replied.

"Well, it's got to stop." She grabbed her dress from the ground and pulled it on over her head. Her motions were jerky with a sudden anger.

Johnny sat up, wondering what burr had gotten under her saddle. "Why? We're both single, consenting adults."

"I don't want to consent with you anymore. Ten years ago I made a mistake, and you've told me that you can't forgive me for that. Well, I love you, Johnny. I've always loved you and I don't know what to do about it. But I know I need to stay away from you so I can somehow learn to stop loving you.''

Without waiting for his reply, she turned and disappeared into the darkness of the night. Johnny stared after her for a long moment.

She loved him.

The words echoed inside his head. She loved him and she didn't know what to do about it. She loved him and he didn't know what to do about it.

He stood and grabbed his jeans and shirt. Dressing quickly, his head spun dizzily as he tried to sort out his emotions where Marissa was concerned.

He couldn't deny that he still entertained strong feelings for her…feelings of desire, and the memories of a shared past. She was the mother of his son, and there was a part of him that would always be with her.

But, he didn't want her love, didn't trust it. The ache he'd carried in his heart for ten long years was too big for her recent confession of love to fix.

Chapter 14

It was a perfect day for a rodeo. The sun shone bright, and the temperature was expected to top out in the lower eighties. A light breeze stirred the dust into swirling devils that danced across the ground. But what was a rodeo without a little dust?

Marissa and Benjamin climbed out of her car at ten o'clock and headed for the Mustang arena, where the rodeo action was set to take place. Outside the arena, a carnival was finishing last-minute preparations for a noon opening.

The air was filled with scents, the sharp odor of animals, the fragrant smell of fresh popcorn, cotton candy and roasting peanuts. Beneath the strong aromas were the more subtle ones that came with a crowd of people...soap and sweat, a variety of perfumes and colognes, and the always present scent of rawhide and leather.

Benjamin's head turned left and right, craned and stretched like a disjointed marionette as he tried to see here, there and everywhere. Marissa knew who he was looking for...his dad.

Her heart skipped a beat as she thought of Johnny. Last night had been like a dream, a fantasy when nothing mattered but the two of them. For a brief time they had relived a special moment from their past. But when the moment ended, Marissa was left with the reality of loving Johnny, and him not loving her.

A huge chunk of her heart would always belong in that clearing where she'd left him. But, somehow, someway she had to get past her love for him, had to get over it. If only she knew how.

The noise level in the arena was deafening. Bulls stomped and snorted, calves bawled their displeasure, spurs jingled and horses whinnied and above it all, shouts and whoops from the people who filled the seats and the rodeo personnel on the ground below.

"You think Dad will find us?" Benjamin asked as they took their seats in the fourth row.

"I'm sure he will," Marissa assured him.

"And he'll find us before he rides the bull?" Benjamin looked at his mother worriedly.

"I promise he will," she said, knowing Johnny wouldn't compete without a word or two with his son.

Benjamin gripped tight to the yellow scarf he'd brought with him. He intended to give it to Johnny for good luck. Like a knight wearing the colors of his lady, Benjamin wanted his dad to tie the scarf around his neck before he climbed on the back of a bull.

"Hey, look, there's Lucy," Benjamin said and pointed to where Lucy jumped up and down and waved.

Marissa waved back, noting that Lucy wasn't alone, but with Derrick. As Marissa watched, Lucy grabbed

Derrick's hand and tugged him toward Marissa and Benjamin.

"Guess what?" Lucy said by way of greeting. She waved her left hand, displaying a diamond engagement ring.

"Oh, Lucy, I'm so happy for you!" Marissa hugged her friend tightly, then gave Derrick a quick hug as well. "So, when's the big day?"

"We haven't decided yet," Derrick replied as he placed his arm around Lucy's shoulder. "We're thinking maybe fall, although I wouldn't mind a small, impromptu ceremony as soon as tomorrow." His eyes shone with love as he gazed at his fiancée.

Lucy giggled. "Isn't he terrible? Actually, I'm thinking maybe September. And, of course, I want you to be my maid of honor."

"I'd be honored," Marissa replied and blinked back tears of happiness. Again the two friends hugged and Derrick and Benjamin exchanged a long-suffering look of male impatience.

"Honey, we'd better find our seats," Derrick finally said.

Marissa released Lucy. "Go on. We'll catch up later."

She watched them go, envying them their obvious love for each other. That was the way it was supposed to work…you love somebody and they love you back.

"Mom, are you okay?" Benjamin asked. "You look like you're about ready to cry."

Marissa laughed and sat back down next to her son. "I'm fine, and I promise you I won't embarrass you by crying."

"Good," Benjamin replied firmly.

The barrel-racing event was first. Marissa and Benjamin settled in to watch the competition. Most of the riders they didn't know. Many of the men and women who would compete in the day's events were rodeo gypsies who followed the circuit from town to town. Only a few of Mustang's own would be competing in a variety of the rodeo contests.

"Hey, there's Dad." Benjamin jumped up from his seat and waved frantically at Johnny, who stood at the bleacher entrance, scanning the crowd. "Dad! Dad!"

Benjamin finally garnered Johnny's attention. With a wave and a nod, Johnny started toward them.

Marissa steeled herself for the encounter. He looked exceptionally good in a pair of tight black jeans and a white western shirt with a touch of black embroidery on either shoulder. His hat was cocked on his head at an angle that made him look slightly dangerous and handsome as the devil.

Marissa was aware of female heads turning to follow his progress toward them. She knew they were looking not because of his infamous stature, but because he was a fine-looking cowboy that made women think of sins of the flesh.

"Hi, partner," Johnny greeted his son, then nodded to Marissa. "You having a good time?" he asked Benjy.

"Great, but I can't wait for the bull-riding event." Benjamin held out the yellow kerchief. "This is my special lucky scarf. I wore it one time when I sang in church and I didn't make one mistake during my song. I thought maybe you'd like to wear it."

Johnny took the kerchief in his hand and stared at it for a long moment. When he looked at Benjamin once again, Marissa saw the depth of his emotions shining from his sky-blue eyes. "I'd be proud to wear your lucky scarf, son." He tied the kerchief around his neck. "How does it look?"

"Great!" Benjamin replied.

"You want to come with me and see some of the bulls?" Johnny asked.

Benjamin turned to Marissa. "Can we, Mom? That would be so cool."

"You go on with your dad. I'll wait here for you," Marissa replied. Marissa knew the less time she spent with Johnny, the better.

She watched as her two favorite men walked off together, their strides the same, long and masculine.

She knew now why she hadn't dated in the last ten years, knew why she'd developed no relationship with any man. Someplace in her subconscious, she'd known eventually Johnny would come home. And so she had waited for him.

Waited for nothing, she reminded herself. For ten years she'd kept her heart for him only to discover he no longer wanted it.

And yet he wanted her physically. There was no way he could fake his desire for her. That, at least, was as strong as ever. Was it possible for a man to make love to a woman and yet not love her? Marissa knew there were plenty of women who believed plenty of men were capable of just that. But she found it difficult to believe about Johnny.

He'd loved her once. Was it possible she could make him love her again? Could she make him love her enough to forget how stupid she'd been in the past? She didn't know. All she could do was try.

With this thought in mind, she got up and went in search of Johnny and Benjamin. She found them at the bull pens, looking at the bull Johnny would ride in the preliminary round.

"His name is Muffin," Benjamin told his mom as she

joined him. "Dad says there's no way he'll get thrown from a bull named Muffin."

Marissa eyed the black Brahman. Two thousand pounds of muscle and temper. "Doesn't look much like a Muffin to me," she said, a sick dread in the pit of her stomach as she imagined Johnny trying to ride such a beast.

As Benjamin ran to the next pen to see the bull, Marissa turned to Johnny. "You don't look nervous," she said. No, he looked at ease, with a confident gleam in his eyes.

"I don't feel nervous," he agreed. He leaned back against the thick fencing and propped the heel of a boot behind him. "It's been a good morning. I met a couple of guys I rodeoed with when I was in high school."

"That must have been nice."

"It was." He reached up and tipped his hat back farther on his head. "I'll tell you what's nice. Unlike the judgmental people of Mustang, rodeo people don't much care where you're going or where you've been. They just want to know how good you rope, or how good you ride."

"Don't judge the people of Mustang too harshly," Marissa said softly. "You've always been far harder on yourself than anyone here in Mustang could be."

Johnny nodded, then frowned as he looked over her shoulder. Marissa turned to see what he was looking at and saw Brad Emery talking to Benjamin. Like a bullet, Johnny shot toward his son. Marissa hurriedly followed, her heart beating a rhythm of fear.

"Benjy, why don't you go get me something to drink from the concession stand?" Johnny said to his son, but his gaze remained fixed on Brad. Johnny pulled a couple dollars from his pocket and pointed to a nearby vendor selling hot dogs and drinks. Benjamin took the dollars and raced toward the vendor.

"Good-looking boy you've got there, Johnny," Brad said, a smirk curling his lips. "Yes, sir. That's a fine-looking young man. Benjamin, right? Be a damned shame if anything bad happened to him."

Marissa gasped, and Johnny lunged forward, grabbing hold of Brad's shirt. The smirk gave way to anger as Brad struggled to free himself from Johnny's grip. "Let me go, you crazy bastard," Brad yelled.

Marissa was aware that they had attracted the attention of the people in the area. Men moved in closer, anticipating a good old-fashioned rumble.

"I'm not the crazy one around here," Johnny said. "And if you ever touch a hair on my son's head, I'll kill you." He released Brad by shoving him backward.

Brad fell to the ground on his back, his face contorted with rage. "Why you…"

"Did you hear me, Emery? You touch my boy, and I'll hunt you down and I'll kill you." Johnny's words echoed in the silence that had fallen among the bystanders.

Johnny took Marissa's arm. "The show is over, folks," he said loudly. Without a backward glance at the man still on the ground, Johnny guided Marissa toward Benjamin, who stood with a drink in hand next to the concession.

"You all right, buddy?" he asked his son.

Benjamin nodded, his eyes huge.

Johnny took the drink Benjamin held and took a long swallow. "Hmm, root beer. My favorite." He smiled reassuringly at Benjamin, who relaxed visibly.

"He didn't say anything bad to me," Benjamin said.

"He was just trying to get under my skin." Johnny smiled apologetically. "Guess he succeeded."

"If you wouldn't have pushed him down, I would have," Marissa replied, her blood still cold as she remembered the way Brad had smirked.

Johnny wrapped one arm around Marissa's shoulder and pulled her close against him. "Don't you let this worry your head. Brad knows better than to hurt you or Benjamin. He's a stupid fool, but he's not a complete lunatic." He placed his free hand on Benjamin's shoulder. "Come on, let's get you two back in your seats. The bull-riding event is the next one up."

An hour later Marissa and Benjamin watched as Johnny rode Muffin for the required eight seconds, propelling him into the final round to take place the next morning.

And the next morning Marissa and Benjamin were back in the same seats, waiting for the final competition that would hopefully win Johnny his seed money.

She and Benjy had only seen Johnny a short time after his win on Saturday. He'd come to where they sat, his eyes sparkling with victory. He'd sat with them for just a few minutes, then told them he was heading home for a long hot soak in the tub.

It had been early evening when Marissa had finally talked Benjamin into calling it a day. They'd gone home, eaten a late supper, then Benjamin had gone to bed and Marissa had been left with her thoughts.

And always…always her thoughts were of Johnny. There were times she felt as if she had been born loving him, and would eventually die loving him.

As she sat next to Benjamin, waiting for the final bull-riding action to begin, she wondered what Johnny would say if she proposed they get married. It really wasn't as crazy as it sounded.

No decent woman would be seen in Johnny's company as long as he was branded the town ex-con. He'd told her time and time again that he liked making love with her. So, they could marry and raise Benjamin together, and she would love him enough to make up for the fact that he didn't love her.

"I hope Dad wins," Benjamin's voice cut through Marissa's insane thoughts.

"Me, too," she agreed. She clutched her fingers together in her lap, nerves bucking and kicking like a wild bronco in her stomach. *Please let him win,* she sent the silent prayer skyward.

She couldn't imagine what he might do if he didn't win the prize money. The very idea terrified her. She had a feeling if Johnny didn't win, he would give up. He'd make himself believe that it would be better if he left Mustang, left Benjamin. She was afraid he'd believe no father was better than a father who had nothing. He'd be wrong, but she didn't know if she had the power to convince him of that.

As the bull-riding finals were announced, both Marissa and Benjamin leaned forward in nervous anticipation. There were six cowboys competing in the finals....five men who could beat Johnny for the purse.

"Okay, ladies and gentlemen, let me introduce our clowns, Timmy and Tommy," the announcer said, the speaker system sending his voice throughout the arena. Timmy and Tommy, the raggedy clad clowns with sad painted faces, waved to everyone, then Timmy took his position inside one of the barrels and Tommy stood ready to roll the barrel.

"Our first cowboy today is Stephen Cottrane and he's

riding an old bull named Raider." The announcer barely finished his statement before bull and rider exploded out of the gate. The crowd went wild, hooting and hollering their encouragement, but the cowboy fell off after only four seconds.

The next two riders suffered the same fate. "Okay, the score is bulls three, cowboys zero," the announcer said. "Let's see if our next rider can change that score. He's a local cowboy. Johnny Crockett riding Diablo."

Diablo was a black Brahman. Snorting mad, the bull twisted and jerked as if trying to dislodge the offending weight on his back.

Johnny's body moved with a fluid grace, one arm up in the air, he rode the bull until the eight-second buzzer rang. The crowd went wild, Marissa and Benjamin adding their screams of excitement to the others.

After the buzzer rang, Johnny untied his hand and hopped off the crazed bull. He grabbed the kerchief from around his neck and waved it at Benjamin and Marissa.

The next two riders met the same fate as the first three, leaving Johnny the undisputed champion and the winner of the prize money.

"Come on, let's go find your dad," Marissa said when the event was over and Johnny had been announced as the winner.

She and Benjamin left the bleachers and went to the bull pens. Marissa saw him in the distance with a couple of other cowboys who were obviously congratulating him.

"Dad!" Benjamin hollered.

Johnny smiled widely and in five quick strides joined Marissa and Benjamin. He swept his hat off his head and plunked it down on Benjamin's. "I told you I'd win," he said as he crouched down and gave his son a hug. He straightened and pulled Marissa into his arms. With a cowboy cry of uninhibited happiness, he bent her over backward and planted a deep, long kiss on her lips.

Marissa was vaguely aware of catcalls and resounding whoops from everyone around them. But, it was difficult to concentrate on anything but the kiss itself.

When he finally released her, the crowd clapped and Marissa's head spun with pleasant dizziness. Johnny laughed and Marissa realized just how relieved he was in winning the money. For the first time since his return to Mustang, his eyes held no shadows and his laughter held genuine jubilation.

"Come on, let's go find a quiet little corner where the three of us can celebrate," he said. He reached out and tousled Benjamin's hair. "We can talk about how we're going to spend my prize money."

"Johnny."

The three of them turned at the deep male voice and saw Sheriff Jesse Wilder approaching them. "Hey, Sheriff, did you see my ride?" Johnny asked with an easy smile.

Jesse didn't return the smile and a fist of anxiety slammed into Marissa's stomach. "No, I'm afraid I missed it," Jesse replied. "Uh…" his gaze flickered from Marissa, to Benjamin, then back to Johnny. "I need to talk to you, Johnny," he said.

Johnny's easy smile fell away and Marissa felt the tension that straightened his spine. "What's going on, Sheriff?"

"I, uh, need to ask you a few questions." Again Jesse's gaze went to Benjamin, then back to Johnny.

"Here…what's going on here?" Marissa's father appeared next to Marissa. "Jesse? Is there a problem here?"

"'Fraid so, sir," Jesse replied. "I need Johnny to come down to my office. I've got some questions that need to be answered."

"I'm not going anywhere until I know what's going on," Johnny replied. He turned to Marissa's father. "Would you mind taking Benjamin to get a drink or some popcorn or something?"

Jeffrey Sawyer looked at his daughter for approval. She nodded her consent, then turned back to Jesse. It was bad. Whatever had brought him here, brought him to Johnny was definitely bad. She could see it in Jesse's dark eyes.

Only when Jeffrey had taken Benjamin out of hearing range, did Jesse say what had brought him. "Johnny, Brad Emery has been murdered."

Chapter 15

"Murdered?" Johnny stared at the sheriff in stunned surprise.

Jesse nodded. "He was found about two hours ago in his barn. Somebody hit him over the head with a shovel."

"So, what's this got to do with me?" Johnny asked. But he knew. He knew with a sick dread where this was leading. "Look, Jesse, I've been here since dawn. If Emery was murdered this morning, then I've got a hundred witnesses that will state I've been here all day."

"The coroner has placed time of death between ten and two last night. Can you tell me where you were at that time?"

"He was with me," Marissa said. She stepped up next to Johnny and grabbed his arm. She raised her chin defiantly. "He couldn't have killed Brad Emery, he was with me all night."

"Marissa." Johnny's heart swelled as he heard her lie.

He couldn't let her do that for him. He looked at Jesse. "I was alone…at home in bed."

"I got a dozen witnesses say they heard you threaten to kill Brad yesterday," Jesse replied.

The sinking sensation in Johnny's stomach intensified. It was like déjà vu, the past all over again. "I didn't kill him," Johnny said earnestly. "I might have threatened him, but I didn't kill him."

"I still need you to come down to the station," Jesse said.

"Am I under arrest?" Johnny's heart beat rapidly as he waited for Jesse's reply.

"Not yet." Jesse gestured toward the patrol car waiting nearby. "Hopefully we can get this cleared up as quickly as possible."

Johnny nodded. Brad dead? Murdered? What was going on? If Brad killed Sydney, as Johnny believed, then who in the hell had killed Brad?

"Johnny," Marissa grabbed his arm once again, her cheeks streaked with silent tears. "Johnny, it will be all right. Somehow, someway, we'll figure this out."

Again he nodded, and felt an insidious numbness creeping over his body. He knew what was going to happen. The same thing that had happened before. He'd be railroaded into a conviction, only this time he wouldn't get ten years. He'd get life.

Gently, he removed Marissa's fingers from his arm. He wished he had words that would take away her tears, but he didn't.

He got into the back seat, hoping that Jeffrey Sawyer had taken Benjamin far enough away that the little boy hadn't seen his daddy getting into the back of a patrol car.

Johnny closed his eyes, wondering why life seemed to

enjoy kicking the stuffing out of him. He'd thought he was on the way up. The euphoria of winning the bull-riding event had just peaked, providing him a glimpse of the possibility of dreams…and now this nightmare.

Brad dead. He struggled to understand what might have happened. He'd been so certain that Brad had killed Sydney…but now the first flutter of uncertainty appeared. Was it possible that the person who had killed Sydney had also killed Brad? But who? And why?

The sheriff's office was just as he remembered it. A small building that housed the town jail. There were two cells in the back and Jesse's office at the front. Thankfully, Jesse didn't lead him back to one of the cells, but rather pointed to a straight-backed chair opposite his desk.

"I'm sorry about this, Johnny, but I wouldn't be doing my job if I didn't bring you in," Jesse said. The sheriff swept off his hat and threw it on the desk. "I was sixteen when you were arrested for Sydney's murder. I didn't believe you were guilty then, and I don't believe it now."

Johnny nodded, still numb. "If I was going to kill a man, I wouldn't be stupid enough to threaten him in front of dozens of witnesses."

"So you say you were home alone last night between the hours of ten p.m. and two a.m.? Did you get any phone calls, have any contact with anyone who can confirm you were at home?"

A ghost of a smile curved Johnny's lips. "Since getting out of prison, my social calendar hasn't exactly been full. Other than Marissa and Benjamin, I don't get any calls…unless you count that crazy hat-wearing social reporter, Millie Creighton. She's contacted me several times wanting a story on adjusting to life after prison."

"I understand that some of Brad's men have been paying covert visits to your place, doing a bit of damage."

"Who told you that?"

"Nobody in particular. I just heard it through the grapevine."

Johnny scowled. "The people in this town do too much talking."

"Johnny, you've got to give me something, otherwise I'm going to have to hold you. Should I call you a lawyer?"

Johnny laughed bitterly. "No, thanks. At the moment I'll take my chances without a lawyer. The last one I had left a bad taste in my mouth. You charge me, arrest me, then I'll think about a lawyer."

"Who do you think killed Sydney?" Jesse asked.

For the next thirty minutes Johnny told the young sheriff his theory of Sydney's murder. He explained to him about all the people he had spoken with, how many had mentioned Brad's physical abuse of the girls and their mother.

"Okay, if I believe everything you say, then it's possible Brad killed Sydney in some kind of a temper fit. But then who killed Brad?"

Johnny sighed and raked a hand through his hair. "I don't know. I don't have a damn clue." He frowned thoughtfully. "Have you checked out Gus Winstead? He hated Bradley."

Jesse waved his hands dismissively. "Everyone in town knows Gus hated Brad. And everyone in town knows Gus is usually too drunk to do anything about it. Gus passed out last night at the Roundup. A couple of the bouncers dragged him into the backroom where he slept it off on a cot. He was still there when I checked it out a little while ago."

Johnny sighed once again, feeling old and weary. "I don't know how to fight this, Jesse. It's just like last time. Everything circumstantial points to me, and I don't have any kind of defense."

"What about Marissa? She said she was with you all night."

Her name brought a deep pain to Johnny's heart, the pain of memory. "No, we weren't together last night. She's just trying to make amends."

"Make amends?"

Johnny nodded, the pain pressing tight against his chest. "Ten years ago, on the night Sydney was murdered, Marissa and I were together."

"But I've read the files and according to them, you had no alibi," Jesse countered.

"I had no alibi I wanted to use. The truth is I was dancing in the woods with Marissa while somebody choked the life out of Sydney."

"Why didn't you tell somebody that?" Jesse looked at him incredulously. "That might have kept you from going to prison, from being found guilty."

Johnny shook his head. "I didn't want to involve Marissa. Nobody knew we were seeing each other. And her father would have read her the riot act. I figured, if she came forward, then fine, we'd go with the alibi. But, she didn't come forward."

"I'm surprised she hasn't wound up dead," Jesse said wryly.

Johnny smiled and shrugged his shoulders. "I loved her." He fell silent for a long moment, remembering all those nights of wondering if Marissa would come forward. He'd been so torn. He hadn't wanted her hurt and so prayed she'd keep quiet. And yet when that had happened, he'd been angry.

"It wouldn't have made a difference if she'd come forward. The prosecution and the jury needed a conviction and nothing said or done was going to save me. I was going to prison whether she came forward or not." Johnny realized as he said it that he'd made peace where this issue was concerned.

Johnny could forgive Marissa for not coming forward to tell the world she'd spent that night with him. What he couldn't forgive her for was the fact that she hadn't come to speak with him at all. He hadn't wanted her alibi...he'd wanted her support, her love, and she'd taken it away from him.

He clenched his hands into fists, knowing the anger that coursed through him wasn't just directed at Marissa, but at the whims of fate that had cast him once again in the position of suspected murderer.

Dammit! He'd just won enough money to begin a new life, make something of himself. He'd wanted to be a good man...for Benjamin...for Marissa. He shook his head, wondering how she had gotten back into his thoughts.

"Sheriff." A deputy stuck his head into the doorway. "You'd better get out to the Emery place. Somebody is up on top of the barn roof threatening to jump."

Jesse and Johnny both sprang from their chairs. "You stay here, I'll be back later," Jesse directed Johnny.

"Like hell," Johnny replied. "Whatever is going on out at the Emery place, I've got a right to know. I'm going with you."

For a moment the two men stood face to face, determined stubbornness on each of their features. "All right, but you stay the hell out of my way," Jesse relented.

Brad Emery was dead. Marissa struggled to make sense of the senseless. Despite the fact that she and

Johnny hadn't been together the night before, she knew
Johnny was innocent. Johnny was not a murderer.

After Jesse left the rodeo with Johnny in the back of
the patrol car, Marissa had asked her father to take Benjamin home with him.

"What are you going to do?" Jeffrey asked, his forehead furrowed with wrinkles of worry.

"I don't know, but I've got to do something," Marissa
replied, fighting off tears. It wasn't fair. Dammit, it
wasn't fair that Johnny was once again on the pointy end
of justice.

"Mom?" Benjamin tugged at her arm, his eyes huge
and solemn. "Is Dad going to be all right?" Without
warning tears spilled onto Benjy's cheeks. "I don't want
him to go away. I don't want him to go to prison again."

"Oh, honey." Marissa bent down and gathered her son
in her arms, remembering that although he tried desperately to be grown-up, he was still just a little boy. A
frightened little boy. "Don't you worry, sweetheart. Your
daddy isn't going anywhere."

Determination overtook Marissa's pressing tears. She
didn't care what it took. She'd make sure Johnny had the
best defense lawyer money could buy. She'd sell the
store, sell her house, do whatever it took to make sure
he wasn't at the mercy of a public defender with too
many cases and too little time for an innocent man.

"Now, you go with Grandpa, and I'll see you later this
evening, okay? Be brave, Benjy. Dad would want us both
to be brave."

Benjamin swiped his tears and straightened his back.
"Tell Dad I love him," he said, then he took his grand-
father's hand and the two of them left.

It took Marissa only a moment to know what she

wanted to do. She got into her car and headed for the Emery place.

If what Johnny believed was true, that Brad had been an abusive monster, then it stood to reason he wasn't just abusive to Sydney, but to the other Emery females as well. She had to talk to Rachel. Perhaps the older woman could offer some clue as to who would kill her stepson. Surely Rachel knew what was going on in Brad's life, surely she would know if anyone else had hated him enough to kill him.

Marissa knew she might be making things worse for Johnny by speaking to the elder Emery, but she had to take that chance. She knew things looked bad for Johnny. Lots of people had heard Johnny threaten Brad the day before, it would be easy to convince those people that Johnny had followed through on those threats.

When she pulled into the driveway of the Emery ranch, she nearly changed her mind. Several patrol cars were there, and in the distance, the barn was cordoned off with yellow crime tape.

She drove only a couple of feet toward the house when a deputy stopped her. "Hey, Marissa. What are you doing out here?" Deputy Alex Baxter crouched down by her car window, a sweet smile curving his lips.

Marissa breathed a silent prayer of thanks. Alex Baxter had always had a crush on Marissa. Although she didn't like it, if necessary she would use that crush to her advantage. "Alex, I need to speak to Rachel."

"Ah, Marissa, I can't let you do that." He looked chagrined, as if there was nothing he'd rather do than tell her she couldn't get what she wanted. "You know we're conducting a murder investigation out here."

"Is Rachel being questioned?"

Alex shook his head. "We did that already. She and

Gillian are in seclusion. They told us they don't want to talk to anyone."

Marissa shut off her car engine and stepped out. "But Rachel wants to talk to me. She called me just a little while ago." Marissa hoped the lie didn't show in her eyes. "You know, Rachel and I have grown close over the last couple of years. She needs me now, Alex."

She stepped close to him, invading his personal space. A light red flush covered his face. "I promise I won't get in the way of your investigation," she said.

He hesitated, looked at the house, then back to her. "Okay. Go on. But you know Jesse will have my hide if you do anything to hinder the investigation."

Marissa nodded, then took off running toward the house before he changed his mind. She had no real idea what she intended to say to Rachel and knew only that she had to try to convince the woman that Johnny hadn't killed Sydney or Brad. Somehow she had to get Rachel on Johnny's side. Surely a jury would listen to the mother of a victim proclaiming the innocence of the defendant. Marissa prayed it wouldn't get that far, that somehow, someway Johnny would be set free long before a trial.

She rang the doorbell, waiting impatiently for an answer. She was afraid one of the other law enforcement officers would see her and send her away. Thankfully, the door was opened immediately by the taciturn housekeeper.

"I need to speak to Rachel," Marissa said.

"Mrs. Emery is not receiving guests."

"I'm not a guest," Marissa exclaimed and pushed past the old woman.

"It's all right," Rachel said to the indignant housekeeper. "Marissa." She invited Marissa to follow her. They went into the same room where they had sat before, on the day Rachel and Brad tried to blackmail Marissa into forcing Johnny to leave town.

Rachel gestured to a chair, but Marissa ignored her, preferring to stand. The first thing Marissa noticed was that for a stepmother who'd just learned her stepson had been murdered, Rachel was coolly controlled, without a trace of sorrow or grief.

"I assume this isn't a social visit," Rachel said. "What can I do for you, Marissa?"

"You can tell me the truth."

Rachel flinched in surprise at the harshness of Marissa's tone. "The truth about what?" she asked, her hand reaching up to linger nervously at her turtlenecked blouse.

"The truth about Brad and his abuse."

Rachel flushed and averted her eyes from Marissa. "I...I don't know what you're talking about. Brad is dead, and there's no point in discussing him."

Marissa balled her fists at her sides, fighting the impulse to take the older woman by the shoulders and shake her. "Rachel, they've taken Johnny into custody for Brad's murder. If you know anything...anything at all that might prove Johnny's innocence, I beg of you, please go to Jesse."

Rachel sank down in one of the chairs and rubbed a hand across her forehead. "I don't know who killed Bradley, but I wish it would have been me." She looked up at Marissa. "I see I've shocked you." She shook her head. "Bradley was a mean, sadistic child who grew into a meaner, sadistic man. He took pleasure in physically hurting us."

"You? Sydney? Gillian?" Marissa sank down on her knees by the side of Rachel's chair. "Rachel, Johnny already spent ten years in prison for a murder he didn't commit. Please don't let it happen again...please.''

Both women turned at the sound of footsteps in the hallway. "Gillian?" Rachel called. The front door whooshed open, then slammed shut.

Rachel turned back to Marissa, her eyes ancient with suffering. "Please...I can't help you. Just go away. I want everyone to go away and leave us alone." She buried her face in her hands.

Marissa stared at her in a combination of frustration and pity. She didn't know if Rachel knew anything that might help Johnny, but it was obvious Rachel's life with Brad had been hell, and even his death seemed to bring her no peace.

"Mrs. Emery." Alma, the housekeeper flew into the room, her normally rigid features twisted to radiate fear. "You've got to come. Gillian is on top of the barn, and she says she's going to jump."

"Oh, God. Dear God." Rachel jumped out of the chair and raced for the door, Marissa barely a step behind her.

Rachel ran like a woman half her age, covering the distance between the house and the barn in a mere couple of seconds. On the ground in front of the barn, half a dozen officers stood, looking up to the peak of the roof, where Gillian sat precariously close to the edge.

"Gillian," the tortured cry ripped from Rachel's throat.

"Stay back, keep away," Gillian cried. "Stay away or I'll jump."

"Calm down, honey. Come on down," Alex yelled. "Come down, and we'll get you some help."

"I don't want help. I just want to die!" Gillian screeched. She scooted closer to the edge. Rachel released a scream of terror and Marissa's heart seemed to stop beating.

"Do something," Rachel said to Alex. "For God's sake do something to get her down."

"Jesse is on his way, Mrs. Emery. Nobody is going to do anything until he gets here," Alex explained. "Every time we try to get close, she threatens to jump. Twice we've tried to put up a ladder, but she goes crazy. I'm not sure she won't jump if we don't stay back."

Rachel broke, sobs wrenching through her. Marissa placed an arm around her shoulders, wondering what was going on, why Gillian was threatening to kill herself.

"She's all I've got left," Rachel sobbed. She shrugged off Marissa's arm and stared up at her daughter. "Somebody has to help her. I can't lose her, too."

At that moment Jesse's patrol car pulled in and squealed to a halt. Before the engine had completely died down, both Jesse and Johnny were out of the vehicle.

Marissa instantly ran to Johnny, grateful to see that he looked no worse for his time in Jesse's custody. "You all right?" he asked her tersely, then gazed up at Gillian.

"I'm fine." Marissa followed his gaze. "We don't know why she's up there, but she won't let anyone near her," she explained.

"Gillian, it's all right, you can come down," Jesse shouted up to the young woman. "Don't worry, honey. We'll get the person who killed Brad."

Gillian laughed, the laughter dancing on the edge of hysterical. "I know who killed Brad. I did. I killed him."

Marissa gasped and Rachel moaned as Gillian continued, "And I don't want to go to prison, but I can't let Johnny go back to prison, either."

"Why did you kill him, Gillian?" Jesse asked, his voice gentle.

"He killed Sydney."

A wave of relief rushed through Marissa at Gillian's words. She looked at Johnny, saw the utter release of torture on his face. Finally…vindication.

"How do you know he killed Sydney?" Jesse asked.

Marissa quickly realized what the sheriff was doing. While he was asking questions of Gillian, several officers were silently getting a ladder up against the side of the barn.

"He told me he killed her. He laughed about it. He said that's what happened to little girls who didn't mind their brothers. He killed her because she was going to tell on him. She was going to tell how he beat us, and tormented us." Gillian, realizing what the officers were doing, screamed a protest. "Get away! I swear I'll kill myself."

Jesse motioned the officers away, then sighed in frustration. "I don't know what to do…I don't know how to get her down."

"Let me try," Johnny said.

Jesse shrugged his consent.

Johnny looked up at the young woman clinging precariously to the edge of the roof. "Gillian, did you know I was friends with your sister?"

"Yes, I found her diary."

"Is that what you were looking for that night I caught you in the shed?"

"Yes. I knew she'd kept one. I was the only one who knew about it, but I never found it after her death. Then, I forgot about it." She began to cry again. "And then you came back to town, and I remembered it, and I knew she used to keep it in the shed. It was buried and I found it."

"Gillian, I'm coming up." Johnny didn't give her a

chance to protest. He knew instinctively that he was probably the only one who could get Gillian to come down.

"Johnny." Marissa grabbed his arm, her eyes shim-
mering with tears. "Please be careful."

He touched her cheek reassuringly, then went inside
the barn. It took him only a moment to realize how Gillian had gotten onto the roof. A window from the loft
led out to the roof. Johnny climbed through the window
and stepped out on the pitched roof. His heart jumped
into his throat as his feet slid down several yards. He
crouched, using his hands as leverage to crawl up to
where Gillian clung to a vent.

"Don't come too close," Gillian warned.

"Okay, I'll stay right here." Johnny hooked an arm
over a section of a brass weather vane. For a long moment neither of them spoke.

"You must hate us," Gillian finally said. "You went
to prison all that time, and Brad should have been the
one behind bars."

"That's over and done with now," Johnny said. "And
nothing can change what's happened in the past. But, I'll
tell you this, Sydney wouldn't want it to end this
way…with you up here. She loved you, Gillian. She
talked about you all the time."

A sob caught in Gillian's throat. "I hated her. I hated
her for dying and leaving me alone. And now I'm either
going to go to prison or I'll join Sydney…and I can't go
to prison."

Johnny's heart ached. How much she looked like Sydney and how he wished he'd been able to help Sydney.
How he wished he'd have known what was going on in
her life.

"Sydney loved you, Johnny," Gillian continued.
"You were the big brother she wished she had. She was

going to tell you about Brad the night he killed her. She knew you'd help her."

Johnny closed his eyes, his soul weeping for the girl who had died, the girl he'd loved like a sister. He opened his eyes and looked at Gillian. "Gillian, you aren't alone anymore. Everyone in town knows how abusive Brad has been. There's a strong possibility you won't have to go to prison." Johnny was rewarded by an ebbing of her cries. Encouraged, he continued. "We'll all testify on your behalf, Gillian. You can plead self-defense. Come to me. Give me your hand." Johnny held his hand out toward her. "Please, Gillian. I couldn't save Sydney. Please let me help you."

With another sob, Gillian reached out and grabbed his hand. Using all his strength, Johnny pulled her toward him, grabbed her around the waist, then half dragged, half carried her back through the window and to the loft.

They were met there by Jesse and his men. "Go easy," Johnny said as Jesse reached for Gillian. Jesse nodded.

Stumbling outside, Johnny was met by Marissa, who flew into his arms and nearly knocked him over. He held her close for a long moment, vaguely aware of Rachel and Gillian being placed in the back of Jesse's car.

"It's over," he said, as much to himself as to Marissa.

She looked up at him, her brown eyes shining with joy. "Yes…finally it's over."

"And I seem to be stuck without a ride home."

"I'd be glad to give a handsome cowboy a ride," she replied.

Johnny nodded and moved out of her embrace. He felt as if he'd just ridden a killer bull. Exhaustion weighed heavily, his muscles ached and his emotions were far too close to the surface for comfort. He felt dirty, weak…as if in exposing the ugly secrets of Brad and his family, he'd also opened a wound and exposed his own negative emotions.

Marissa seemed unaware of his somber mood. As she drove him to his place, she rattled on about the prize money, his new start, the clearing of his name and how wonderful it all was.

"Johnny, are you all right?" she finally asked as she pulled up in front of his house.

"Fine. Just tired. It's been a long day." He got out of her car, somehow unsurprised when she did the same. He'd just faced one reckoning and he knew instinctively he was about to face another.

He sank down on the front stoop and motioned for her to join him, a weary resignation stealing over him. She sat next to him, as always smelling of the floral perfume that had always stirred, not only his body, but also his heart.

"You told me not too long ago that you could never forgive me for abandoning you when you needed me most," she began. A nervous tick appeared at the corner of her mouth, and he wanted to cover that mouth with his own, kiss her until the tick stopped and she moaned pleasure instead.

"That's right," he said, knowing he couldn't follow through on his impulse. He had to stop thinking of making love to her, had to stop imagining her kisses, her touch. It wasn't fair to her…to want her and not love her.

"So, there's no chance for us." The words held such wistful yearning, Johnny could feel it like a palpable force around him.

He steeled himself against it, didn't want to be affected by it. His heart ached with too many losses, and he couldn't separate them out. "Marissa, you'll always be special to me. We share a past…we share a son." He knew how inadequate the words were, saw the pain on her face, but he didn't know what else to say.

He drew in a deep breath. "Marissa, I can't trust that you won't hurt me again."

She bit her lip for a moment, stilling the nervous twitch. "So, you will take a chance on a two-thousand-pound bull in order to get money to fix the ranch, and you'll climb up the steep slope of a barn roof to save a poor, helpless young woman, but you're afraid to love me again?"

"I knew neither the bull nor Gillian would hurt my heart. You did, and I can't risk it another time. Hell, Marissa, sooner or later you'd figure out that you're better off without me." He offered her a wry grin. "Have you forgotten? I'm that poor, fatherless Crockett kid."

She stared at him for a long moment, then stood. "That's always been your problem, Johnny Crockett. You've always been your own enemy, expecting that people would think the worst of you. I loved you ten years ago, and I did a very stupid thing. I'm finished apologizing for my sins of the past. I love you now, but I'm not your problem, Johnny. You are. And until you figure out that you're worthy of loving, then you don't have a chance in hell of happiness."

She didn't wait for his reply. She stomped off the porch, got into her car and drove off without looking back. A yawning black emptiness filled Johnny as he watched the last of the dust from her tires swirl away.

"Crazy," he muttered. She was fool crazy if she thought the reason he refused to love her again was his problem. She'd left him...he'd never forget those days and nights, waiting for her to come by, waiting for her to call...send a note...anything.

He'd sat on this very porch...wishing and hoping. He

frowned and rubbed his forehead tiredly. No...that wasn't right. He hadn't been sitting on the porch, he'd been sitting in jail.

He was just tired, bone and soul weary. That's why he felt such a black hole inside him, that's what made his heart ache with something akin to regret. Tired. He'd go in and hit the bed. Everything would look better in the morning.

Chapter 16

How could a sunshine-drenched morning look so bleak? Marissa wondered as she watched the morning sun seeping around the edges of her bedroom curtains. She didn't want to get up, didn't want to go into the shop. She wanted to stay in bed forever, hide beneath the blankets and never have to face the fact that Johnny Crockett didn't love her.

She rolled over on her back and stared at the ceiling. She didn't really have to get up. Benjamin had spent the night at her parents' house and she was to collect him later that evening after she'd closed up the flower shop. She'd spoken to him briefly the night before, letting him know that his dad was safe and sound.

Irritated with herself and her wallowing self-pity, she rolled out of bed. Of course she would open the shop, and she would be friendly and cheerful to the customers and she would forget Johnny Crockett was ever a part of her heart.

Somehow, someway, she'd get over loving him. They would share custody of Benjamin and that would be the extent of their interaction. No more dancing in the woods, no more making love until near dawn. She would find a way to get over Johnny Crockett.

Dressed and ready to face the day, Marissa performed one task before leaving the house. The pink wildflower she'd dried and kept for ten long years she crushed and threw in the garbage. Without a backward glance, she left the house and drove to the shop.

The morning was sheer torture. Although no customers came in to order flowers, it seemed as if half the town dropped by to talk about the Emerys and Johnny's exoneration. Marissa wanted to scream at them all, tell them she didn't want to hear Johnny's name mentioned ever again in her presence. But, of course she didn't do that.

She smiled and corrected rumor with truth, or filled in the blanks for those who didn't know the whole truth. If there was one thing the people of Mustang liked to do, it was gossip. If the gossip was going to be about Marissa, Johnny and the Emerys, Marissa was determined that the facts would at least be correct.

At noon the doorbell tinkled announcing yet another customer. Marissa left the backroom and went up front to see Millie Creighton. She wore a hat with little plastic horses on it, apparently her tribute to the rodeo just passed.

"Ah, Marissa, I'm so glad you're in today. I have a hundred questions to ask you about everything that has unfolded. My readers love scandal, and from what I've heard my next column will be sensational."

"Millie, I'm sure you've heard about everything that happened yesterday. You don't need my input."

"On the contrary, I've only heard secondhand about everything. You were actually there when Gillian climbed up on the roof. It must have been horrible." Millie's eyes shone with excitement, like a vulture picking at other people's despair.

"I'll tell you what I think is horrible," Marissa replied, narrowing her eyes as anger swelled inside her. "I think it's horrible that most of the people in this town knew how abusive Brad could be, but nobody came forward to say it might have been him that killed Sydney. I think it's terrible that Rachel and Gillian suffered Brad's abuse all these years and nobody in this town did anything to save them."

Millie looked shamefaced. "You're right, and perhaps I'll write a column on that very issue." Her shame faded quickly. "But you must feel wonderful about Johnny being innocent of Sydney's murder. You were the only one in town who really believed in him."

Marissa's heartache swelled. "Yes, I'm glad Johnny is innocent and now can get on with the rest of his life." Without me, she mentally added, fighting desperately against the pain the mental words brought with them.

They both turned as the bell rang. Marissa stiffened as Johnny strode through the door. He looked like hell. Whisker stubble covered his cheeks and his eyes were slightly red, as if he hadn't slept. "We need to talk," he said without greeting, his voice holding a hard edge of anger.

"We have nothing to talk about," Marissa replied, grateful that her voice remained cool and calm.

Johnny eyed Millie, who stared at them both with obvious interest. "Get out," he ordered the older woman. "This shop is closed for the moment."

"I beg your pardon?" Millie sniffed with indignation. "I was here before you were."

"And you're leaving before I do if I have to tie you up like a calf and carry you out to the sidewalk." Johnny's threat sounded very real as he gazed menacingly at Millie.

She hesitated only a moment, then moved to the front door. Johnny followed her, giving her a gentle shove to hurry her along. When she was outside, he locked the front door and turned the Open sign to read Closed.

When he turned back to face her, his eyes blazed with blue flames of anger. As he advanced toward her, Marissa was vaguely aware of Millie peeking in through the front window.

As Johnny drew closer, Marissa backed up. She had no idea what had him so spitting angry, but she wasn't about to air it here where Millie could get an eyeful. She retreated to the backroom. Johnny followed her and calmly closed the door.

"What do you think you're doing?" Marissa demanded.

"Why didn't you tell me you lost the prom account because of me?"

So that was his problem, Marissa thought, trying not to admit to herself that even whiskered and sleepless, he still made her heart beat the rhythm of love. She shrugged. "It was none of your business."

"The hell it wasn't," he said firmly. He drew a steadying breath. "Anything that happens to you or Benjamin is my business."

"Who told you about that anyway?" she asked.

"I stopped in the diner for breakfast. Lucy filled me in."

"I'm going to kill her," Marissa replied, angry with him, angry with Lucy, angry with everything and everyone in her life.

He leaned against the sink and placed his black cowboy hat on the counter. "Tell me what the account was worth, how much profit you expected to make, and I'll pay you."

"Don't be ridiculous," Marissa replied. "I don't want your money." That's the last thing she wanted from him. She just wanted him to go away and leave her alone.

"Then there's only one way to make it up to you," he said. "I guess I'd better marry you."

Marissa picked up a white carnation from her work bench and threw it at him. "Damn you, Johnny Crockett, that's not funny." Tears blurred her vision. How could he be so cruel? Didn't he know his words were like taking a knife and plunging it into her heart?

He picked up the carnation and sniffed it, the anger that had glowed in his eyes gone. He threw the flower into the sink and stepped toward her. "I didn't intend it to be funny. I intended it to be forever."

Marissa stared at him in confusion. "I know what you're trying to do. You're trying to make me crazy, and once I'm totally insane, you'll take custody of Benjamin."

He laughed, the deep chuckle dancing up her spine,

making goose bumps of pleasure raise up on her arms. "I don't want custody of Benjamin unless I get custody of you as well."

His smile faded and he looked at her somberly. "I did a lot of thinking last night, Marissa." He raked a hand across his whiskered jaw. "Hell, I sure couldn't sleep after you left. I tossed and turned, your words going over and over again in my head."

He sank onto one of the metal folding chairs and Marissa leaned back against the work counter, wondering where he was going with this, if she could really trust his words.

"At dawn I got up, angry with you for keeping me awake all night. But still, I couldn't get what you'd said to me out of my head. I sat on the porch and watched the sun come up and thought of all the things I intended to do to the ranch with the rodeo money. Then I thought of all the things I wanted to do for Benjy with the rodeo money. Funny, winning that money finally made me feel worthy to be Benjamin's father."

"But you were always worthy of being Benjamin's father," Marissa protested.

He nodded. "You believed that, but I didn't. Then I realized something else...I was punishing you for something you had nothing to do with."

"What? I don't understand?" Marissa had no idea what he was trying to tell her, but she wished he'd get to it before her heart exploded from stress.

Johnny averted his gaze from her and instead stared at the cut flowers in the nearby cooler. "I loved my dad, Marissa. He was my partner, my hero, my world. When he left Mom and me, I was absolutely devastated. Even though Mom tried to tell me different, I knew it was somehow my fault. If I'd gotten better grades, not spilled my milk at dinner, been a better son, he would have stayed."

"Oh, Johnny," Marissa said softly, wishing she could go back in time and somehow ease the heartache of a little boy whose father had deserted him.

"The problem is when you didn't come to the jail to see me, when you didn't show up at the trial to support me, it all got mixed up together. My dad's desertion and yours became one big ball of anger and pain inside me and I couldn't separate the two."

He stood, the pain that had lined his face gone. "I'm not Johnny Crockett, the poor, fatherless boy who went to prison, anymore. When I first returned to Mustang, all my dreams were for Benjamin. I thought I'd lost the ability to have my own dreams. But you gave them back to me."

"I'm glad," Marissa whispered, unable to stop the tearing of her eyes.

"This morning I recognized my dreams…the ones you once shared with me. I want to build my ranch, turn it into a productive success, but I can't do it alone. I need you to help me. You see, Marissa, I tried to fool myself, but the truth is, I love you, and I don't quite know how to stop loving you."

He opened his arms to her, and she flew into them, her tears becoming sobs. He held her tight and stroked her hair. "I figure if I love you, and you love me, and neither of us can stop the way we feel, why not get married and build a life together?"

Marissa laughed through her tears. "That's the worst proposal I've ever heard."

"Okay, how about this?" He stepped away from her, so she could see the vivid blue of his eyes, the sweet emotion that softened his features. "I love you, Marissa. I've always loved you. I can't think of living without you. Marry me. Be my wife. Let me fill your days with laughter and your nights with love."

"Yes…oh yes," Marissa replied.

Once again he pulled her into his arms and his lips claimed hers with all the hunger, all the love, all the devotion that was in his heart. And she responded with the same emotions.

When the kiss ended, Johnny took her by the arm and led her out of the backroom and into the front shop area where Millie still had her nose pressed against the glass.

He unlocked the front door and guided Marissa out onto the sidewalk. "Millie, you want a story?" he asked. The older woman nodded, the horses on her hat appearing to gallop in excitement.

"I just proposed to Marissa, and she just said yes." Again he pulled Marissa into his arms. "Tell your readers Johnny Crockett is the luckiest person alive and he's going to spend the rest of his life loving Marissa, raising Benjamin and building a ranch that will be the envy of all of Mustang."

Marissa giggled as she watched Millie frantically scribbling on a tiny notepad. The giggles stopped as Johnny kissed her once again. He'd had her heart for the past ten years and she intended he keep it for the next hundred. "You were wrong," she whispered against his neck.

"Wrong about what?" he murmured, his lips nipping at her throat.

"You aren't the luckiest person alive…I am."

He scooped her up in his arms. "Let's go to my place and we'll show each other just how lucky we are." His eyes flamed with the sweet fire of love and passion, and Marissa saw her future there…a future built on love and dreams and happily-ever-afters.

*   *   *   *   *

Look for another exciting adventure in Mustang,
Montana, in Carla Cassidy's next book,
WIFE FOR A WEEK, coming your way
from Silhouette Romance in October 1999.

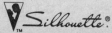

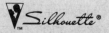

THE MACGREGORS OF OLD...

#1 *New York Times* bestselling author

NORA ROBERTS

has won readers' hearts with her enormously popular
MacGregor family saga. Now read about the MacGregors'
proud and passionate Scottish forebears in this
romantic, tempestuous tale set against the bloody
background of the historic battle of Culloden.

Coming in July 1999

REBELLION

One look at the ravishing red-haired beauty and Brigham
Langston was captivated. But though Serena MacGregor
had the face of an angel, she was a wildcat who spurned
his advances with a rapier-sharp tongue. To hot-tempered
Serena, Brigham was just another Englishman to be
despised. But in the arms of the dashing and dangerous
English lord, the proud Scottish beauty felt her hatred
melting with the heat of their passion.

Available at your favorite retail outlet.

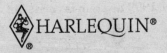

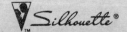

Coming in June 1999 from
Silhouette Books...

Those matchmaking folks at Gulliver's Travels are at it again—and look who they're working their magic on this time, in

HOLIDAY
Honeymoons

Two Tickets to Paradise

For the first time anywhere, enjoy these two new complete stories in one sizzling volume!

HIS FIRST FATHER'S DAY   **Merline Lovelace**
A little girl's search for her father leads her to Tony Peretti's front door...and leads *Tony* into the arms of his long-lost love—the child's mother!

MARRIED ON THE FOURTH   **Carole Buck**
Can summer love turn into the real thing? When it comes to Maddy Malone and Evan Blake's Independence Day romance, the answer is a definite "yes!"

Don't miss this brand-new release—
HOLIDAY HONEYMOONS: Two Tickets to Paradise—
coming June 1999, only from Silhouette Books.

Available at your favorite retail outlet.

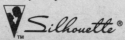

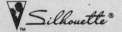